Winter Wonderland

HEIDI CULLINAN

Finding Mr. Right can be a snow lot of fun.

Paul Jansen was the only one of his friends who wanted a relationship. Naturally, he's the last single man standing. No gay man within a fifty-mile radius wants more than casual sex. No one, that is, except too-young, too-twinky Kyle Parks, who sends him suggestive texts and leaves X-rated snow sculptures on his front porch.

Kyle is tired of being the town's resident Peter Pan. He's twenty-five, not ten, and despite his effeminate appearance, he's nothing but the boss in bed. He's loved Paul since forever, and this Christmas, since they're both working on the Winter Wonderland festival, he might finally get his chance for a holiday romance.

But Paul comes with baggage. His ultra-conservative family wants him paired up with a woman, not a man with Logan's rainbow connection. When their anti-LGBT crusade spills beyond managing Paul's love life and threatens the holiday festival, Kyle and Paul must fight for *everyone's* happily ever after, including their own.

This book is a work of fiction. The names, characters, places, and incidents are products of the writer's imagination or have been used fictitiously and are not to be construed as real. Any resemblance to persons, living or dead, actual events, locale, or organizations is entirely coincidental.

Heidi Cullinan, POB 425, Ames, Iowa 50010

First publication 2015
www.heidicullinan.com

Dedication

For Linda Lytle
who will someday sing me "Valley-High" again.

Thanks to

Lillie for all the proofing in this and every one of my rereleases this year. Thanks for giving me a polish and organization we both know I would never be able to manage on my own. Thanks also to my family and friends who have barely seen me as I've tried to put my catalog back on the shelf. I promise someday I'll come out of my office again.

Thanks to my readers who keep sending me emails and letters of encouragement, and sweaters, and GIFS, and candy, and hugs, and jewelry, and all the amazing things you do to cheer me up. And above all, thank you for buying the books, even the second (and third!!!) editions. You are absolutely the best.

Thank you as always to my patrons for helping fund this massive republication machine, for being my lighthouses and my campfires, and for always being the first readers of every release. Thanks especially to Pamela Bartual, Rosie M., Tiffany Miller, Kaija Kovanen, Marie, Sarah Plunkett, and Sarah M.

Chapter One

A TEN-FOOT-TALL SNOW penis towered over Paul Jansen's front steps. Again.

He perched on the edge of his sofa, sipping his coffee as he kept the curtain pulled back with his foot so he could assess today's phallic offering. It was pretty good. It had a bulging vein down the front, but it wasn't as defined as usual. Big balls, but they'd clearly been joined to the shaft in a hurry. The glans had a nice contour—the snow artist usually took the most time there.

He'd give it a B+. Putting his mug aside, Paul tightened his robe before stepping into his boots. Opening the front door, he squinted into the sleet and wind. Saluted the penis. Snapped a photo for posterity.

Then he took aim with his right foot, braced himself against the doorframe and kicked the sculpture into pieces before reaching inside for his shovel so he could deal with the balls.

This was the third snow penis he'd dismantled of

the season—the very *early* snow season, as the first squall had come through in late September. After the October tenth storm, they'd had snow cover ever since. The snow penises had started shortly after the blizzard. The first time had him laughing, and he'd left it up for a few hours. But it upset his neighbor on the other side of the duplex. It also made it tricky to get out the front door. So after taking a picture, he'd kicked it down and told his friend Arthur once he got to work, "Very funny, but stop upsetting Mrs. Michealson."

Arthur had only blinked at him. "What's funny?" So Paul showed him the picture on his phone, and Arthur laughed. "That's pretty good! But how'd you do it? The snow is way too fine to pack."

"I didn't. You think I'd put a penis on my own front steps?"

Arthur shrugged as if to say, *Why not?* He squinted at the photo. "Seriously, this is a work of art. It's almost a sculpture."

"Well, it's gone now." Paul frowned. "I thought for *sure* you'd put it there."

"Nope, sorry." Arthur passed Paul his phone. "Let's get to work on this bookshelf."

Paul had put the snow penis out of his head and focused on his job. Logan Design and Repair had only been open for eight months, and while they weren't about to go bankrupt, they worked like dogs to break even. Paul had gotten his electrician's license over the summer, and Arthur was working on plumbing. They didn't do anything big, but they could fuss with a water heater, a fritzing stove, a garbage disposal. Right now they were assembling custom bookshelves for the new pastor's study at the Lutheran church.

Paul did the books, which often kept him at the shop late. When that happened, dinner usually appeared, delivered by Frankie, Paul's other best friend's fiancé. Sometimes it was stew or something homemade, sometimes it was a hot beef sandwich from the café. Sometimes he got hauled off to Arthur's house to have dinner with the whole gang: Frankie and Marcus, Gabriel and Arthur. Hauled off was the only way they got him there, because Paul hated being the fifth wheel.

Though he was equally tired of being alone.

The day the first snow penis showed up they'd *tried* to get Paul to come to dinner once they were done ribbing him about his secret admirer, but Paul refused to go, opting to eat his dinner from home at the shop as he caught up on some paperwork.

Shortly after he settled in, his mother called.

"Paul. I'm glad I caught you." The clipped, irritated tone made it clear *glad* was a figure of speech and nothing more. "I heard about the incident on your porch. I hope you told Arthur it was in poor taste and I won't have to hear about this happening again."

Arthur's name dripped with disdain as it came out of her mouth. "Actually, I have no idea who did it."

His mother clucked her tongue. "What a scandal. Have you told the police?"

About a snow penis? Paul entertained himself for a minute with the idea of trying to file that report. "It's only a prank, I'm sure. Probably won't happen again."

"I certainly hope not." She paused, her tone promising she was about to segue into the real reason she'd called. "I wanted to know if you were coming to church this Sunday."

Oh, hell. Whenever Mary Jansen told her son she wanted to know if he was going to church, it was code for *I have someone I want you to meet.* And this someone would not, under any circumstances, be male.

Paul fumbled for a lie. "I'm due to go hunting with the guys this weekend."

"You've hardly been to service lately. What will Pastor think?"

"I went a few weeks ago, but I promise I'll go again soon."

"Let me know when, and I'll have your favorites for dinner after."

His favorites and an eligible young lady. "I will," Paul said. This was also a lie.

She'd ended their call shortly after that, but the exchange put Paul off finishing his supper and distracted him enough he mostly stared, frowning at the totals on the computer screen until it was just past midnight. Giving up, he headed home.

A new penis blocked his front door.

The second one had been something else. Not quite as tall, but it curved carefully to the right, and it had all the veins detailed like it was going to be used for an anatomy lesson. This one was uncircumcised, and the balls had hair—dried grass fused into the snow.

He took a picture of this one too, sending it to Marcus, Gabriel, Frankie, and Arthur as a group text. *Fess up. Which one of you is the artist?*

He had his money on Frankie, since he was the *stylist*, but either they were all practiced liars, or it wasn't any of them. They all replied laughing, insisting it wasn't them, dying to know who it actually was.

Paul had no idea.

He wracked his brain, crawling through his most recent hookups, but none of them fit the penis-sculpture bill. None of them lived in Logan, either, and while he did live on the edge of town, whoever was giving his front steps dick was putting in serious effort at weird hours in questionable weather. This had to be somebody local.

Everybody in town ribbed him about his snow sculptures. Some people, usually older women, clucked their tongues and seemed to blame him for disgracing the town, but most people thought it was funny. Someone had snagged a picture of the second one, and it wasn't uncommon for Paul to stand up from selecting a can from the bottom shelf at the grocery store to find someone grinning and showing him a Facebook photo of his front steps with a penis on it. Not knowing how exactly he was supposed to respond, Paul would chuckle or roll his eyes, basically *aw-shucks* his way out of the awkward.

His mother, of course, kept urging him to report the "indecency" to the authorities. His elderly neighbor hounded him with fears this meant they were about to see a home invasion. His sister, Sandy, sent him several Facebook messages explaining to him in self-righteous disdain how embarrassing the situation was to the family and how it was Paul's responsibility to keep it from escalating.

Paul wasn't sure what there was for him to do. He'd figured the first two for kids distracting themselves from the fact that they were getting full-on blizzards this early in the year. This third one, though, tipped him into annoyance.

The night following the third penis, after the little old lady behind the library checkout desk flashed him a snow-penis photo before she scanned his card, Paul complained to Gabriel, Logan's librarian and Arthur's fiancé. "Why just me?" he complained as Gabriel stood with him in the vestibule while Paul put on his coat. "It can't even be a gay thing. You and Arthur aren't getting it, and neither is Marcus or Frankie."

"We're too far out in the middle of nowhere. If anyone showed up on our lawn, Arthur would meet them with a shotgun." Gabriel rubbed his chin thoughtfully. "But yes, you're right, Marcus and Frankie should be fair game in their new house, if it's a gay thing. Though maybe they're afraid to target a lawyer who looks like a grizzly bear."

Paul sighed as he wrapped a scarf around his neck. "I thought about rigging up a video camera to catch them, but I don't have one. Plus it's so cold and snowy, it would probably fog over or plain not work."

Gabriel grimaced at the parking lot, which was a wasteland of snow and drifts. "It's ridiculous how early the snow came this year. Frankly I'm terrified of January at this rate. Everyone's worried, talking not about *if* we'll lose power, but *when* and *how often*. Your snow-penis adventures are almost comic relief."

"My neighbor doesn't find them funny."

Gabriel waved this idea away. "Edna Michealson loves to complain. Every time I run the Bookmobile, I have to mark out a half hour for her stop. Not to discuss books, but to listen to her itemization of the things she's angry about that day."

Paul didn't enjoy listening to his eighty-nine-year-old former fourth-grade teacher lecture him about *inappropriate snow organs*. "They were cute at first, but enough is enough."

Gabriel's lips twisted in a sly grin as he leaned into the wall beside the coat rack. "I'm having fun watching Arthur attempt to replicate them. He's finally figured out he needs to add water, but he doesn't have the ratio correct and either ends up with soup or crumbs. Yesterday he managed an obelisk, but it cracked in half when he tried to add a testicle."

Paul tugged his stocking cap into place, arranging it so the hole from the nail he'd caught it on wasn't over his ear. "My family is convinced it's Arthur."

"I know we've been teasing you about it, but maybe it's true. Maybe it's a secret admirer."

Paul snorted. If the snow-penis artist truly *was* an admirer…well, honestly, Paul wasn't sure what he thought of that. Why not message him on Grindr and ask to meet for coffee? Anybody whose idea of courtship was cock-blocking his front door…

Okay. It was a *little* cool. And even when the balls were glued on and he had to chisel them off the stoop, he laughed.

Paul waved goodbye to Gabriel and went home, stopping at the café to grab dinner. Unwrapping his hot beef sandwich, he sat in front of his television with the movies he'd checked out from the library.

It was admittedly too early, but Paul was already on his second round of Christmas movies. Gabriel had built up quite a collection, and there were enough new ones Paul had a lot of ground to cover before the actual holiday.

He loved the Hallmark and Lifetime movies. The first movie, *Christmas with Holly*, reminded Paul of the year he, Arthur, and Marcus had lived together at Arthur's cabin—that was the Christmas where Marcus and Frankie met, when Frankie got stranded in Logan. That holiday the four of them had become a family.

The second one, *Christmas Lodge*, wasn't as good. It was sweet and cute and had that squishy quality Paul favored, where all the problems evaporated and

Christmas was amazing. But it had a heavy Christian bent, and Paul couldn't sink into it the way he wanted. While nobody in the movie was overtly homophobic, Paul knew the movie producers would tell him he didn't deserve a gooey Christmas miracle because he was gay. He loved, though, the way the heroine found the perfect guy in the perfect place in the mountains. He knew real life wasn't like that, but he adored sinking into the soft feeling where things *did* work out, especially at Christmas.

He could use a good Christmas. He could use a perfect guy showing up on his front door with a wreath and a wry smile, ready to move into his life. It hadn't happened *exactly* that way for either Marcus or Arthur, but…well, it hadn't escaped Paul's notice that the last two years were like they'd taken turns getting Mr. Right for Christmas.

Three years, and three of them. *The three bears,* Frankie teased them. That made Paul baby bear, he supposed, which was fine. But he'd been trying to find his Goldilocks all year long, and he'd pretty much dated or bedded every gay man in the county and then some. Unless someone else got stranded during a blizzard, he couldn't see how he'd be getting a happily-every-after for Christmas.

He checked his Grindr in case he could hunt down a different kind of happy ending, but there was only the usual nudge from PrinceCharming1990. Paul had no idea who the guy was, or even *where* he was—he had his location turned off. Wherever Prince Charming lived, he had some kinky ideas of what he wanted to do with Paul, and he was damn persistent about them.

Tonight PrinceCharming1990 played it coy. *Let's play in the snow.*

Paul ignored the request to play in the snow the same as he had all the other not-really-veiled innuendos.

1990. That was probably the guy's birth year. Paul would turn thirty-nine in June. When Prince Charming had been born, Paul was entering high school. That was just…no. The thought alone made him feel like a child molester. Even if this particular child could curl his toes with some of his sexual suggestions.

Prince Charming wasn't on a sex app and wasn't crafting snow organs on his doorstep. Paul put ice penises and Grindr out of his mind and one of the disks from the ten-pack of holiday romances into the player.

He'd been looking forward to this DVD set ever since Gabriel had ordered it for him, and he'd saved it for last in his current checkout binge only because the other two were due the next day. He had every intention of watching at least two of the ten movies, but he'd gotten up too early, and he fell asleep five minutes into the first one. One minute the first movie was starting, and then he opened his eyes and found himself staring at the silent home-menu screen.

Listening to the *scritch, scritch, scritch* of something on his front porch.

Paul sat up slowly, blinking at the door. It sounded like a raccoon. Or a bear.

Swish, swish, swish. Scritch, scritch, scritch.

Scrape. Shuffle. Scrape.

That wasn't a bear. That was somebody on his front porch.

That was somebody *assembling a snow penis* on his front porch.

He scooted to the edge of the couch, checking the urge to rush to the door. If he made too much noise, whoever it was might run off. If he tiptoed to the door, he could pull it open and catch them by surprise. Halfway to the door, though, it occurred to him he should maybe have a weapon. Nothing lethal, but…well, if it *wasn't* a couple of kids, he should be ready.

He didn't have a baseball bat, though. He had his hunting rifles in the closet, but those were hardly appropriate. He also didn't have a lot of time. A peek through the curtain revealed the penis was nearly assembled.

One guy. Not a kid, and not a bruiser. All Paul could make out was a dark-colored parka and a knit hat with earflaps. The pants were different. Kind of like the things they wore in hospitals. What did you call them? Scrubs. Something about them rang a bell, but he couldn't figure out why.

In the end, he went without a weapon. Whoever this was, Paul could take him, though he doubted it would come to that. Drawing a deep breath, he steeled himself for God only knew what and put his hand on the doorknob.

He managed to flip the light switch *after* he yanked, which meant as the dim bulb illuminated the porch steps, he got a good look not only at a seriously articulated frenulum but the face of a bright, blue-eyed young man, cheeks pink from cold.

Paul stared. "Kyle? Kyle Parks?"

Kyle's lips closed, pressing into a thin line. Then, bold as you please, he lifted an eyebrow, and his sly smile made Paul shiver in a way that had nothing to do with cold.

Blowing Paul a kiss, Kyle stepped off the porch and into the night, leaving Paul to stare at the snow penis, which he saw now came with a piece of printed card stock hanging by yarn cemented into the sculpture.

The card read, *Let's play in the snow.*

Paul lifted his gaze to the intricately crafted penis, seven feet tall, flared glans gleaming like an icy jewel in the porch light. He thought about Kyle Parks, the nice night nurse standing out here on his porch, carving the penis, shaping all those veins.

Sending him all those PrinceCharming1990 Grindr texts.

Kyle. Little Kyle. Offering to lick his…

Paul shut his eyes, but he still saw the wicked smile from Kyle mixed in with PrinceCharming1990's naughty suggestions.

Letting his breath out in a ragged huff, he opened his eyes and yanked the card off the penis. He kicked the sculpture over, not taking a photo, not lingering to watch it crumble in his haste to get inside and flip off the light.

But he lay in bed for hours, staring up at the ceiling, so far from sleep he wasn't sure he'd ever get there again.

That couldn't have happened. Of all the people who might have mounted a snow penis on his porch…

Let's play in the snow.

To his shame, Paul got a little hard.

He buried his face in his pillow, groaning into the stuffing. He couldn't act on this. He needed to block PrinceCharming1990 *right now.*

He didn't, though. He lay in bed until the wee hours of the morning, the cheesy Christmas movies mingling with Kyle Parks's wicked smile, until they tangled together and he dreamed of sweet Kyle standing outside a picturesque log cabin, smiling and welcoming Paul home.

Flanked by an army of well-endowed snow penises.

EVERYONE IN LOGAN thought they knew who Kyle Parks was. Everyone in Logan was wrong.

The problem of growing up in a town of less than one thousand was people couldn't seem to let go of your youth. They remembered Kyle selling Boy Scout popcorn or sitting in their Sunday school class or wetting his pants in their backyard when he wasn't quite potty-trained, and somehow all those memories meant they couldn't accept he *wasn't* that kid anymore. In their heads, he was still the leggy little boy with a bad haircut. And everybody, *everybody* still talked about how he'd had such a habit of tottering around in his mother's makeup and heels. *Shouldn't that have been our first clue?* Except even there he wasn't a gay *man*. He was a gay *kid*.

It didn't help, Kyle knew, that he *looked* like a kid. Not only did he get carded everywhere he went, but more often than not people argued with him. *You can't be twenty-five.* Out of town they talked about his baby face, but in Logan the people who'd known him since he was little insisted he still *was* little. The general consensus was he might, possibly, be almost twenty, but that was as far as they'd go. The State of Minnesota's decree on his license that he'd been born in 1990 had to be a mistake. Someday Kyle supposed he'd be grateful for his youthful looks, but right now, he'd give anything for a few gray hairs. Or the ability to grow more than peach fuzz for a beard. Or a hometown where people were willing to believe he wasn't Peter Pan.

As he drove away from Paul Jansen's duplex, heart beating too fast, memory of Paul's shocked, slightly horrified face burned into his brain, Kyle hated his youthful appearance more than he ever had.

In his head, making the snow sculptures combined with Grindr taunts had been the perfect flirtation. It was true, he couldn't get Paul to give him so much as a second glance in person, but he'd assumed that was the whole *you're too young* thing again. Possibly the *I only date big, hairy bears* thing, though he'd seen Paul with a few svelte men. Kyle had already tried to alter his own type—for a week he ate nothing but fatty food and drank whole milk, but he ended up losing weight because he got sick from all the junk. In the end, he'd reasoned all he had to do was get Paul to see him as a fun, sexual object. And available. And willing. Ergo, Grindr. Except Paul had at best nibbled on his lures.

The first snow penis had been a lark, but he'd gotten more mileage out of that than a pile of dirty direct messages, so he figured what the hell—lather, rinse, repeat. If he'd thought Paul would catch him in the act, he would have dressed for the occasion, or worn something he could have *un*dressed in more quickly. Though from the look on Paul's face, it wouldn't have mattered. Dammit.

The drive between Paul's house and his own home was brief, but no one else was awake at this ungodly hour, so Kyle was able to continue scowling to himself as he put away his coat and pulled material out of the refrigerator to make a sandwich. In deference to his shitty mood, he added an Angry Orchard cider. Putting the whole business on a tray, he shuffled around the corner to his room.

As he ate, he wondered, not for the first time, if it would help if he got his own place. It was possible Paul would reject him at any age and in any locale—which hurt—but…well, Kyle was willing to try anything.

He finished off his sandwich quickly but nursed his cider as he poked around the internet, turning the volume down as he indulged in some shameless porn-clip surfing. Since he was cranky, he didn't go for his favorites but instead fed his bad mood by searching for his kink in free two-to-six-minute teasers.

Because even in his porn he was "too young". He'd bet his ass none of the guys in the bear-twink sections were twenty-five, and Christ, if he was dumb enough to go to the daddy-kink section, he got alarmingly young boys and men who reminded him of his grandfather. Which, he wasn't casting any stones. But could a guy get a thin, handsome young man with a cute, cuddly bear who was either his own age or only a *little* bit older?

He knew better than to hope he'd stumble on the twink doing the bear. Oh, those videos existed, and you can bet your ass he had them bookmarked. But when he was in a mood like this…well, he didn't know *why* all he wanted to do was drive home how impossible he was, but it's what he reached for. In case he had some idea his problem was because he lived in a teeny-tiny town in the middle of nowhere. No way. He was a freak in every direction. Long, narrow feet. Skinny body and long legs. Baby face. Feminine mannerisms.

Nellie bottom tattooed on his forehead against his will.

He had a nice haircut, and an excellent dye job, since Frankie Blackburn had moved to town and opened up a hair salon. Other than that, everything was miserable, and he might as well have a second cider.

He didn't, because at this point it was six in the morning, and his mother was almost up. It didn't matter how many times he told her it was *different* to drink in the morning when you'd been up all damn night, she still clucked and fussed. Which he supposed was another argument to move into his own place.

I'll scan the ads tomorrow, he told himself as he climbed under his covers and drifted off to sleep.

His dreams were a fucked-up mash of porn, Paul, and work. Which got weird when his brief foray into medical porn clips inspired dreams of Kyle giving a naked Paul a prostate exam in a nursing home bed. Had he been awake, he'd have shut his imagination down, but as it was, he woke hard and came in the shower with the *very* pretty image of naked Paul Jansen on all fours, begging for Kyle's cock.

His mother was in the kitchen as he came out, cooking pork chops for lunch, and she smiled and murmured, *"Good morning,"* to Kyle as he emerged. A country station played in the background, and Daryl Parks sat at the table, reading the paper. Kyle's brothers sat across from each other, scanning through mobile phones. At the smaller table by the sliding door, three of Kyle's nieces and nephews fought over who had more chicken nuggets and tried to spill each other's milk.

Kyle peeked around the corner to the dining room and the TV room beyond before frowning at his mother. "Where's Linda Kay?"

"I don't know." Jane Parks's tone was heavy singsong, her eyes wide as she nodded toward the cupboard.

Kyle made a big show of scratching his chin and frowning. "Oh, no. Do you think she moved out?"

"It's difficult to say." Jane's voice played along, but she returned her focus to lunch preparations.

"That would be a shame. It snowed again last night, and I was going to make a new fort. A big one." He sighed dramatically. "I suppose I'll just make a small one for the kids."

The door to the pantry opened as two hundred pounds of beaming, gleeful woman emerged. Linda Kay enveloped Kyle first in a wide smile with her tongue protruding past her lips before wrapping arms around him and squeezing him. "I got you, little brother."

Kyle hugged her back as best he could, and his smile, if not as beautiful and pure as hers, was heartfelt. "You got me all right. Does this mean you'll make a snow fort with me?"

Linda Kay squinted her eyes shut tight and shook her head hard enough to flap her brown hair into his face. "*No.* I want to make a *dragon.* Breathing *fire.*"

"A fire-breathing dragon?" Kyle repeated, his brain already running ahead of him with the possibilities.

"That fire will be made out of snow, not the propane tank," Jane remarked dryly from the stove.

Damn. Kyle grimaced at Linda Kay. "Our mother is *no fun*."

Linda Kay got a wicked look in her eye as she leaned in and whispered loudly in Kyle's ear, "I'll sneak it out of the garage."

"You will *not*, Linda Kay."

When Linda Kay pouted, Kyle kissed her cheek. "We'll find a way to make it cool. Let me get something to eat and a cup of coffee, and it's on."

Linda Kay followed Kyle around the kitchen as he made himself a pod of decaf in the Keurig, and when he leaned on his mother's left shoulder to peer at his breakfast/lunch, his sister took up a similar position on the right side.

Jane sighed. "You *two*. Can't you wait ten more minutes?"

"We're *hungry*." Linda tried to pinch off a corner of a pork chop only to laugh as Jane swatted her away.

This was because after twenty-five years as Kyle's twin, she knew the drill. While she made her feint, Kyle stole a piece of bacon from the plate by the stove. He took a bite before surreptitiously passing Linda Kay the rest behind Jane's back. As his sister scuttled off with a wicked chuckle, Kyle leaned on the counter and sipped his coffee while he chatted with his mother.

"Do you work tonight?" she asked him. "I know the schedule has been a mess lately, and I've lost track of your rotation."

He nodded. "The late-late shift. Eleven-to-seven. But tomorrow I have off, because I'm day shifts over the weekend."

Jane clucked in disapproval. "It's not healthy for you to work such irregular hours. It's bad enough with all those overnights."

"Somebody has to work them. Though, there's good news." He grinned as he set his coffee aside. "I hear Dolorianne is thinking of retiring."

Jane nearly dropped her spatula in joy. "Oh—does that mean you could take her shift? The regular days-only one?"

Kyle rolled his eyes. "God, I wish. No, this would mean I could have the three-to-eleven one if I wanted it."

She frowned. "But, Kyle, you can't *possibly* go back to school with those hours."

Not this again. "Mom, I don't *want* to be a registered nurse. I'm fine with being an LPN."

"But you'd have so many more career opportunities as an RN, and you'd make more money."

Kyle didn't want to have this argument for the eightieth time, so he changed the subject. "How was your circle meeting yesterday?"

She brightened. "Oh—it was wonderful. The Ruth Circle *and* the Hope Circle met at the church, and the library board came over too, even Mr. Higgins. The fundraiser is on for sure."

"So more sleigh rides with Santa and dancing after?"

"No, this year there will be more. A craft fair, an ice-skating rink, and all the local businesses will have open houses. *And.*" She elbowed him and waggled her eyebrows. "I told them you'd make snow sculptures."

"*Mom.*"

"Don't complain. You love doing it, and Linda Kay will get such a kick out of helping."

"They're something special I do with her." *And until I got caught, on Paul's front steps.* Kyle glowered into his coffee. "Am I going to get paid, at least?"

She swatted him hard enough to make him yelp. "Kyle David Parks! Of course you won't get paid. All the funds go to the *library.*" She aimed a wooden spoon at his nose. "And when you stop by to talk to Gabriel Higgins about what kind of sculptures, don't you dare bring up money."

Kyle held up his hands in self-defense. "I swear I won't."

Mollified, she added some cheese to the eggs she fixed for Kyle because she insisted people needed eggs for breakfast, whenever it happened. "It's going to be something special. There will be charter buses from the Cities and Duluth, a Santa village, and reindeer. They even have a theme this time. Winter Wonderland."

That wasn't a theme so much as a cute, generic title, but Kyle wasn't going to argue. "Sounds great. I'll stop by the library tomorrow, see if Linda Kay wants to go along."

"If it snows the way it's supposed to, that will work out nicely. She has designs on going to Eveleth to see Kenny, and she'll be upset if the weather cancels her plans."

"Okay." Kyle pushed off the counter to get plates and glasses for the table, but his mother caught the edge of his T-shirt and held him in place.

"I also heard at the meeting there was another *sculpture* on Paul Jansen's front porch this morning."

Kyle grimaced, his black mood returning with a vengeance. "Yeah, well, it'll be the last one."

"I should hope so. He's too old for you."

"He's thirty-eight, not seventy. Besides, our age difference is only three years more than the one between you and Dad."

Jane pursed her lips and became focused on over-seasoning Kyle's eggs. "I don't understand why you can't date someone your age, is all I'm saying."

"Because the men my age are idiots. Also, there are five of them on my team in the whole county." He pushed his toe into the loose section of a floor tile. "It doesn't matter. He's not interested. Nobody's interested."

She hesitated. "I bet there are more gay men your age in Duluth." When Kyle gave her a hurt look, she kissed his cheek. "Don't pout. I'm not telling you to move out. I'm trying to help you be *happy*."

"I want to be happy *here*. If I move out, it will be to an apartment downtown."

Linda Kay stuck her head around the corner where she'd been eavesdropping, her face a picture of betrayal. "You can't move out!"

"I'm not moving out." Kyle pulled out a stack of plates and passed them to her. "I'm setting the table, and you're helping."

She grumbled, but she helped all the same. When they sat down to eat, she leaned in close and whispered, "How did the snow penis go?"

He shook his head. "Busted. And he didn't like it."

Linda Kay flipped her wrist in a dramatic throwaway gesture. "Please. No taste."

Grinning, Kyle leaned over and kissed her hair. "I love you, Linda Kay."

"That's because I'm awesome." She stole a piece of his bacon and winked in her delightfully clumsy way. "We'll give our snow dragon a *big* penis."

"Mom would have a fit."

She gave him a *please, don't be stupid* look. "So we *hide it*, obviously."

She held up her hand for a high-five. Kyle gave her one, then ate his eggs, his black mood getting buried under plans for an elaborate, ice-breathing dragon with a hidden dong.

Chapter Two

THE MORNING AFTER he discovered the snow-penis artist, Paul stumbled into the shop groggy and clutching a mug of convenience-store coffee. When Arthur made a snide remark about how rough he looked, Paul almost literally snarled at him.

"Whoa." Arthur put down the chair clamp he was holding and turned to face Paul. "What's going on with you?"

Paul had left the house with every intention of keeping quiet, but all it took was for Arthur to give him *that look*, the concerned, *let me take care of you* one, and Paul folded. "I caught the person making the sculptures. Gabriel was right. It was an admirer."

"I was what now?" Gabriel emerged from the shop office holding a ceramic mug with a tea-bag tag draped over the edge. He had the studied casualness and rumpled appearance of someone who didn't want anyone to know he'd been recently well-fucked over a desk.

Paul put his travel mug aside and sat on a stool, defeat crawling over his skin. "You were right. The person leaving snow cocks on my steps was trying to get my attention. He's been sending me Grindr messages too. Last night I met him."

"And? Who is it?"

Arthur slipped an arm around Gabriel's waist as he asked this. Gabriel leaned into the embrace with the same unconscious attraction. The sight of them so settled together made Paul happy and ache all at once, especially in light of his current nightmare.

Paul grimaced as he ground out his confession. "It's Kyle."

Arthur frowned. "Kyle who?"

"Kyle Parks. Daryl's youngest."

Arthur's eyes bugged practically out of his head. "*Kyle Parks?* Holy shit."

Gabriel frowned. "I'm sorry, what am I missing here? Why are you two acting like this is the end of the world? Is he an ex or something?"

Arthur turned to Gabriel, horrified. "Of course he's not Paul's ex. He's a *baby*. Christ, is he even out of high school?"

Gabriel swatted Arthur. "Stop being dramatic. Yes, he's a little younger than you two, but so am I. So is Frankie."

"Yes, but he's what, *nineteen?*"

"I sincerely doubt it." Gabriel pulled out his phone and punched at some apps. "Facebook says he's twenty-five."

"There's no way Kyle Parks is that old," Arthur insisted.

Paul had been about to point out the PrinceCharming1990 handle as evidence, then realized that *was* twenty-five years ago. Which made him feel older than ever. He rubbed at his neck. "Even if he is, he's still pretty young."

Gabriel arched an eyebrow. "I'm thirty-two. Frankie is thirty. What's magic about the six years between us and Kyle? Especially since of the three of you, Paul is the youngest."

This whole conversation was freaking Paul out. He threw up his hands. "I'm *not* thinking about Kyle Parks that way, no matter how old he is."

Gabriel tipped his head to the side. "What's so horrible about him?"

Paul fished for another excuse. "He's not my type."

Arthur kept glowering. "There's seriously no way he's twenty-five."

"What's your type?" Gabriel pressed.

The hell if Paul could figure that out. "When he was born, I was in high school."

"When I was born, Arthur was in third grade. None of us are in school now."

"He *looks* young. Too young for me." Except every time Paul remembered the wicked smile on Kyle's lips, he fogged over. That confidence. His brightness, so stunning and yummy and—"He…he…he's too femmy."

Even before Arthur winced, Paul realized it had been the wrong thing to say. Gabriel rose to his not-inconsiderable height and glared at Paul through his glasses. "*Too femmy.* Goodness. I didn't realize you had a butch test, Paul."

"I didn't mean it like that." Paul slouched forward and rested his elbows on his knees so he could cradle his head in his hands. "I'm grabbing at excuses because the bottom line is thinking of Kyle Parks sexually freaks me out. And he's sending me sex messages and mounting erections on my porch."

"Then be an adult and tell him thank you but no thank you." Gabriel scooped up his mug and went back to the office.

Rising from the stool, Paul downed a scalding swallow of coffee and shuffled over to the workbench.

Arthur clapped a hand on Paul's shoulder. "For what it's worth, I'm freaked out, and he's not even hitting on me."

"He really isn't my type." His cheeks colored as he stared at the worktop. "I mean, what, two bottoms?"

"You gotta go with your instinct. Just because you're the last two gay men in Logan doesn't mean you gotta be dance partners. There are other towns." Arthur winked. "We'll find you somebody. Don't you worry."

Don't you worry.

Why that stuck in Paul's craw so hard, he couldn't

say, but it did. Probably because they'd been saying it to him for a year. Probably because they acted like there was some secret barrel of gay men they could crack open. Paul knew better.

It wasn't fair. The others were paired up, and not a *one* of them had been looking when they met their Mister Right. In fact they'd all been disengaged from romance. If Paul thought for one minute not searching was the magic bullet, he'd do it. Frankly he hadn't tried to date at all lately.

Except the Christmas magic hadn't held for him, because he hadn't found anyone. And he still wanted. He *always* wanted.

It was dark when he drove home, and it was snowing again. Big, fat flakes whose crystal shape he could identify on the windshield before the defroster made them melt away. He told himself he was driving through town instead of heading home because he wanted to stop at the store, but he didn't stop. He didn't pull in at the muni, either. He drove all the way to the north end of Logan, where the care center sat like a snug oasis amidst the trees.

He knew, intellectually, he couldn't see Kyle because of the way the rooms were set up and the blinds pulled against the draft, but Paul sat there all the same. To put the more usual image of Kyle in his mind, not the one where Kyle looked wicked.

But Kyle wasn't visible. He might not even be at work at all.

Paul drove home. He put his truck in the garage, but he hadn't shut the door before Edna Michealson stuck her head out the back door of her side of the duplex.

"Paul?" She huddled into her housecoat as she wrinkled her nose at him. "Thank heavens. I thought you'd never come home. The walks are a mess. I nearly killed myself trying to get the mail."

The walks weren't that bad, though she was right, they needed doing. Technically he was only responsible for his side of the property, but whoever Edna's son had hired to take care of her side was falling down pretty heavily on the job.

Paul grabbed the shovel and the ice pick he kept in the garage. "I'll take care of it right away, Mrs. Michealson."

She wrapped her housecoat tighter and lifted her chin, acknowledging he was doing his duty but reserving the right to tell him he was doing it badly. "You shouldn't leave it until dark. You can't see the ice as well."

Normally Paul was able to let her barbs roll off his back, but tonight it was hard work not to take her personally. "I'll check it again in the morning, if that makes you feel better. I'll put some sand down too, and salt, if the air temperature warms up enough for it to work."

She didn't smile, only kept watching him work. When he came close to her landing, however, he saw the shame mixing with her indignation. "I'll call Hans tomorrow and tell him he needs to find someone better to do my walk. I'm sorry it keeps falling to you."

Funny, a little acknowledgment was all Paul had wanted, but now he felt sorry for her and nothing else. He leaned on the ice pick a bit, resting from his exertion. "Don't worry about it. I can pinch-hit until you find someone better. I don't mind helping, but my hours aren't always the best."

Edna averted her gaze. "Thank you. That's very kind of you."

"Not at all. Just being a good neighbor." Paul saw her shiver and frowned. "I think you should head inside. Wouldn't want you to come down with a cold. Don't worry about this. I'll take care of it."

With another "Thank you", she disappeared into the house. He shoveled her walk and his own. Once he escaped inside too, he pulled a frozen meal out of the freezer and punched the appropriate time into the microwave. He queued up the holiday romance he'd fallen asleep to the night before.

The movie, much like the microwave meal, wasn't great. But they both did their part to carve away the ache in his gut. That, he told himself as he went to bed, was better than a poke in the eye.

There wasn't a snow sculpture on his front steps the next morning. Which should have been a relief. Except mostly it made him wish he could put in another movie instead of going in to work.

AS PREDICTED, LINDA Kay was upset she couldn't go to Eveleth. Eventually she decided going to the library with Kyle was an acceptable substitute, but not until he tossed in lunch too.

"I wanted to see my boyfriend," she complained as Kyle drove them at a snail's pace through the blowing snow.

Kyle kept his focus on the road. The plow had been through, and he didn't have far to go, but he wasn't taking any chances on putting his car in the ditch, especially with Linda Kay along. "Hey, at least you have one."

She sighed heavily. "Are you giving up on Mister No-Fun?"

"He looked pretty unhappy to see it was *me* flirting with him, so yeah. I'm out."

"He's an idiot. You're the best guy he could find in the whole state. You're funny, smart, and handsome, and you're nice. What's he so picky for?"

Kyle bit back a retort that she should ask Paul. Linda Kay would take him literally and march over to the repair shop to do it the second she got out of the car. "Hard to say." He ruffled his hair with his hand. "Maybe I shouldn't have dyed my hair."

"If he doesn't like you because of your hair, he's a bigger jerk."

Ironically, Kyle had chosen ginger because Paul's most famous ex was a legitimate redhead. Though maybe that reminder only made things worse.

The library was busy, which at first surprised Kyle, but what else was there to do in a snowstorm in a small town? Most people were checking out movies, but plenty of families with children were in the play area, drifting there from what looked like a story time finishing up. Kyle loitered amidst Gabriel Higgins's throng of adoring fans, waiting for the crush to subside, but when the librarian saw Kyle, he smiled, waved, and extricated himself.

"Thanks for stopping by. Let's go to my office."

The din of the main library area dulled as the door closed them into the small space. Kyle sat in the chair with its back to the door as Gabriel indicated. "Mom said you wanted some help with snow sculptures for the fundraiser?"

Gabriel waved this idea away as he sat. "Oh, if it happens to snow and you feel you have the time, yes, certainly. As I said to Corrina over and over, the library doesn't *need* a fundraiser, but I agree the event gives a shine to the town and possibly a boost to the economy. I'd love to have your help with design, if you're willing to give it. Arthur and Paul can build anything our library board and city council dream up, but they won't be much for making it pretty. I heard you were something of an artist in high school, so I was hoping you'd be willing to reprise that role." His lips quirked. "And if we *do* get snow, we already know you have talent in the snow-sculpture department. Though perhaps we'll keep them G-rated in deference to the younger attendees."

Kyle grimaced. "He told you."

"He did." Gabriel leaned back in his chair and crossed his legs. "But why are you looking like that? Surely you're not giving up."

Gabriel was on his side? "Easy for you to say. You didn't see his face when he caught me."

"Oh, he's not horrified of *you*. But he—and Arthur, oddly enough—is obsessed with this idea that you're too young."

"I'm so sick of everyone thinking I'm some infant. I can't believe Paul thinks so too. I shouldn't be surprised, but it doesn't stop me from being disappointed."

"So it's not simply a lark? You have feelings for him?"

Kyle squirmed in his seat, but Gabriel showed no sign of letting him worm out of this inquisition. "What if I did? You have some *other* objection, if it's not my age?"

"I have no objections whatsoever—unless this is simply a game to you. Paul is looking for a partner. A serious partner." Gabriel sighed. "And though I know it's not the truth, I always feel as if I took his fallback plan away from him. So let's put it this way. If you were laying Grindr bait and planting penises on his front porch because you were bored and snaring Logan's last bachelor seemed like a good time, then please consider this excitement concluded. If there's something more to it than that…" his smile practically glinted, "…then

I'd be happy to help you plot round two of your campaign."

Kyle's eyes went wide. "You'd help me? Seriously? Why?"

"Because I've seen you with your sister. I know you'll say, *but she's my twin, of course I'll take care of her*, but it's not every twenty-five-year-old man who would devote so much time and attention to a young woman with Down syndrome. In public you give off an air of flirtation, devilishness—which doesn't help your age issue, I will say—but underneath you're kindhearted and loyal. When you interact with Linda Kay, you're another person entirely. An amazing one. Of course I want that for Paul. But first I want to know *why*. Partly because I'm curious, but also because your answer will help me figure out how to help you."

Kyle stared at the edge of the librarian's desk as he finished his confession. "Well, obviously I don't *know* we'd get on. But I've always felt like we could. It started out…okay, this doesn't help the age thing either, but when I was in middle school, I'd see him…and he was so perfect. He smiled at me one day, helped me when I'd fallen on my ass on some ice, and my type was set. I always wanted big blond guys with slightly curly hair. I chased Paul clones all the way through community college when I lived in Duluth. Then I came back and settled in, and…"

Kyle glanced up at Gabriel. "You aren't the only one who noticed Paul wanted a real relationship. *I* knew Arthur was wrong for him, so I bided my time. I kept trying to catch the eye of Marcus or Arthur, thinking it might make him jealous or at least *see* me, but that was a bust. When he and Arthur broke up and Arthur got hung up on *you*…well, I thought, it's now or never. But I still couldn't ever get him to so much as notice me. So I tried seducing him online. A few times we sexted, but that was about it. I never had the courage to tell him who I was. Then one day on the way home from work it had snowed, and I had this crazy urge to put a penis on his porch. I don't know why or what I thought it would do, but it got me more traction than anything else, so I kept it up. I thought maybe I'd lure him in slowly, then do a big reveal—but he caught me. And *recoiled*."

"Not from *you*. From the *idea* of you."

Kyle huffed. "How is that better?"

"Because you can still show him who you are. The real you, not the kid he imagines you still are—or the mincing fop you present."

Kyle drew up short. "I'm not a *fop*."

"I know. Stop acting all affected in front of him, so he can see it too."

Kyle blinked. "I don't act affected."

Gabriel flipped a limp wrist and adopted a lisp. "*Darling*, every time I see you in public, you act like Carson Kressley." When Kyle frowned in confusion, Gabriel rolled his eyes. "*Queer Eye for the Straight Guy*. Look it up on YouTube."

Kyle knew *Queer Eye,* vaguely. Carson must be the blond one who was a walking gay stereotype. "I'm not that bad. I just…play it up a bit because the act makes things easier. People expect it. It's like a wall."

"Yes. Tear it down for Paul."

The very thought made Kyle's stomach lurch. He wrapped his arms over it, slouching. "And be what? Don't you dare say *yourself.*"

"Well, what is it you want him to be interested in?"

Kyle hunched more. "I was basically me when he caught me making the penis. He's not interested, whatever I am."

A silence expanded between them. Gabriel tapped his finger on his desk as he pondered something. "I'll admit I don't have an idea of how to help, exactly. Or rather, I have *one* idea. But I warn you. There's no putting this gun back on the rack. And when I say gun, I mean siege weapon."

Kyle raised his eyebrows. "Siege weapon?"

Gabriel's eyebrows waggled. "How well do you know Arthur's mother?"

Chapter Three

P AUL WAS ON his back, head cocked sideways as he put a screw in the underside of a shitty prefab desk, when the bell over the door of the shop opened. Swallowing a curse because he'd almost had the damn thing finished, he smiled at the pressed wood so his tone wouldn't sound pissed. "Be right with you."

"Oh, don't bother, sweetheart. Take your time, we'll wait."

That was Corrina Anderson's voice. Arthur's lovely but managing mother. With a *we*. Paul set the drill and screw aside and shimmied out from beneath the desk. "How can I help—?"

The words died on his lips.

Kyle, to his credit, looked uncomfortable. He smiled weakly at Paul before averting his gaze to land on anything but the man in front of him. Corrina, either oblivious or uninterested in this, carried on in her breezy, bossy way.

"I have the most wonderful news. Jane Parks talked

Kyle into helping us with the Winter Wonderland project. He's such an amazing artist—he can *paint* those lovely Scandinavian folk-art decorations instead of stenciling them."

Kyle held up a hand. "Actually, they still need to be stenciled. But I can design the stencils, yes."

Corrina beamed. "See? This is why we need a *real* artist on the team. And since you're in charge of building, Paul, I wanted the two of you to get together as soon as possible to lay out your plans."

Paul panicked. "Building? When did I get put in charge of that?" *I can't get together with Kyle.*

"Oh, darling, you've always been. Did Arthur not tell you?" She shook her head as if to say, *Isn't that just like my son.*

"Corrina, I'd love to help, but we're slammed with orders, what with Christmas—"

"But don't you see? That's why Kyle is here." She patted them both on the shoulder, beaming proudly. "I've already given Kyle your phone number, so you can set a time to get together and discuss. I thought maybe something at the café. Oh—Kyle, sweetheart, send a quick text to Paul so he has *your* number."

Kyle pulled out his phone and obediently texted. Paul felt his own phone buzz in his pocket.

"*Wonderful.*" Corrina rubbed her hands together. "Well, I have some shopping to do before the grocery store runs out of everything. You two make your plans. But, Paul, don't keep Kyle too long. He has his sister over at the library to think about."

Waving over her shoulder, Corrina pulled the hood of her coat over her head and bustled out the door. Leaving Kyle and Paul to stare at each other. Awkwardly.

Kyle broke the silence with a heavy sigh. "Sorry. If I'd have known where she was dragging me, I'd have made an excuse to stay away."

Paul blinked. He would have? "Oh—it's okay. I know how Corrina gets."

Kyle's blush was pretty on him, which Paul had never noticed before, so why he'd started now was anybody's guess. "It's just that I hadn't worked out how to apologize to you yet. For...everything."

He was apologizing? Paul frowned. "It's okay," he said automatically, not exactly sure what he was offering reassurance about. It *wasn't* okay for Kyle to sext him and leave penises on his porch. It confused him, though, that Kyle felt bad about it.

"No, it's not." Kyle squared his shoulders and stood straight, looking for everything like a schoolboy taking his lumps. Except...no. For once Kyle *didn't* seem boyish. "If we're going to work together, I don't want any awkwardness between us. I apologize for being so pushy and inappropriate when I knew you weren't interested. I took advantage of you, and I'm very sorry."

Took...advantage? Pushy? Well—yes, but... "It's not that I'm not interested, but you're too young for me—"

Kyle held up a hand. "Please. It's fine. You don't have to make excuses. I'm a big boy. I can handle a guy not being into me."

"But it's not that at all, it's just—"

Kyle lowered all his fingers but one, aiming his pointer at Paul. And winking.

Paul felt a funny hitch inside.

Kyle held up both hands, smiling sadly. "It's fine. If you aren't too upset with me, nothing more needs to be said, and I promise it won't happen again."

Paul felt dizzy and off-kilter. "I'm not upset at all, but I don't want you to think…" Paul didn't know how to finish his sentence.

Kyle had his phone out, swiping through his smartphone screens. "I apologize in advance for my schedule. Lots of night shifts. The best time for me would be Tuesday evening, but if you have plans, I can certainly find another window."

No, Paul had no damn plans. "Tuesday's fine."

"Great. Would seven be okay? A little late for dinner, I'm sorry, but I don't get off until six."

"It's fine." He felt like all he said to Kyle is *fine* and *it's okay.*

"In my calendar now. Where did you want to meet? The café, as Corrina suggested?"

That seemed safe and neutral, and it was public. "Sure."

Kyle put his phone away and pulled his gloves from

his pockets. "Wonderful. I can do most of the stencil cutouts at home, and at that point anybody could finish things off. Or I could come when you're not working."

Now Paul felt like an ass. "It's not a big deal."

Kyle was embarrassed and reluctant and…cute. Which Paul needed to stop noticing. "Thanks. That's…kind of you."

Despite his panic over whatever switch had been flipped making Kyle inappropriately attractive, Paul couldn't stand how awkward Kyle felt. "Honestly, it's not. The sculptures were amazing. And the—" *He* blushed as he stopped himself from saying the sexting had been hot. "It's fine. It's okay. I mean it."

Now Kyle's eyes sparkled, a secret, knowing manner that made him seem like the kind of guy who would send Paul texts detailing how he'd blow him until he couldn't stand. A smile left Paul slightly hard and sent all his admonitions to not think Kyle was cute right out of his head. This wasn't cute. This was…hot.

It wasn't possible that campy Kyle Parks was hot, but fuck, he sure was.

Kyle saluted and winked. "See you Tuesday." He left.

Flustered and confused, Paul pulled out his phone. Saw he had a new text from an unknown number. It was an Emoji—one of those picture things Frankie sometimes texted with. A little snowman.

Why the fuck that got Paul the rest of the way hard, he couldn't even remotely begin to explain.

CORRINA APPEARED FROM beneath the overhang of the empty building beside Logan Design and Repair as soon as Kyle cleared the line of sight of the front door. She grinned at him like he'd escaped with a bag of money. "So. It went well, don't you think?"

Kyle wasn't sure. He rubbed at the back of his mitten as he glanced over his shoulder at the building. "It felt weird. Basically, I lied."

"Oh, *pish*. Paul's a bit of work, is all. You're not lying. You're laying pipe." She took his arm and leaned in conspiratorially as they shuffled through the snow toward the library. "Now it's time for phase two."

Kyle still couldn't get over how military this campaign was. "*Gleaning intelligence,* right? I'm still not sure what you mean."

"It means you need to take a crash course in Paul Jansen. Learn his likes and dislikes."

That was hard to argue with, especially since Kyle's usual tactic of *wear something nice and flirt* wasn't getting him anywhere. Except he almost thought Paul was interested, especially there at the end. "Okay. Where do we start?"

"Most of it I can send you in an email, but for a good chunk of it, we need the library."

"The library?" Kyle repeated, but Corrina waved him forward, as if whatever waited for them would expire if they didn't arrive fast enough.

When they entered the building, Gabriel rose from the circulation desk, grinning at them as they shook snow from their coats. "So? How did it go?"

"An excellent start." Corrina draped her sodden stocking cap on the rack above the coats. "Did you prepare the items I requested?"

"I did indeed, and checked them out in Kyle's name." Gabriel gave Kyle a look over the top of his glasses. "I can't give them to you, though, until you pay your fine, as it's over ten dollars. Library policy."

"What items are you giving me?" Kyle asked.

"DVDs." Corrina patted Kyle's shoulder. "Paul loves Lifetime Original Movies all year long, but he becomes very indulgent at Christmas."

"Corrina made the selections—I don't want you thinking I'd violate patron privacy by revealing his favorites myself." Gabriel pursed his lips. "I'm quite serious about the fines as well. You owe, in fact, over *twenty* dollars."

Kyle pulled his wallet out and handed Gabriel a twenty. "So I have to watch a bunch of sappy romance movies?" *And Paul likes those?*

Linda Kay had watched a movie in Gabriel's office while she waited for Kyle, thrilled at her special treatment, and she flirted with Gabriel as they said goodbye. Kyle left the library with his sister, his stack of DVDs and a receipt for his fines, a red circle around a notice that he still owed $5.65.

They stopped by the café for lunch, where Linda Kay alternated between relaying the plot of the children's movies she'd watched while she waited and singing her favorite show tunes. Once they were in the car and heading back home, Linda Kay sifted through the DVDs Kyle had checked out. "Why do you have all these movies?"

Kyle wasn't sure how to explain. "Gabriel wanted me to try them."

"They look boring."

Kyle had to agree. "I'm going to give them a try all the same."

He began his first one that evening, as he thawed out from sculpting a fairy princess (with wand) to go with the snow dragon. Corrina said *The Christmas Card* was one of Paul's top five. Kyle plugged it into the DVD player, curled up with an afghan, and prepared to get to know his crush.

Twenty minutes later, he'd stopped trying to talk himself into it not being so bad and mostly did his best not to vomit. When his mom came in and asked what he was doing, he fumbled to quickly turn it off, as if he'd been caught watching porn.

He finished the movie in his room, and over the next few days he dry-swallowed the rest. He dropped them off on his way home from work on Tuesday, along with the money for his remaining library fine.

Gabriel wasn't in, but Corrina was, and she beamed at him. "So. What did you think?"

Kyle tried to bite his tongue, but after days of garbage, he didn't stand a chance. "What did I *think*? Oh my God. They're *hideous*. Was this some kind of joke?"

"Not at all. These are some of Paul's favorites. I even confirmed with Arthur, though I didn't tell him why I wanted to know." Corrina regarded him archly. "What didn't you like about them?"

Where did he start? "For one, half of them were creepily religious. Going to church is fine," he added quickly, as Corrina had taught him fifth grade Sunday school, "and you know I attend when I don't work, but they're so…*in your face*. And *cheesy*. And *cardboard*. These aren't even cartoons, these characters. And what's up with there always being a fiancé or boyfriend who gets thrown over? I mean, it happened in *every single movie*." He tried to stop there, but he couldn't. "How in the world are *these* Paul's favorite movies?"

"Something for you to meditate on, yes?" Corrina nodded at the clock. "You're still on for dinner with him tonight? At seven?"

"I'm running home to change now."

"Good. Wear something nice but not too nice. Not too *tight* either, Kyle. Leave some things to the imagination."

Kyle was starting to regret enlisting Corrina. "I wasn't planning on club clothes. We're only going to dinner at the café."

"That's right. But remember, darling. *No matter what*, I don't want you to kiss him tonight."

Kyle laughed. "I'm pretty sure it's not something in the realm of possibility."

She aimed a finger at his nose. "I'm serious. *No.*

Kissing. You can come *close*, but that's all. It's of vital importance."

"Got it." It had *definitely* been a mistake to involve Corrina. He smiled his flirty smile and waggled his fingers. "Wish me luck."

It had started snowing while he'd been in the library. Only a flurry, but after so many other snows it was demoralizing, doubling his drive home. During the blizzard a few years ago, his brother had snowmobiled him to work, and after that experience Kyle had ponied up and bought a Ski-Doo of his own. He'd only used it for recreation so far, but something told him this year things would change.

He didn't take super care in dressing for his dinner not-date, but he did make sure his hair wasn't sticking up, wore a dark gray sweater he thought brought out his eyes, and splashed just a *hint* of Kenneth Cole Reaction on his pulse points.

His mother sashayed her hips and made a *woo-hoo* noise as he dashed through the kitchen. "You didn't tell me you had a *date.*"

"I don't." Kyle turned away and became busy wrapping his cream knit scarf around his neck. "I have a meeting for the Winter Wonderland thing."

"So you're teasing the old ladies by looking and smelling so good. I see. But you should eat quick. I saved you a plate in the oven."

"The meeting's at the café. I'll eat there." He kissed her on the cheek as he swiped his keys from the dish above the microwave and grabbed his hat. "See you later, Mom."

He wished he'd have taken her up on the food as he drove into town, stomach grumbling. His only solace was that by seven the café would be starting to clear out, as most people would eat at six or even five. Except when he pulled into the parking lot, he found it full to bursting. In fact, he had to drive around twice before he could find a place to park.

Paul stood inside the front door, clearly flustered. Every single seat was taken, and people lined along the windows waiting to be seated.

Three-quarters of the seats were taken by women wearing red hats. One of them was Corrina Anderson, who saw Kyle and waved.

Oh. No.

Paul gestured helplessly at the crush. "The Red Hat Society is having a dinner meeting here, and there's a forty-minute waitlist. On a *Tuesday*. They've never *had* a waitlist before. Ever."

Kyle's guilt at his unwitting part in this was drowned out by his legitimate hunger. "I can't possibly wait forty minutes to eat. I don't mean to be a princess, but I'm not kidding. I had to swipe a meal bar on the fly for lunch, and that was at eleven. I'm starving."

"We could order to go, but at this rate, God only knows when it'd be ready."

Goddamn you, Corrina. "You know what, there's no rush. We can try again another day. Maybe meet in the library or something." And this time, he wouldn't tell his *helper* when his meeting time was.

Paul rubbed the back of his head in a self-conscious gesture. "I hate having you go hungry. We could have them fire up a pizza at the muni."

The municipal liquor store had a small bar at the back and for a ridiculous fee would heat up a frozen pizza in a seldom-cleaned toaster oven under the counter. Kyle stifled a grimace. "I'll find something at home."

After frowning in the general direction of the kitchen, Paul held up a hand. "Give me five minutes."

Kyle wanted to point out in *fifteen* minutes he could be home stuffing cereal into his mouth, but he nodded instead and crowded into the coat rack, miserable in his now-ravenous hunger while surrounded by other people's food. He waited for Corrina to come over and explain herself, because he longed to rip into her over her ridiculous plans. She didn't so much as glance at him a second time, however, too busy eating her hot beef sandwich over Texas toast. Which was what *he* would have ordered. He always ordered it. He'd be less than ten minutes away from eating it now, if Corrina hadn't done this. And *why* the hell she'd done this he'd never—

"Here."

Kyle blinked as Paul reappeared and thrust a stack of Styrofoam takeout boxes at him. The smell of grease and meat and potatoes and bread hit him in the gut. "What—how?"

"Went into the kitchen and pulled a favor. Two people will wait five minutes longer for their orders, but they got to sit down, so it's all good."

Paul's possessive, self-satisfied look made Kyle melty. "Where will we eat, though?"

It was then he realized Corrina's plan. Somehow she'd known this was how it would go down. Somehow she knew wiping out the café would leave them eating at the bar on the highway, the muni, the shop, or Paul's house. *Oh, Corrina. You're a master class.*

Except Kyle could tell Paul was nervous about bringing him home, and frankly Kyle wasn't sure he was ready to stand on the steps where he'd been so soundly rejected. Ignoring the voice in his head warning him Corrina would cluck her tongue, Kyle gave Paul a bone. "Would it be okay to go to your shop? I assume you have the plans there anyway."

The relief came off Paul in waves. "Yeah. That's a great idea. I mean, I don't have any plans yet. I barely understand what's going on with this Wonderland thing. Though it's not very comfortable seating at the shop."

Kyle shifted the boxes so he could hold up one hand. "Seriously not needing fancy right now. I could happily eat this with no silverware under the street-light."

"I can do you better than that for sure." Paul grinned, and it made Kyle's heart flip over. "Come on. I'll give you a ride, and you can pick up your car after."

See, Corrina? I can be even smarter than you. Kyle beamed. "Thanks. Sounds great."

Chapter Four

KYLE WAS ACTUALLY a really decent guy.

Paul had known this for years. Before Marcus's mother had passed away, Kyle was one of the kindest nurses at the care center, helping Mimi cling to whatever dignity she could manage before Alzheimer's took it all. Everybody knew he was great with his twin sister. He was friendly too. And yes. He was cute. Paul had eyes, and he'd taken note, as one did.

But this was the second time in a row Paul had witnessed Kyle being…well, not steeped in camp, to put it bluntly. Frankie always made self-deprecating comments about his swishiness, which Marcus usually got defensive about, but Kyle was something different. He often, especially at the care center, did the singsong goodbye thing in a way that said *Here I am doing the singsong goodbye*. He never went out without looking like some kind of gay fashion plate, which was damn weird in a micro-town in the North Woods. Even his scrubs somehow managed to be gay as hell, and not because they were covered in rainbows. Somehow everything about Kyle was twinkling, fabulous gay.

To be blunt, Paul had long suspected Kyle of doing it on purpose. And though he tried not to be bothered by it, it *did* bother him.

Tonight all that stuff, while still present, was toned *way* down. In the shop, Kyle peeled away his bright blue puffy parka with matching knit hat, scarf and mittens, revealing a close-fitting gray sweater and equally snug jeans. If Paul wanted to imagine what Kyle's ass was shaped like, he didn't have to anymore. But the usual affected gestures were absent. No trills, no flirty-yet-sexless hip-wiggles. When he flipped open his to-go container, yes, he did it with a graceful, delicate air. When he ate, even though he was almost clumsy in his eagerness to get food in his mouth, there was no denying the femininity of his movements. These gestures, however, all seemed natural. They *fit* the man in front of Paul.

For the first time in basically ever, Paul looked at Kyle and admitted this was indeed a *man* in front of him. Not a kid playing around, flirting with Paul and making him feel weird. Gabriel had pointed out over and over that Kyle wasn't as young as Arthur and Paul insisted he was—and Paul could finally see it.

Kyle, catching Paul staring, blushed and reached for a napkin with the same smooth grace. "Sorry, do I have potato on my lip? I shouldn't have eaten so fast."

He didn't, but Paul couldn't admit why he *had* been

staring. "Just a little, but you got it." He felt bad for lying, so he touched his beard and mustache ruefully. "Don't worry, I'm sure I'll catch more than you before I'm finished."

Kyle eyed Paul's beard wistfully. "I keep trying to grow a beard, but it looks terrible. After a week I'm still nothing but messy fuzz."

Paul was about to say a beard wouldn't suit Kyle, but then his imagination kicked in, and…Christ, with his dyed hair, Kyle would look a hell of a lot like Arthur before he'd filled out.

Clearing his throat, Paul became focused on his hamburger.

Kyle wiped his mouth again, leaving a grimace. "Do you have disposable cups anywhere? I didn't think to grab a drink at the café."

Paul rose, embarrassed at his rudeness. "Sorry. We have pop and beer in the mini-fridge. What's your pleasure?"

"It's no trouble. I can get water from the bathroom faucet."

Paul was pretty sure if Kyle got a look at the shop's bathroom, he wouldn't want to drink water from it. "We don't have any clean cups. I can run across the street to the convenience store and get something bottled."

"I don't want to bother you. Pop or beer will be fine."

They toured the fridge, where the choices were

Mountain Dew, Red Bull, and Fat Tire. Kyle's gaze flitted between them, and he bit his bottom lip absently as he tried not to frown.

Paul closed the fridge and reached for his coat. "I'll be right back."

"No, I'll go." Kyle bustled to his own coat and hurried into it. "I'm so sorry. I get erratic heartbeats when I drink too much caffeine, and I don't care for beer."

"I'll come with you." Paul zipped up his coat. "It's my fault for having such poor choices."

"Well, it's not like you knew you'd have company." He tugged his hat over his ears.

It was the same stocking cap Kyle had been wearing the night Paul had caught him making the snow penis. To cover the fact he was studying Kyle too closely again, he said, "Nice hat."

"Thanks." Kyle's cheeks stained. "I made it."

Paul's eyebrows lifted, and he paused in putting on his gloves. "Seriously?"

"There's a lot of down time on the night shift. I've gotten pretty quick with my needles, and now I go a little crazy making winter gear." He pulled back one of the earflaps. "I knit the outside and sew in a fleece lining. *So* warm."

Paul could imagine. "That would be handy while hunting."

"It is. I've knit hats and fleece collars for my dad and my brothers. They were all eye-roll about it until they tried them out. Now when theirs start to get worn, they expect me to make new ones."

"That's nice of you. I tried to get the guys to knit one winter. The other two couldn't even cast on, and I ended up with a sagging oblong rectangle with holes all over."

"Oh, it's not hard, once you get the hang of it. If you want, I'll teach you sometime."

They walked across the street together to the small convenience store. The older woman working gave them a quiet "Hello" as they came in. Kyle got a Sprite, and Paul picked up a two-pack of chocolate cupcakes. As they walked back, though, it occurred to Paul they had caffeine. "These okay?"

"Oh, yes. It's only coffee and soda and energy drinks. I drink decaf coffee when I wake up, and I eat chocolate all day long." He looked abashed. "Sorry. This is the only place I'm high maintenance. Well, that and beer. I drink hard cider, though."

"Everybody's got something. Frankie feels sick if he eats red meat. Gabriel can't stand black coffee. Arthur gags on coconut."

"What about you?"

"Peanut butter and chocolate. Love both alone, can't stand them together."

Kyle's smile looked good on him. "Noted. No Reese's for Paul."

They finished their food, and as Paul unwrapped the cupcakes, Kyle glanced around. "Have you started building the frames yet?"

"Frames?"

"For the Winter Wonderland booths." Kyle gestured in the air. "Little hutches, Corrina said. Six of them. Places for vendors on the square. That's what I'm supposed to stencil."

Paul grimaced as he passed over a cupcake. "I haven't heard much detail about any of this, to be honest."

"According to Gabriel, this is how these things go. The library board gets wild ideas, usually late in the game, and everyone scrambles to fill in their gaps." Kyle took a bite of cupcake, then daintily wiped his mouth as he finished chewing. "He said we should feel free to do whatever we think seems feasible, and if it doesn't match their beatific vision, he'll steer them around to reality."

"How big are these hutches supposed to be?"

Kyle sipped his Sprite, looking thoughtful. "Well…they have to all fit on the square, to start. And speaking personally, I think they should be able to have space heaters inside. Honestly, it would be better if they were closed off. Even a few hours is a long time to stand in the cold."

"That's a lot of building in a little time. And a waste if this ends up snowed out and nobody can come."

Kyle rubbed his chin. "I don't know why they're not having it in the old school gym again."

Paul could guess. "Corrina wants it to be bigger, better. The elementary gym barely fit the event last year. She wants to branch out."

"I'd say let's table this until I get more information, but I'm afraid if I go to Corrina for clarifications, she'll make it bigger in her attempts to explain what she wants."

Paul had to agree. "You know, last year it seemed like Marcus and Frankie did a lot of the organizing. It was Marcus's friends Ed and Laurie who gave lessons. And Frankie knew the stylists. A lot of Gabriel's friends came up too. Maybe all six of us should have chili and conversation at Arthur's or something. I could see if they're around this weekend."

Kyle winced. "Sorry, I work evenings, and Saturday is kind of Linda Kay's day for what I'm awake of it. But I could come by Sunday before I go in to work at seven."

"Sure. I'll talk to the guys and get back to you."

With the cupcakes finished and the reason they'd gotten together in the first place punted to Sunday, Paul should offer to drive Kyle to his car and let him go home. Instead, he stared at Kyle again, and once more, he was caught.

Kyle touched the side of his hair self-consciously. "Why do you keep looking at me that way? You make me feel like I've grown a unicorn horn."

Paul fumbled with what excuse to give, which somehow led him to confessing the truth. "You're different tonight."

Kyle frowned. "Different than what?"

"Than you usually are. Though, I guess we haven't spoken much before."

Except for the mostly one-sided sexting.

Paul cleared his throat. "So, uh. Stencils and snow…stuff. I didn't realize you were so into art."

Kyle nodded, relaxing somewhat. "I've always been creative. I did more sculpture than painting in school."

"You're good. The snow dicks were…lifelike."

Kyle gave Paul another sideways look, as if to ask, *Why are you bringing this up?* "I enjoy making snow sculptures. Linda gets one every fresh snowfall. At the rate this winter is going, we'll have to branch into a field to house them."

"How did you make them so fast? The ones on my porch?"

"Oh, I'm pretty clever when it comes to cock."

The quip came with Kyle's affected voice, except instead of simpering affectation, it was a whip crack. It startled Paul, inspired him to sit a little straighter. Kyle didn't blush, simply stared Paul down.

Paul tried to regain his ground, but between Kyle's sharp gaze and the mental image of Kyle being good with cock, it disarmed him. He reached for a familiar wall. "I—Sorry. I didn't mean to start anything again."

Kyle's lips pursed as he stood up. He reached for his coat. "I should be heading back."

Paul rose too. "Kyle, I didn't mean it like that."

Kyle waved a hand at Paul, a gentle flick of a slight wrist. "Enough. Message received. I won't flirt with you anymore, even for fun."

Paul hurried after him, eventually cutting him off. "Look. You're a great guy."

"But you're not interested, I know. I was making a damn joke."

"It's not that I'm not interested. But you're too—"

Kyle's gaze flashed a half-second warning before he whipped out a hand and covered Paul's mouth. When Paul stumbled away, Kyle came with him, until Paul's back went flat against the door.

"Don't say another word." Kyle stared angrily down at him—*down*, yes, because he was a little bit taller than Paul, though decidedly less than half his width. It didn't seem to matter in that moment.

"Don't say I'm *young*. Don't say you're *old*. Don't fucking say a word because I don't want to hear it. It's demeaning to us both. I've already figured out you're not interested. I'm a big boy—*all grown up*—and I've moved on. Personally, I think it's your loss because I have it on several authorities I'm absolutely *wicked* in bed. Not quite as intense as Arthur, maybe, but then that didn't exactly work for you, did it?"

When Paul startled, Kyle grinned a grin that made Paul's guts churn with want.

"Go ahead and think I'm some infant twink wiggling my ass at you, hoping to get plowed by a sweet teddy bear." The grin faded, leaving only feral heat. Kyle didn't stroke Paul's face, but he could swear he tingled simply from the focused gaze of the man before him. "I'm not an infant, I can't help my body type, and if I got you in the same room as a bed, it wouldn't be *my* ass sore in the morning."

Paul couldn't speak, his breath coming in erratic staccato bursts. When his shock bled away, it left him still paralyzed, but with want, not fear. *That can't be right,* his brain kept telling him, except as he stared at Kyle, really looked at him, he was pretty sure his brain was wrong.

Paul also suspected, with the way Kyle kept leaning closer, a fiery warrior closing in on his prey, he was about to get kissed. To his surprise, he was *ready* to be kissed. By Kyle Parks. Against the back of the shop door. An angry, *I'll show you* kiss that already had Paul melting inside.

At the last second, however, Kyle stopped. He drew away, averted his gaze. Then he zipped up his coat and pulled his hat and mittens from his pockets with shaking hands. "I—I should go."

Don't go. That was insane, so Paul swallowed it. "I'll drive you."

Kyle jammed the hat over his hair. "It's fine. I'll walk."

No, *that* was insane. "It's a mile plus to the café, and it's ten degrees outside."

"Sounds perfect." Kyle wrapped his scarf around his face and saluted Paul with a fat mitten. "Text me about Sunday."

He pushed Paul aside and opened the door, and

Paul watched him trudge through the falling snow into the dark night.

THE SECOND KYLE was out of sight of the shop, he called Corrina, whose phone went to voicemail. He hung up, considered sucking it up and walking, then caved and called Gabriel. "I'm sorry to bother you, but are you still in town? If so, is there any way I could talk you into giving me a ride to my car?"

"Yes, and sure—but where are you, and why do you need a ride? Did you have car trouble?"

"I'm walking to the café from Paul and Arthur's shop. It's a long way, and I'm freezing."

"I'll be right there."

Gabriel appeared in a green Nissan, and it slid a little as he braked in the thick snow. Kyle climbed in, shaking as much snow from himself as he could. "Thank you *so* much."

"I'm kind of glad you called." Gabriel squinted through the fat snowflakes on his windshield, looking uneasy at the sight of them. "I was caught up in something and wasn't paying attention to the weather. Frankly I'm surprised Arthur hasn't called me to scold. But then, he's babysitting Thomas and the girls, so he might not have the luxury of paying attention to what's happening outside." Gabriel spared a glance at Kyle before focusing on the business of driving through snow. "So. Explain why I'm picking you up like this."

"Because Corrina told me not to kiss Paul. I'm pretty sure the kiss would have turned into fucking him against the door, so I took off."

"Why did she tell you not to kiss him? And why in the world did you listen?"

Kyle tipped his head to stare at the ceiling. "I don't know. I almost went back twice. I guess I thought she was right about the café, so maybe I should trust her."

"What about the café?"

Kyle spent the rest of the ride telling Gabriel about the dinner date, about Corrina's Red Hat Society meeting, about the intimate dinner for two in the shop. He also filled him in on the new plan for the Winter Wonderland project. "Mostly we decided we didn't understand what was going on, and Paul's going to see if all of us can meet somewhere on Sunday afternoon. All of us being him, me, you, Arthur, Marcus, and Frankie. He says you guys solved last year's clusterfuck, so maybe that can happen again."

"That should work. I'll talk to Arthur."

"No, don't. Paul's going to ask you. Act surprised."

Gabriel smiled. "Sure. So explain to me now how you were nearly having sex against a door."

"He kept staring at me. At first I thought I had stuff on my face, and he said I did, but now I wonder. I was *different* tonight, according to him. I still don't understand how, because all he said was *than usual.* Which is annoying, because mostly I was nervous and self-conscious, but *that* was when he looked at me like he finally understood I was a male human. *Then* he looked like he was about to tell me I was too young again, and I kind of went postal on him."

"Interesting. Go on."

"Well, I told him I *wasn't* too young, said I'd burn up his sheets, and he'd need an ice pack on his stool in the shop the next day."

Gabriel laughed, a delightful trill reverberating inside the car. "I wish they had surveillance in the shop. I'd rewind it to watch his face." He glanced across the seat at Kyle, gaze dancing with devilry. "Are you really that toppy?"

This was a weird conversation to be having with his local librarian. Kyle became focused on a loose thread on his mittens. "Just because I'm skinny and limp-wristed doesn't mean I want to bend over."

"No, and I don't mean to stereotype. I will say it surprises me, though now as I truly think about it, maybe not. I can see what Paul means about you being different, if you were letting that side of you out."

They were at the café now, which had barely any cars left in the lot. Gabriel pulled in beside Kyle's car. As Kyle released his seat belt, Gabriel turned to him with a smile. "I think you and I need to get to know one another better. Frankie too. When we meet on Sunday for this get-together I don't know about yet, let's discuss a time the three of us can escape to Duluth." He waggled his eyebrows. "Or maybe even the Cities. We could do some early Christmas shopping."

Kyle hadn't been to Minneapolis in forever. "That sounds great."

Gabriel winked and made gentle shooing motions at the door. "Go on. Drive safe, all right?"

"You too," Kyle said, and hurried out of the car.

It took him an extra fifteen minutes to get home, and when he pulled into the garage, he let out a heavy sigh of relief. As he stomped snow off his boots and hung his things in the mudroom, Linda Kay's worried, bespectacled face appeared at the window. When he opened the door, she enveloped him in a tight hug, pressing her face into his chest. "Kyle David, you scared me half to death. You should have come home hours ago."

Kyle hugged her back, kissing her hair. "I'm sorry, sweetie. I didn't mean to upset you. I was on a date."

She lifted her face, worry evaporating to interest. "Oh? With who?"

Kyle's lips quirked. "Paul."

Her face screwed up into her beautiful, squinty smile. "You *devil*. Did you make it to third base?"

"I didn't even get to first. I'm playing hard to get."

Linda Kay let go of him and rolled her eyes. "Well, *that's* got to be a first. Is it working?"

Kyle remembered the way Paul had looked at him, back pressed against the door. "Maybe."

"Then keep your zipper shut, buddy." She took his hand and pulled him toward the kitchen. "Let's celebrate with hot cocoa and marshmallows."

Kyle followed her, smiling and feeling loved and warm and home. "Sounds perfect."

Chapter Five

PAUL TEXTED ARTHUR, Gabriel, Frankie, and Marcus in a group message about getting together on Sunday. Arthur replied immediately, said it was fine and offered to host. But when Marcus responded, he said *he* wanted to host because they wanted to show off the new house, which Paul knew was Marcus believing *Frankie* wanted to show off. Arthur complained *he* had plenty to show off too, because they'd settled on the plans for the cabin remodel.

For three days Paul's phone buzzed as Arthur and Marcus argued, until Gabriel suggested they bring the cabin plans along, enjoy Frankie's cooking, and plan another event at the cabin soon. Frankie thought this was a wonderful idea and offered to make chili, and why didn't everyone else bring a dish to pass? There was some argument over who would bring what sides, but eventually Paul was able to text Kyle.

We're meeting to discuss the Winter Wonderland thing at 2:30 at Marcus and Frankie's place on Sunday. Does that work for you? Frankie was trying to not wake you up too early but leave enough time before your shift.

It took Kyle half an hour to reply, during which time Paul mostly paced his living room worrying that strange, awkward end to their dinner Tuesday night had messed everything up. After which he would remind himself there wasn't anything between them to mess up, and that was the way it had to be. He was in the middle of trying to phrase a new response nudging to see if Kyle was upset with him when the text came through. *Perfect. Thanks. Should I bring anything?*

Paul let out a heavy sigh of relief and deleted the draft he'd been slaving over. *You and I were supposed to bring dessert, but I can do it since you're probably busy.*

I like baking, and Linda Kay loves to help. If that's okay?

It was, because Paul had planned to pick up a package of cookies from the grocery store. Now he didn't have anything to bring, though. He'd bring some beer. And Sprite for Kyle.

Sounds great. Thanks. He sent the text, and then on an impulse sent a second. *Do you want me to give you a ride?*

He blushed and scolded himself for stupidity. Why had he offered that? Wasn't he supposed to be *not* engaging with Kyle?

I don't want to pull you away from your friends. I'll have to leave by six to go home and get ready for work.

Paul relaxed, realizing what had been his subconscious drive to make the offer. *Actually that works out perfectly. Gives me an excuse to leave early. It's nothing against them, but they get kind of*—he hesitated, trying to figure out how to word it—*coupley.* Except autocorrect switched it to *couple* as he sent, so now he sounded like an idiot. He tried again. *I mean that they're all caught up in each other, and I'm the odd man out.*

Sounds like every family gathering with my siblings. Sure, I'll take a ride. Thanks. When should I be ready?

Marcus would bitch if they got there too early. *How about I come around 2:15 and you show me the snow sculptures?*

I'll be ready. With dessert.

There was nothing lewd about that comment, but Paul was still ridiculously aroused when he put the phone down and went to the shower. He jacked off, thinking he needed to get sex out of his system, but as he leaned on the wall, hot spray beating into his chest as he stroked himself, all he could think about was the night before. When Kyle had backed him into the door. When Kyle had been angry and cocky.

If I got you in the same room as a bed, it wouldn't be my ass sore in the morning.

Paul's decidedly empty ass clenched at the memory, but his cock only got fuller. None of the frustrated, empty masturbation sessions that had plagued him lately. Even the ache at knowing he'd be the odd man out at the potluck had faded. In the safety of his fantasies, he let that saucy promise play out. Imagined Kyle pushing him onto his bed. Looming over him as the guy who had told Paul off, not the winking, cheerful innocent who waved at visitors from behind the nurses' station at the care center. When this imaginary Kyle pushed Paul's legs back, real-life Paul leaned on the shower wall. When Kyle teased his entrance, Paul's balls drew up. When Kyle pushed inside, Paul let out a huff of breath and stroked himself faster.

When Kyle kissed him, hard and demanding as he buried himself to the hilt, Paul came all over the wall. He made such a mess he had to get out paper towels and dig splooge out of the grout and the crevices of his hot water handle. He was glad for the chore, because it gave him something to focus on other than the fact that he'd just gotten off to imagining Kyle Parks fucking him.

Paul got off to a Kyle fantasy again on Saturday morning, one so intense he was late for his scheduled visit to his parents. After bailing on them the week before, he'd promised he'd come by for Saturday dinner, and though the overnight snow squall had stopped, the plows hadn't been down his parents' road, making it clear he should have left twenty minutes *earlier* to be on time. This meant as he pulled up to the farmhouse, his father was outside, ostensibly fussing with the sidewalk to make sure it was clear, but mostly being available to watch for Paul and deliver the greeting Paul had known was coming.

"You're late. Your mother's been worried sick."

"Sorry. I texted." Paul held out his hand. "Here, Dad, let me do that for you."

Larry waved this offer away. "It's fine. Tim came by early this morning. Plowed the drive, cleared off the walk."

Tim was Paul's brother-in-law, who lived a few miles over and farmed the land Larry no longer could. There was no logic in Paul, who didn't have a tractor with a snowplow attachment, to drive seven miles out of town on unplowed roads to shovel a ten-foot walk, but his father's tone made Paul feel guilty all the same.

They went inside together, Paul taking care to not only wipe his boots but line them up the way his mother liked, hanging his coat on the peg that had always been his while Larry called out, "Mother, Pauly's here."

Paul's mother emerged from the kitchen, frowning as she wiped her hands on a dishtowel. "Land sakes, we were worried sick." Mary kissed Paul's cheek and patted his arm. "Come eat. The pork chops need to come out of the oven, or they'll get tough."

After stopping to wash his hands in the bathroom by the kitchen, Paul took his place as his mother laid out a dish of peas, a bowl of mashed potatoes, pork chops, dinner rolls, and gravy. His father tucked a cloth napkin in his lap and poured milk into his glass from a gallon jug. "How's business? You breaking even yet?"

Paul nodded as he accepted the milk from his father. "Doing fine. Nice and steady."

"Probably the Christmas rush. You best put plenty by for the long winter months."

"I will." Paul poured his mother's milk as she sat.

"Thank you." Mary draped her own napkin. "Will you say grace, Dad?"

Larry said a short prayer, during which Paul murmured along but mostly let his mind wander, thinking how it drove Arthur nuts how Paul's parents called each other Mother and Dad.

Mary passed him the potatoes. "I heard at Circle you were helping with the Winter Wonderland festival. What will you be doing?"

"Still sorting that out. I'm meeting with Arthur and the guys tomorrow to make plans. Some kind of display area, which Kyle Parks is going to stencil. The guys are helping out too."

Mary pulled a face. "Let's hope there are no *displays* like last year."

The display upsetting her almost a year later was Arthur's grand proposal to Gabriel, in a Santa suit. Paul didn't reply, pushing his peas around his plate.

Dinner proceeded along, alternating between inquiries about his life and reports of his parents' comings and goings. Larry's hip was giving him trouble, according to Mary, but he insisted it was fine. Mary had started a new afghan she intended to give to the donation basket at church. She also had made great progress on some squares for the quilt her women's circle was making.

"Sandra and Tim are coming over tomorrow for lunch after church. Dad will probably take the kids up to the hill to go sledding, if his hip is okay."

"My hip will be fine, Mother."

Mary gave Paul a look that said she clearly wasn't convinced of this, but time would tell. "You should come sit with us at church, Paul, and eat lunch after."

"I'll do my best," Paul lied.

He'd let his mother parade eligible women past his nose before he'd spend time voluntarily with his sister and brother-in-law. Anytime they were around, he had to listen to hate speech about somebody, usually gays but not necessarily limited to that demographic. Sandy particularly hated Gabriel and what she called his *progressive agenda*. "He always has books about black and Hispanic kids. And Asian kids. You want to know how many of those we have in Logan? Zero. And thank God. Probably he'll have a book about Islam next. Trying to turn our poor innocent children into Jihadis."

There was no Gabriel-bashing today, thankfully. After dinner he offered to do some odd jobs, but they didn't have any because Tim had done them all. Or they had some and knew if they got too complicated, Paul would try to come back with Arthur. So he watched some hockey with his dad until Tim came over to do chores. Paul hurried into his coat, making noise about how he couldn't stay because he had lots to do at home.

When he did get to his house, he pulled a micro-wave meal out of the freezer, and while it heated, he cracked a beer and dug out the holiday romance DVD set.

A Boyfriend for Christmas sounded like a great thing to be busy with for the evening.

WHEN CORRINA STOPPED by the care center Saturday evening, Kyle leaned over the nurses' station, looked her dead in the eye, and said, "I want to kiss him."

"You will, dear. But if you want to kiss him more than *once*, you'll do as I say." When Kyle protested, Corrina, still in her winter gear, aimed a red-gloved finger beneath her no-nonsense expression. "Don't give me any guff, young man. You may have fantasized about him since you were old enough to know you could, but *I* have been mothering that boy since he started hanging out with Arthur. I know what it will take to win him."

It was hard to argue with that, which made Kyle fantastically grumpy. "*Why* can't I kiss him? And how long is this moratorium going to last?"

"It's difficult to say how long exactly. With proper attention, you should be kissing by Thanksgiving for sure."

Kyle groaned and slumped forward onto the station.

Corrina patted him on the arm. "There, there. It might be earlier. I was giving you worst-case scenario. You have to understand how skittish and contrary Paul can be. The more he can't have something, the more he wants it. And in addition to his hang-ups he has about your age, he was most unfortunate in his parental lottery." She looked at him over her half-rim glasses. "Are you still watching the Christmas movies?"

"I figured I had the general gist of them, so no."

"Can you tell me why he watches them yet?"

Kyle fumbled for a response most likely to get him out of more movies. "The romance?"

Corrina tweaked his nose. "I'll tell Gabriel to pull you a new set."

A patient call button rang, and Corrina waved goodbye to him as he went to the intercom system to answer. It was *one of those nights*, where everyone was agitated and needed special attention. Mr. Haverson, a ninety-two-year-old man with Parkinson's and severe dementia, kept triggering the alarm on his chair because he was convinced he had to go out and check his cows. He scolded Kyle for making him sit in his chair, called him Bobby and told him it was well past time he got his act together and got a job. Bobby Haverson was his son, dead of a heart attack five years ago.

Kyle didn't point this out, only patiently told Robert Senior over and over that he was doing his *best* to do his job, but for that to happen, Mr. Haverson had to stay in his chair. About the time that nonsense settled down, Hettie Lansing started screaming because her roommate was moaning in her sleep. During all of this, nice Mrs. Matherson, who was perfectly lucid but needed care while she recovered from the flu, waited forever for a cup of water because her throat was dry, all because she wasn't a melting-down mess like the rest of the care center.

The CNAs and the other nurses on staff did their best to help, but there was so much chaos, they all ran themselves ragged. His shift was technically over at three, but it was quarter to four in the morning before he was able to trudge to his car. When Kyle finally got home, he peeled out of his clothes, left them in a heap, and fell asleep as soon as he crawled under his comforter.

He slept without dreaming until he woke because someone was gently but insistently tapping him on the arm. He opened his eyes to see Linda Kay's face peeking over the edge of his mattress. Smiling sleepily, he fumbled a hand out from the blankets to honk her nose. "Hey, pretty lady."

She rose enough so her chin could rest on the blankets. She *wasn't* smiling. "Mom said I can't wake you. But there was an accident."

Kyle sat straight up, holding the comforter to his naked waist. "What happened? Is anyone hurt?"

Linda Kay's eyes filled with tears. "Dad and Rob threw snow over the fence and wrecked the dragon and the ice princess."

Kyle allowed himself a moment to drift down from the adrenaline. Once his heart wasn't slammed against the back of his throat, he wiped away Linda Kay's tears with his thumb. "Hey, no worries. We can fix it."

The door to his bedroom opened, and their mother

came in. "Oh, Kyle, I'm so sorry. I told her not to come in here."

Linda Kay tipped her chin up. "Mom, he was *awake*. I was only *watching* to see so I could tell him right away."

Kyle fumbled with his phone until he could depress the home button to reveal the time. Eight thirty. No wonder he felt like marinated hell.

His mom leaned in the doorway. "Kyle, honey, go back to sleep. It's far too early for you to be awake."

It was, but thanks to Linda Kay's accidental intimation someone in the family was hurt, there was no way he'd fall asleep again before ten. He shook his head. "If I'm going to fix the sculptures before I go to Marcus and Frankie's, I should get started."

Jane leveled a glare at her daughter. "She can wait until tomorrow, or another time when you can build new ones."

Intellectually Kyle knew Linda Kay made the sad, kicked-puppy-dog face because she knew it would slay him. That didn't stop the look from doing exactly what it was meant to do. "It's okay. If I start now, I can maybe get a nap in."

He slugged some decaf and stared out the sliding door to assess the damage to his work while his mother hurried to cook him bacon and eggs. His dad and brothers heaped snow from the drive behind the garage, but they'd started piling high because they anticipated they'd need a lot of space. They'd overshot, however, and a huge section had come crashing into the backyard and onto Linda Kay's snow garden. He'd have to inspect closer to be sure, but he was pretty sure he'd have to rebuild the dragon and the princess both. Which would take him hours. Plus he'd be exhausted afterward.

Jane brought him his plate and wagged her finger. "Do *not* make yourself too tired to go this afternoon. I know you're looking forward to it. She *can* wait. She won't like it, but she can do it."

Kyle darted a glance to the couch, where Linda Kay knelt, face pressed to the window. "I can make it work."

"You spoil her." Jane sighed and kissed his cheek.

Kyle kissed her back and took his plate to the table.

It turned out he could save most of the dragon and the princess too, but the repairs were delicate and time-consuming, and in the end he spent almost more time fixing them than if he'd started completely fresh.

"You need to finish later," his mother called out the door. "It's after one. You'll want to shower before Paul comes to get you."

Yes, he very much did. But he hadn't finished the princess's face, and Linda Kay stood next to him, breathless as she waited to see if her brother could rehang the moon. "It'll only take another minute," he insisted, and picked up his carving knife.

WHEN PAUL ARRIVED at the Parks farm, Daryl Parks got off his tractor and came over to shake Paul's hand. "Good to see you, Paul. How's business?"

"Going well, thank you."

"Say, do you guys repair iPods? The one we use in the shed stopped working, and I can't even find a way to open the thing up."

"Well, I can repair them, but I'm not certified. And I have to tell you I'm about a one-to-one ratio, fixing vs. breaking it more."

Daryl chuckled. "That's a sight better than I've managed. Would it be okay to give it to you today, or should I bring it by the shop?"

"I can take it, sir."

Daryl grinned and slapped Paul on the shoulder. "Come on. Kyle's in the back. I'm coming along to watch, because he never stopped to take a shower like Jane told him to, and he'll be fit to be tied now that you're here."

Paul wasn't sure what to say to that, so he followed Daryl Parks.

The farmer gestured to the far side of the yard. "We were clearing snow this morning and accidentally busted the dragon and the princess. Linda Kay sobbed like you wouldn't believe. Guess this was a very special princess. Jane told her to leave him be, but Kyle wouldn't hear of letting her wait. That boy's soft as jelly for his sister."

Daryl led Paul to the side of the garage, where Kyle

crouched diligently over a five-foot sculpture. Linda Kay stood bundled beside him, watching intently—until she saw Paul approaching. Then she poked Kyle in the arm and whispered, loud enough for them to hear in Logan, "Hey. Your boyfriend is here."

Kyle had been in a kind of work trance, but at this he startled and rose, giving Linda Kay a look that said there would be retribution later. "It can't be two fifteen already, can it?"

"It's two twenty, actually," Daryl said with a grin.

Kyle winced and clutched at his hat. "Oh my God, I haven't showered or *anything*."

"Which is your own fault, because your mother called you at least four times." Daryl glanced at Paul and indicated the sculptures with his head. "So, what do you think? He's not bad with a pile of snow, as far as I reckon."

As understatements went, this one was a whopper. Behind Kyle was a dragon, at least ten feet long and four feet high. Its tail wound around a real rock, which had been painted to look like a gold nugget. Its head rested on a stump—subtly, as the dead tree was clearly for support only—and it breathed snow-fire that arched across a small snow-brick wall. It was so alive it looked ready to leap across the fields. The scales, the eyes, even the fine detail on the flames were stunning.

But the dragon was nothing compared to the snow princess who stood beside him. She was a *sculpture*, carved out of a single, solid block of snow. Her shoulder-length hair blew in unseen wind. Her snow-cape billowed over a poufy gown with intricate beads and folds. Her crown sat boldly on her head, and in her hand was a star-shaped wand with gold beads in the center. What caught Paul by the edge of the heart, though, was the face. It was a beautiful, wide-smiling face, with a stubby nose, slightly slanted eyes, and bit of tongue protruding past the lips.

In short, it was an ice princess with Down syndrome.

Paul realized they were waiting for him to respond, but all he could do was shake his head and keep staring in wonder. "Amazing," he managed at last. "I've never seen anything like it."

Kyle used a mittened hand to shield his eyes from the weak afternoon sun as he looked back at the house. "I really do need to shower. Do you think they'll be mad if we're a little late? I can be fast."

Paul would see to it they weren't. "You go get your shower. Don't rush."

Kyle blew him a kiss then pointed the knitwear at his father. "Help her mist them down so they freeze hard tonight. Just a *mist*."

Daryl waved his son off, and Paul stayed to watch as Linda Kay, carefully supervised, misted her snow sculptures with the large spray bottle she'd been clutching. Several times she cackled, a noise both wicked and charming at once. At one point, as if seized by sudden joy, she held the spray bottle aloft, tipped her head back and sang loudly and in no key whatsoever, "*Valley high, I call yoooooooou.*" Then she resumed her spraying, until her father told her she needed to stop or she'd wreck them.

She relinquished her bottle to Daryl, but she tugged on Paul's arm when he tried to leave. "Take my picture," she said, beaming. "With the snow princess. Because we're both pretty cute, right, sexy man?"

"Linda Kay." Daryl's tone was a warning.

Linda Kay chuckled again, sticking out her tongue. Laughing, Paul got out his phone and urged her to get closer to her doppelgänger. He took several pictures, one with her standing at attention, one with her mimicking the pose, and one with what Linda Kay called her baby-eyes pose, which Paul assumed was supposed to be bedroom eyes. In each photo, her tongue protruded.

After four more photos, Linda Kay attached herself to Paul's arm. "Okay, hot stuff. Let's go get hot chocolate and snuggle, okay?"

He couldn't help but laugh with her, and though Daryl tried to get him out of his role as escort, Paul gave him a nod to let him know this was fine. She had such *joy*. Plus, she was all kinds of saucy and smart. A little inappropriate, missing several social cues, but on the whole, delightful.

Once they were in the house, she showed him where to put his boots, made them each a hot cocoa in a Keurig machine, and tugged him toward the den.

"Come on. The babies are all sleeping, so we have the TV to ourselves. We'll watch a movie while you wait for slowpoke."

Jane Parks appeared from around a corner. She smiled briefly at Paul and greeted him before turning to her daughter. "Kyle will be ready in a few minutes. You do *not* have time for a movie."

Linda Kay crossed her arms over her chest. "Fine. I'll show him just the *valley high*."

She plunked Paul on a soft brown sectional and bustled to the DVD player. Soon the opening titles of *South Pacific* played on the screen. Tongue out in concentration, Linda Kay punched at the remote until she queued up a scene. She bounced and giggled as she pushed play. "Here we go. *Valley high*."

The scene was a bunch of soldiers on an island—well, an island movie set, because it was an old movie, from an era when there was no such thing as green screen or special effects. A black woman started to sing about a lonely island, and when she got to the chorus, Paul realized she was singing *Bali*, not *valley*. A quick check on his phone revealed this song was "Bali Ha'i", where the matriarch of an exotic island lures the lead so he can fall in love with her daughter. Linda Kay, however, was clearly singing *valley high*. Singing it at the top of her lungs, from the bottom of her belly. She sang to the woman on the screen, to the far side of the room, to the window. She sang with abandon, and with no clear words ninety percent of the time. Until the song called for *valley high*.

As the song wound to an end, abruptly a bright tenor filled the room, sending a tingle down Paul's spine. Kyle—hair artfully styled, green sweater making his complexion glow, jeans snug enough to show off his slim hips—sailed into the room, arm extended as he joined Linda Kay in an unusual duet. When he sang with her, she hit more of the words, but mostly she garbled along until she got to the good parts.

Paul noticed Kyle got all the words right, except like Linda Kay, he sang *valley high*.

When they finished, Linda Kay clapped and pulled her brother down to kiss him on the cheek. "I love you, Kyle David."

"I love you too, Linda Kay." He kissed her forehead. "I'm going to go with Paul for a while. I'll be home around dinnertime, and I'll kiss you before I go to work. Okay?"

She swatted him playfully and stuck out her tongue with mischievous glee. "Go on, you lovebird. I'll catch your act later."

Kyle raised apologetic, slightly helpless eyebrows at Paul. "So. Should we go?"

Paul rose. "Ready when you are."

Chapter Six

P AUL FOLLOWED KYLE outside and held open the door to the truck for him. Once they were inside, Kyle all but melted into the passenger seat, embarrassed. "I'm so sorry. For making us late. For my sister and her bald innuendos."

"We're not that late, and your sister is charming." He glanced across the seat. Kyle looked exhausted. "How much sleep did you get last night?"

"Three hours? Maybe four." He ran hands over his face. "I should have listened to my mother and done the sculptures another day."

Three hours, and he had to work tonight. "We can reschedule. The guys won't mind, I swear."

"*No.* Thinking about going with you today was the only thing that got me through my horrible shift last night." He yawned, tried to swallow it and failed. "It's times like this I wish I could mainline caffeine the same as everybody else."

Paul's cheeks stained at the *going with you* remark.

"Does sugar help you at all? I know it's short term, but it's better than nothing."

"A little. That's a good idea. I'll grab a big bag of candy before I go in tonight." The next yawn he managed to tame, sliding it into a smile. "So. Tell me about *your* Saturday."

Paul thought back to his awkward meal with his parents, and his night of watching movies he was embarrassed to talk about. "Not very exciting."

"Well, that's no fun."

The image he'd been working to ignore since Tuesday night, Kyle intense and pressing Paul into the door of the shop, rose from the mist. Determined to bottle those odd feelings up again, Paul nodded at the grocery bag and reached for a more inane line of discussion. "What did you end up baking?"

"Cupcakes." Beaming proudly, he withdrew a bakery-style box, opened the lid and revealed a tray of frosting Santas. "It's a little early for Christmas, but Linda Kay feels we can start celebrating as soon as there's snow. So we've had Christmas music on since late September, and we make Santa cupcakes."

The cupcakes were as artistic as Kyle's snow sculptures, with details Paul longed to examine more closely once he wasn't driving. "They look great. What flavor?"

"Red velvet for Santa, naturally, and cream cheese frosting for his beard." He licked some frosting off his finger after he closed the box and put it back in the bag. "Where is their house again? I wanted to say it was on Maple. The old Carlson place?"

"Yeah. We helped Marcus fix it up all summer, and then he and Frankie painted it. They only moved in a few weeks ago, and they haven't let us visit yet because Frankie was still decorating." He smiled and rubbed his jaw. "I think Arthur's sore about it, because he's dragged his feet about redesigning his cabin, and now Marcus beat him."

Maple Avenue was one of the two nicer residential streets in Logan, though that was a relative term. One hundred years ago the house Marcus and Frankie had bought had belonged to one of the mill owners. Back then Logan had been something to write home about, and this was the street you'd tell stories of. Big, straight trees, wide boulevard, fancy streetlights. The house they'd bought had fancy gingerbread on the eaves and lattice windows, and shutters, and heavy woodwork inside above hardwood floors. Of course, most of it had been a mess when Marcus bought it.

Now it shone once again like a pretty jewel in the center of its block. Several evergreen bushes decorated the walk. A white wrought-iron fence lined the property, as well as a quaint little gate whose hinges Paul had oiled himself. The house itself was painted a mint green with light brown shutters a shade darker than the sharply pitched roof.

"It's *beautiful*." Kyle stood in the center of the walk, spinning around, taking it all in. "I can imagine how this will look in the summer, full of flowers."

The front door opened, and Marcus stepped onto the wide porch with a wave. "Hey. Good to see you, Paul." He bear-hugged Paul before engulfing Kyle's small hand in his meaty paw. "Kyle. Welcome to our home. Come on in, both of you. We've got cider and coffee on."

Kyle kept smiling. "This is *beautiful*. My God, if you had stenciling on the woodwork, I'd think this was Mormor and Morfar's house."

"Who?" Paul asked, frowning.

Marcus's lips spread inside his dark beard. "If my high school Swedish holds, that would be Kyle's maternal grandmother and grandfather."

Kyle nodded. "There's this little house behind the main house on our farm, closed off by some trees. The farm originally belonged to my mother's family, the Hults, and they had a big Swedish-heritage thing going on. I think we have about fifty Dala horses on the property. When I was young, my great-grandmother and great-grandfather lived in the cottage. They came over to the main house to eat sometimes, though Mormor cooked all the time too. Mom and Grandma did their laundry. They were both born in Minnesota, but their parents had been the original immigrants to the area, and they felt it was their job to keep the Swedish flame alive. So they were Mormor and Morfar. Their house is a bit smaller than this, and it's nothing but storage now. Linda Kay thinks it's her castle, but Dad locks it so she can't explore." He took a deep breath and smiled. "I remember it smelling like this. Meat and sugar and spice."

Frankie appeared in the doorway from the dining room, wearing an apron and beaming with pride. "Welcome, Paul, Kyle. Marcus, will you take their coats? Can I get either of you anything to drink? Ooh, and is that the dessert you brought, Kyle?"

Kyle showed off his Santas, Paul passed over his assorted beverages, and once they had their winter gear off, Marcus ushered them into a well-appointed living room where Gabriel and Arthur waited, sipping coffee. Frankie brought in coffee for Paul and mulled cider for Kyle. Gabriel and Arthur had claimed the love seat, though they weren't snuggling so much as casually touching one another. Kyle took a wing-backed chair by the fireplace, and Paul the edge of the full sofa. Marcus perched on a settee near the parlor, rising occasionally when Frankie called him from the kitchen.

They chatted about the weather, about the repair shop, about the remodel. When Arthur unrolled blueprints onto the coffee table and explained the upgrades he wanted to do to the cabin, Frankie hurried in, wiping his hands on a dishtowel as he *oohed* and *ahhed* with everyone else.

"We finally decided we'd go with four bedrooms, not three," Gabriel said.

"Why so many bedrooms?" Kyle asked.

Arthur gave Gabriel the kind of gooey, besotted look Paul hadn't thought his old friend and former lover capable of. "Because we intend to fill them with kids."

Kyle blinked. "Wow, really?"

Gabriel smoothed a hand tenderly over the cabin plans. "We're applying to be foster parents. We talked about surrogacy or adoption, but there are so many foster kids who need good homes."

Arthur put an arm around Gabriel, looking proud and content. "We're starting with two, but I figure the worst thing an extra bedroom means is somewhere else for people to escape for peace and quiet, or to store things."

"I think it's wonderful." Frankie leaned on Marcus, smiling.

Kyle, Paul noticed, still reeled a bit from the revelation. He glanced at Frankie. "Do you two want kids too?"

Frankie glanced at Marcus. "Probably not. We'd love to play uncles, but that's it." He raised an eyebrow at Kyle. "What about *you?*"

"I guess it would depend. It's not a lifelong dream or anything, but with the right guy, I'd consider it." He grinned wryly around his mug of cider. "Honestly, I feel like I've already put in more parenting than most actual parents. All my nieces and nephews who Mom babysits, and of course Linda Kay. *She* is my kid who won't ever grow up." He shrugged. "It really would depend."

For a second, Paul figured that would be the end of

it. Then Kyle looked him straight in the eye. "What about *you?*"

Paul stammered out a non-answer. "I—I guess it would depend for me too."

That wasn't a lie, exactly. He honestly didn't know if he wanted kids or not. His fantasy relationship was always *full*, people everywhere, and maybe some of them were young. But he wasn't sure he wanted the everyday business of *his* kids underfoot. Which seemed awful, like kids were accessories to pull out of the closet when he was in the mood.

Yet if Mr. Right came with an army of children, Paul knew he'd morph into Mr. Mom on a moment's notice.

Frankie declared it was time to eat, and they moved the house party into the dining room, where a beautiful oak table decked with fall colors looked like the spread out of a fancy magazine. A small orange Dutch oven full of red chili sat on one side of a leafy centerpiece, while a yellow pot on the other side held what Paul supposed was Frankie's white chicken chili. Cut, garlic butter-coated French bread steamed in a basket on the side by the venison chili, a glass bowl of dark-leaved salad on the other. On a buffet by the kitchen were Kyle's Santa cupcakes, lined up to watch them eat.

Everyone effused over how delicious everything smelled, and as they began eating, how wonderful it tasted. Frankie declared the salad the best he'd ever had, and Gabriel confessed it was pecan kale parmesan, and he'd email the recipe. Arthur had a helping of the red chili and asked Marcus if this was his venison. The meal was a tornado of domesticity and friendship…and partnership.

Kyle sat across from Paul, next to Gabriel. In so many ways, he fit right into the group. As much as Marcus, Arthur, and Paul were of the slightly more burly persuasion, Frankie, Gabriel, and of course Kyle were all…well, *delicate*. Gabriel was mostly lanky and had librarian stamped on his forehead, and when you heard Frankie was a hairstylist, it fit. They were good matches for their fiancés: sweet, gentling Frankie tamed Marcus's grumpy bear. Sharp, no-nonsense Gabriel evened out Arthur's rough edges.

Tidy as it was, though, Paul still didn't think any kind of a relationship was a good idea. His dating adventures in the past year had largely been him finding someone great to cuddle and hang out with or someone to realign his solar system in bed, but never the two together. More than once he'd been told he was too complicated to date, and he'd decided, quietly, that was true.

After Tuesday night, part of him had dangerous fantasies about how maybe Kyle was his Goldilocks after all. Not too hot, not too cold. It was stupid, because he was basing everything on that one moment. One defiant exchange.

He wished it weren't only that one moment. He wished he could see that Kyle now, though he acknowledged it would make no sense here at the table with everyone else. Shouldn't there be a hint, though? All he saw was Kyle basically falling in line with Frankie and Gabriel.

"So." Gabriel wiped his mouth with his napkin. "Let's discuss this Winter Wonderland business. I think we've let the board pretend they have a sense of direction long enough."

He outlined the plan they all essentially knew about: have a fundraiser similar to the one last year in order to raise money for the library. The year before, Corrina's initial plan to raffle off sleigh rides had become, at Marcus, Arthur, Frankie, and Gabriel's direction, a ten-thousand-dollar profit for the town. The city council enthusiastically approved funding to help the library board host the event again, and of course everyone dreamed of it being bigger, brighter, better. The problem was no one seemed to have a clear idea of how to make that work.

"There are two issues." Gabriel ticked them off on his fingers. "One, we must attract people here, without them getting snowed out or in, and we must provide them with something meaningful to do which will cost them money but not us. Corrina seems hell-bent on some kind of vendor fair and has all the neighboring counties in on making crafts, etcetera. I can't see that being what draws people here from out of the area, though, which is what brought us all the success last year."

"What made last year special was the quaint, small-town feeling." Frankie sipped white wine and tapped the side of the glass after. "Even for locals, last year's sleigh ride event felt like the small town everyone thinks they remember. If we can find a way to make *that* happen, we'll have it sorted."

"It doesn't change the problem of the weather," Marcus pointed out.

Frankie shrugged. "We could talk to the hotels in Eveleth about making up a special. If the snow is so bad they can't get from there to here, we'll have to postpone anyway. That's the thing—this is a *winter* wonderland. If it's before December twenty-fifth, yes, we can hang wreaths and so on, but post holiday we could…I dunno. Do snowflakes."

"No." Kyle smiled, and Paul shivered because *there* was a little of that look from Tuesday night. "You do Scandinavian folk art. Dala horses. A grandma or grandpa sitting in the corner doing history lessons—*Oh.*" He beamed at Gabriel. "No, *you* telling stories. Like the one about Saint Lucia. If it's before Christmas, we have a *julbord.* Hell, even post-Christmas, because nobody will know what it is or that it's meant to be on Christmas Eve. We should include some Norwegian nods too, as some people in town have that heritage, and a lot of visitors will. But lean on stencils and folk art for the theming, and add or remove wreaths and snowflakes as needed. For the kids, you can have a *Frozen*-themed area. Because clearly that movie won't die down anytime soon. They could feel as if they're in Elsa's palace." He stopped, and his smile arrested Paul. "Oh, *wait*. I'll *make* Elsa's palace."

Marcus frowned. "You can't call it that. It's copyright infringement."

Frankie waved this away. "We'll call it the snow queen's castle."

Arthur slapped the table. "*Hey*. I got it. We don't build any of these weird little hobbit houses. We decorate the *businesses* on the square. Put on false fronts with the gingerbread and the stencils. We get Marcus to talk to the city and get those empty storefronts open for these vendors. Who knows, maybe some of them will end up opening shops permanently."

Gabriel had the determined look in his eye too. "You do realize if this works, the next step is to make those false fronts full-on remodels. Logan can become a *real* Christmas village. Do it right, and it could be one all year long."

A vision bloomed in Paul's head. "We need to build Santa's house. For this year we could turn the gazebo into something, but next year…"

For the next few hours, their plans flew like lightning. Paul tended to sit back and listen, absorbing and thinking before interjecting an idea or pointing out a flaw someone had missed. Marcus did much the same, and in his own way, so did Gabriel. Kyle, Arthur, and Frankie dreamed big, and the rest of them built castles under them as fast as possible.

Marcus got out a legal pad and began making notes about people he needed to call, permits they needed to square away. Frankie wanted Corrina to talk to the woman who had made Gabriel's and Arthur's costumes from the year before about ordering traditional Scandinavian clothes for as many people as possible—even something as simple as hats. As they broke into the cupcakes and had more coffee and cider, Kyle said he and his mother could sew anything as soon as they had a pattern, and one of his sisters-in-law could help too. Kyle also took on the task of designing a flyer, which Marcus would distribute locally, regionally, and in the Twin Cities as soon as the full program was approved and locked down. The room buzzed with plans and pleasure and potential.

But when Paul rose to get a second cupcake, he glanced outside, saw how dark it was and checked the clock on the wall. "Kyle, what time did you say you had to leave again?"

Kyle glanced at his phone and pushed to his feet. "Oh no. I need to go. I'm so sorry."

They made their hasty goodbyes. Kyle refused to take the extra cupcakes, and they hurried to the truck.

"I love my job." Kyle huddled, tucking his mittened hands between his thighs as Paul started the car. "But times like this I also hate it."

Paul could understand. He also noticed Kyle had barely enough time to toss on scrubs and get to work. They'd just eaten, but would he be hungry later? Should he drive, as tired as he was going to be? At three in the morning?

Kyle's groan interrupted his woolgathering, and when Paul asked what was wrong, Kyle held up his phone. "Snow again tonight. Another seven inches, then blowing snow all day tomorrow. Due to start right in the middle of my shift. I'm going to have to pack a bag and sleep in the lobby until my dad can come get me with the tractor in the morning. And I'm going to have to ask him to stop chores and take me in tonight so my car's not stuck in town. I bought a Ski-Doo for just this moment, but I'm not driving it in the middle of the night, especially when I'm so tired."

The worry in Paul's gut stopped expanding and exploded into a decision. "I'll take you in. And I'll pick you up too."

Kyle put his phone down and turned to Paul, his expression unreadable. "You'll pick me up? At three in the morning? And take me home in the middle of a blizzard?"

Paul shoved his nerves aside, telling himself this wasn't about a fantasy. This was practical help for a friend. "Yes, I'll pick you up at the end of your shift, and I'll take you home. To my house."

He could feel Kyle staring at him. He braced himself for a *you don't have to do that* or *I don't want to put you out*, and he got ready to argue his case. Only silence reigned, though, until Kyle finally said, "Okay."

"Okay," Paul echoed. Though privately he wondered why the simple capitulation put nervous butterflies in his stomach.

KYLE WASN'T SURE how to explain to his mom he was, for lack of a better term, sleeping over with Paul once he was done with his shift. Frankly, he barely understood what was happening. Was this a come-on? Were they friends now?

What was he supposed to pack in his overnight bag?

By the time they got to the house he had twenty minutes to throw a few things together and get to town. He emerged with his bag to talk to his mother, but it turned out Paul had done the explaining for him.

"That's so nice of Paul to give you a place to stay." She handed Kyle a soft-sided lunch tote and his thermos. "If it's bad, don't rush home. Stay tomorrow night too."

He couldn't decide if her sending him off to stay overnight with another gay man so easily came out of eagerness to hook him up, a desire to keep him safe from a snowstorm, or a sense of surety Paul would never make a move. He decided not to think about it too much. "I'm pretty much assuming I'll get called in to work tomorrow night. Which sucks, because I really need my day off." Kyle yawned, further punctuating his point.

His mother pursed her lips, but after glancing at the

clock, she kissed him on the cheek. "You'd better get going."

Kyle craned his neck toward the TV room. "I didn't say goodbye to Linda Kay or let her know where I'll be."

"Don't. She'll be upset and she'll delay you. Let me deal with it."

Kyle hated the idea, but she was right. He kissed her back, hugged her, and turned to Paul.

Paul had hovered near the fridge, but when Kyle approached, he pushed off and pulled his hands out of his coat pockets, holding them out to accept the things in Kyle's hands. "Ready to go?"

"Ready as I get." Kyle didn't need Paul to take his lunch and tea thermos, but he didn't argue because it was nice to be cared for. "I really appreciate this. Do you want me to drive so you don't have to come get me in the middle of the night?"

"I don't mind coming to get you."

"It'll be at three in the morning, remember."

"That's fine."

Okay then.

Kyle followed him to the truck, letting Paul stow his bag behind the front seat with the rest of Kyle's things. He yawned again as he climbed into the front seat. Paul frowned at him. "We should have put off the meeting with the guys."

Kyle shook his head. "I'll push through. Though I warn you, I'll pretty much face-plant when this is over."

"Understood." Paul turned onto the road leading to town.

It was crazy in the way work was before a major storm—half the staff worried about how they'd get home, and the manager ran around trying to find people to cover the shifts of nurses and aides who couldn't make it in during the storm. Kyle ended up with a 3 to 11 shift on Monday, as predicted. The good news was he'd have the two days after free instead, and therefore a faux weekend in the middle of the week.

By eleven the snow had started, and by midnight it came down in sheets. The wind had picked up as well, and soon the windows on either side of the doors were whited out with blowing snow. At first the blizzard was enough excitement to keep Kyle distracted, but by midnight he swayed on his feet. When he took his break, sipping tea from his thermos and eating the sandwich his mother had made him, he thumbed through his phone, hoping for a text from Paul even though he knew he wouldn't get one. He did have a text from Corrina.

Don't sleep with him tonight, and remember the movies.

Kyle grimaced at the screen before deleting the message. He'd sleep with Paul in a hot second, no matter what she said, except he was pretty sure once his shift was done he'd be too tired to get it up, even for Paul. He did wonder if the whole town knew he was staying at Paul's place.

Then he remembered Corrina was Logan's biggest

gossip, so if the town hadn't known, they would now.

Taking a break had been a mistake, as now all he wanted to do was sleep, and he had hours to go. Trina, the aide working with him at the nurses' station, did her best to keep him awake, chatting with him about workplace dish and musing over what she might get her boyfriend for Christmas. "I don't know what to get exactly. We haven't dated long, and I'm pretty sure he's not The One. He's more The One Who Is Handy Right Now."

Kyle swallowed a yawn and shrugged. "What's he into?"

"I don't know. Hunting? But I don't know what kind of hunting stuff to get him and what message that sends."

Kyle didn't know either. "Ask him, maybe."

Trina said she couldn't possibly, and Kyle began to tune her out, wondering what he'd get Paul if they were boyfriends.

It was a harder question than it should have been. Cologne, maybe, but he didn't know what kind. He didn't know what movie either, except the horrible Christmas romances, which he'd do over his dead body.

Maybe a knitted hat? Was that too weird? It might be, but the idea, once lodged in Kyle's head, wouldn't let go. He'd make one of the fleece-lined ones, with a dark variegated wool for the outside. A scarf and mittens to match, but not too closely. He mentally indexed his yarn stash for likely candidates and scoured Ravelry after he helped set up the morning med trays.

While the imaginary gift hat felt perfect in theory, dreaming it up led Kyle into an unexpected musing on what Gabriel had asked him. Why was he so caught up in Paul in the first place? Was Paul, like Trina's boyfriend, The One Who Was Handy Right Now?

The thought worried Kyle, though it also roused his stubborn streak, made him want to vigorously defend his attraction. Paul wasn't simply handy. He was…hot. Sweet. Sexy. Kind.

Also, he was local. That didn't mean *handy*, it meant *similar values*. They were both determined to stay in Logan, with their roots.

Except as the shift wore on, Kyle wondered. Was Paul not actually staying because he was determined to? Was he more stuck? Kyle wanted to say no, because why would he have a business if he didn't *want* to stay. It made sense, and it might be true.

The problem was Kyle didn't *know* any of this was right. He didn't *know* anything about Paul, outside of his address and his Grindr handle and the thing about peanut butter and chocolate. He had Corrina's cheat sheet, which would tell him a lot, but he hadn't even looked at it, afraid it would be full of more stuff like the movies.

Which was stupid, really. It meant he *was* imagining Paul to be someone he wasn't, or at least hoping he remained Kyle's dream man, not a real man.

At 2:50 a.m. the door buzzer sounded, Paul swept into the vestibule, and Kyle's heart skipped a beat. Coated with blown snow, Paul glittered with ice crystals from head to toe as he stomped off his boots and shook off his gloves and hat. The gloves were thick workman's suede, but the hat was ratty and awful.

Paul, however, was as handsome and glorious as ever. His beard and mustache shifted as he lifted one side of his mouth in a self-conscious smile at Kyle as he came out from the nurses' station. "Sorry I'm early. It wasn't as hard as I thought to get here."

All worries about whether or not he was approaching this potential relationship for the right reasons fled his thoughts, because when the man himself was in Kyle's line of sight, he had no doubts whatsoever. "It's okay. I'm just about done."

Trina stuck her head out from behind the med cabinet. "You go on. I've got this under control."

Kyle wanted to kiss her. "Are you sure?"

"Ann will be back from rounds in a second anyway. Go on. Get some rest, because something tells me tomorrow night is going to be a real party."

Kyle blew her a kiss and hurried to the break room to grab his jacket. It was a pretty bright blue with yellow piping, complemented with the bright orange scarf and hat he'd made himself out of worsted Merino. His gloves were a combination of the blue, yellow, and orange, double knit for an extra layer of warmth. Which he very much appreciated as he pushed open the door to the care center and got hit with the biting cold of the blizzard's wind.

It was beautiful outside, though. The air was blasted with white, whorls of wind visible because of the ice crystals it carried. The storm was just getting started, but it was already powerful enough to shut down the town. They had to fight their way to Paul's truck, and once inside, they both exhaled in relief, as if they'd scaled a mountain, not crossed a parking lot.

"I have the house stocked," Paul said as they put on their seat belts. He hadn't turned the truck off, so it was cozy warm inside. "I have a generator too, if we lose power. Won't let us run everything, but it will keep the duplex's heat on."

"We have one too, but mostly Dad uses it for the farm. If we lose power, we use the wood stove. Sometimes he'll hook the generator up long enough for lunch or to run some hot water through the pipes." Kyle rubbed his gloved hands together in front of the heat vent as he stole a glance at Paul. When he caught the man looking at him, he smiled. "Thanks again for letting me stay."

Paul blushed. "No problem."

The drive to Paul's house wasn't terrible, but this was largely because they only had to turn down a few side streets and then head over on Main. Paul frowned. "This is already more drifted than when I came to get you." He glanced at Kyle. "Did I hear you say you have to work tomorrow night?"

"Yeah, unfortunately. No one else lives close enough to town." He stopped. "Oh. I, ah, guess I need to ask you for another ride to work. Sorry."

"Not a problem." He shifted his hands on the wheel. "You can stay again tomorrow night, if the weather's still bad."

God, the man was cute when he blushed. "Thanks."

They reached Paul's house, and conversation stopped as they climbed out of the vehicle and made a beeline for the door. Kyle huddled to the side until Paul joined him, unwilling to go inside without his host. Paul held the door open and ushered him in, and they unbundled together in the warmth of the mudroom, stomping boots and hanging up gear. Once that was done, they headed into the kitchen and stood awkwardly together.

"Do you want something to eat or drink before you go to sleep?" Paul gestured to the fridge. "I got you some hard cider, but I can make cocoa too. I have ham for sandwiches, and some deer sausage."

Kyle had been about to insist he wasn't hungry or thirsty, but he wasn't sure how to behave, and a beverage might be a good buffer. "Cocoa sounds great. Thank you. Can I help you make it?"

"No, I'm fine. You go get yourself ready for bed. Bathroom's just off the bedroom."

Kyle shouldered his pack and followed the direction Paul gestured.

The duplex was plain from the outside—one-story, yellow siding, a cluster of evergreens blocking the wind on the north side—and the inside was much the same. It was a rental, Kyle knew, and it looked it. It felt like a place a man in his thirties put his things and slept and ate. It wasn't bad, but it wasn't good either.

Kyle's heart sank a little as he saw the bed made up on the sofa, then chided himself for thinking Paul would simply tumble him into the sheets. Still, he looked longingly at the comfy queen in Paul's bedroom as he changed into his pajama pants and a sweatshirt, sitting on the fluffy comforter as he tugged on a pair of wool socks. His phone buzzed, which surprised him. Maybe a weather alert? He pulled it out of his jeans, rolling his eyes when he saw the notification. Another text from Corrina.

I'm serious. No hanky-panky. Not yet.

Kyle punched a text back. *Why are you up at three in the morning?*

I set an alarm.

For crying out loud. *Go to bed, Corrina.* Anticipating her next text, he added, *I'm headed there too. Have to work again tomorrow night.*

Give my love to Paul.

Kyle deleted the texts, shaking his head with a reluctant smile. Like he could walk out there and tell Paul Corrina said hi. Because then he'd have to admit he got middle-of-the-night texts from Corrina Anderson warning him away from sex with his crush.

When he padded out into the living room, Paul handed him a mug of steaming chocolate milk, but his gaze stayed focused on Kyle's socks. "Those are cool. Where did you get them?"

Kyle wiggled his toes proudly. "I made them."

Paul's eyes went wide. "You did? That's amazing."

"Not really. It's a variegated yarn, so the pattern makes itself. Socks are easy. I can make them in a weekend." He saw the longing in Paul's gaze and melted. "I'll make you a pair as soon as I have a day off, as a thanks for letting me crash here."

"You don't have to do that," Paul said in tones making it clear he wanted someone to make socks for him.

Kyle settled into the sofa and patted the other side to urge Paul to follow suit. "What colors do you like?"

Paul sat, curling his hands around his own mug, hunching his shoulders a little as he sipped it. "Oh, I'm not particular. Whatever you have is fine."

Kyle wasn't going to admit how insane his yarn stash was. "What's your favorite color?"

Paul shrugged. "Orange. Like the scarf you have." He blushed. "But you don't have to make them. I was only admiring."

Oh, Kyle was *making* Paul some socks. "I have just the skein. I only wish I'd brought it with me. A blizzard is the perfect time to knit."

"Where do you buy it? There's no shop in town anymore, is there?"

"Heavens, no. It closed before I was out of high school. There used to be a passable store in Eveleth, but it closed. There's another in Hibbing, but I don't often get over that way. Mostly I order online, unless I can get to Yarn Harbor in Duluth."

Paul nodded, clutching his mug. The conversation ran dry, and they sipped in silence. Kyle tried to rally his charm and work up a flirt, but he was so tired he felt drunk. He stifled a sigh. "I wish I had tomorrow off. I'm going to be a horrible guest. Sleeping, showering, taking off again."

"Don't worry about that." Paul held his mug tighter. "Sleep as late as you want. I'm giving you my bedroom."

Kyle stared at the couch, trying to imagine Paul's big body fitting on it. "No way. I'm not letting you sleep here."

"It's no problem. I've fallen asleep on the couch a million times."

Kyle shook his head and set his cocoa aside. "No. I seriously will not let you."

"*You* can't sleep on the couch. You're way too tall."

This was true. But Kyle couldn't handle the thought of Paul making himself uncomfortable on his account. He put his hand on Paul's thigh. "Come sleep in your bed with me. I promise not to molest you. If I stay awake long enough to hit the pillow, it will be a miracle."

He got ready for a round of arguments, to barrel

dizzily through them, but to his surprise, Paul blushed and nodded. "All right."

Kyle wondered if he'd caved too quickly about promising no sex as he brushed his teeth, his dick perking up at the sounds of Paul undressing in the other room. Corrina's warning floated back to him, which was annoying, but honestly he was afraid he'd embarrass himself if he tried to start anything. Wouldn't that be something, to finally seduce Paul into some action only to find out his libido had gone to sleep.

It woke, though, as Kyle climbed beneath the sheet where Paul's body radiated heat. The sheets were crisp and clean, smelling of laundry soap, but the scent of their owner overwhelmed the detergent and engaged all Kyle's senses. Paul faced away from him, which let Kyle stare at his back, imagining himself curling around it, running a hand over that muscled thigh.

Yep. His libido, his cock, everything was pretty wide awake.

Kyle arranged himself carefully on his side as he tried to decide how to initiate contact. A foot on his leg? No, too obvious. Snuggling close? Too weird.

The bed was so soft, so warm. The wind howled outside, but Kyle was snug, wrapped in heavy blankets, surrounded by a furnace of a man. Inhaling his soft, spicy scent. He wanted to sink into Paul too. Pull him close after fucking him hard, drift off to sleep sated by sex.

He shut his eyes, telling himself he'd think of the

perfect way to seduce his host as soon as he rested his eyes a second.

The second expanded, and the next thing he knew the bed shifted, the room lit by the thin light of morning as Paul climbed beneath the comforter, the only sound in the house the wind howling outside and the toilet filling in the bathroom. Kyle turned to Paul, blinking in the confusion of being half-awake.

Paul smiled at him, sleepy-eyed and shy. "Sorry to wake you. Go back to sleep. It's only seven."

He's so pretty. Unthinking, Kyle stroked Paul's whiskered jaw.

Paul didn't flinch away. If anything, he relaxed into the touch, his eyes closing briefly in a long, slow blink.

Heat expanded in Kyle, sloughing off slumber, taking him to where he'd left off before falling asleep.

Forget Corrina's warning. Paul wanted this. He'd invited Kyle to stay over. Gave in with one urge to share the bed. Lay there now all soft and vulnerable, so sexy, waiting.

Kyle wanted this. More than ever, more than the dreamy, distant longing for the man he'd harbored for years. Right now in Paul's bed, surrounded by blizzard—this wasn't fantasy. This was real. No flirtations, no setups. Just the two of them together in this bed, safe against the snow.

Putting a hand on Paul's shoulder, Kyle pushed him on his back and brought their lips together as he climbed aboard his man.

Chapter Seven

PAUL TRIED TO say no. He really did. He put his hands on Kyle's arms to push him gently but firmly away. Yet somehow he pulled instead of pushed, drawing Kyle closer. Before Paul could realize what he'd done, Kyle pinned him to the mattress and braced his hands into the pillow on either side of Paul's head. For a moment they held still, Paul staring up at Kyle looming down, his face shadowed and mysterious in the early morning dark, eyes dancing with promise.

Then those eyes closed as Kyle leaned closer and took Paul's mouth with his own.

It was a slow, sensual assault. The sound of their lips smacking together—sealing, releasing, reclosing—echoed in the bedroom, muffled by the snow outside. Kyle's fingers were long and clever, sliding into Paul's hair, trailing down his cheek, tucking behind his shoulder. Kyle's body was hard and intent with purpose as he ground it meaningfully, lingeringly against Paul's own. His mouth nipped, sucked, teased at Paul's, sometimes stealing a tongue inside, but mostly kissing, as if he had nothing else to do in the world.

We shouldn't. The words were there in Paul's mouth, but they couldn't escape through the kiss, and soon they drowned entirely.

He hadn't forgotten Kyle's aggression and innuendo against the shop door—he had, in fact, dreamed about it often, sometimes while still awake. That same forcefulness was back now, and it made him shiver. Gone was Kyle's playful, swishy demeanor—he was all business now, and his work was coaxing Paul into pleasure. When Kyle pushed Paul's T-shirt high enough to expose his nipples, he shivered and arched into Kyle's touch. He held still as Kyle shoved his sweatpants down, palming the naked globes of Paul's ass.

When Kyle's naked cock brushed against his own, Paul shut his eyes and groaned.

"That's right." Kyle took them both in hand as he kissed his way up Paul's neck. "Relax and let me make you feel good."

It all felt a little too good. Paul hissed and clutched at Kyle's waist, trying to slow him down.

Laughing wickedly, Kyle kissed his way along Paul's neck. Pushing Paul's legs until they bent at the knees, he mouthed a hot, wet trail down the center of Paul's chest, pausing to swirl his tongue in a whorl of hair, making Paul gasp for air as Kyle nipped with just a hint of teeth at his belly. He kissed his way around Paul's groin, teasing the rigid length of his cock before diving in to suck gently on his balls. The more Paul writhed, the slower Kyle went, until Paul shook with want as Kyle lazily laved his way along Paul's thigh to brush a kiss at his knee.

Shuddering, whimpering, Paul held still, unsure of how to behave, so he waited to be told. He wasn't disappointed. Kyle lifted his head and smiled sweetly at Paul before bending to kiss him with the same patient languor he'd given Paul's balls.

"Tell me what you want." Kyle kissed Paul's cheek, his chin, the side of his mouth, as his hand idly stroked Paul's length. "Do you want me to suck you? Fuck you? Do you want to suck *me?*" He nipped at Paul's trembling Adam's apple. "Do *you* want to fuck *me?*"

Fuck him? "I—I thought…"

Words left him as Kyle purred against his pulse point. "You thought I was so toppy I wouldn't bottom?" He laughed and bit the place he'd been kissing. "Honey, I can drive from *anywhere.*"

Paul's dick throbbed, aching to spill, but his brain felt broken. He didn't know what Kyle meant, only that the way he said it made Paul want to get on his knees and pant. "I—I don't understand."

"Let me show you."

The bed shifted, and for a terrible moment, Paul was alone. Only a moment—as quickly as he realized his condition, Kyle was back, holding a tube of Astroglide and a condom in his hand. He placed them on the bed beside Paul, leaned over and kissed his quivering abdomen. "Where do you keep your toys?"

Paul blushed hotly. He would have lied and said he didn't have any, but something about the way Kyle looked at him broke everything inside him. "In…in the bottom drawer of my dresser."

He blushed more as Kyle vanished, turning even more scarlet when Kyle reappeared with the big black dildo he knew more intimately than he wanted to admit.

Kyle pushed the silicone against Paul's lips and slipped the dildo inside.

Paul's body jolted—in shock, in shame, but most of all in liquid-silver pleasure. He held still as Kyle pushed the fake cock deeper, until it filled his mouth.

Looking him coolly in the eye, Kyle said, "Open your throat."

God help him, Paul did.

Shirt tucked under his armpits, pants tangled on one ankle, cock weeping and hole clenching, Paul let Kyle fuck his favorite dildo in and out of his mouth. Into his throat far enough to trigger a gag reflex—a reflex Kyle patiently waited out, until Paul relaxed enough to let Kyle fuck him with the toy however he wanted.

"That's right. Suck it good, honey." Kyle had shed his own pants and his shirt. While he fucked Paul's mouth with one hand, he lubed Paul's fingers with the other. "Keep sucking while you prep me." He guided a lube-slick finger to his own ass. "Push in. Don't be shy.

I like it—" He stopped, shut his eyes and sucked in a breath, then smiled as Paul did as he was told. Then he opened his eyes and regarded Paul with so much self-possession he almost glowed. "Rough. I like it a little rough. Fuck me with your fingers, honey, while I fuck your throat."

Paul did. One, then two fingers into the hot, slick warmth of Kyle's pert little ass while Kyle stroked his cheek and fucked his mouth unforgivingly with the dildo. When Paul whimpered, Kyle kissed his nose and told him to go deeper, fuck harder. He told Paul to add a third finger, then left the dildo hanging from Paul's lips while he reached around and slipped a condom on Paul.

"Keep sucking, honey." He gently pulled Paul's fingers from his own ass, smiling fondly at Paul as he aimed his hole over Paul's ready cock. "Suck on the cock for me, and hold still. I'm going to take you for a ride. Don't come until I tell you, please."

Then he slammed his ass onto Paul's dick, driving the dildo deep into Paul, and fucked himself up and down.

Drooling around the dildo, Paul watched helpless, drugged on shock and pleasure as Kyle rode him. He held still as Kyle worked himself, enjoying the delicious heat of Kyle's tight hole, but mostly sinking into the unexpected control he was more than happy to let Kyle hold over him. Especially…this way. His brain kept breaking, feeling like Kyle had oh-so-casually solved one of the greatest logic puzzles of his life.

Kyle kissed his nose and licked the lips straining around the dildo as he kept riding. "Nice fat cock. *Mmm.* My favorite." He pushed the dildo in and out, gently. "Do you like fat cocks too, baby? How about I put this in your ass so I can kiss your mouth while I fuck myself on you?"

Groaning, Paul drooled more. He didn't move his hands because he hadn't been told to, not until Kyle greased it and put it into his hands.

"Put it inside yourself." Kyle tugged on Paul's bottom lip with his teeth. "Reach around and push it in deep."

It was a difficult order to comply with—Kyle kept kissing him, occasionally moving up and down on his cock while Paul tried to cram the dildo blind into his back door. He groaned as the tip breached him, shivered as Kyle's pinch helped distract him. He shuddered as the length filled him, panted when it was buried to the hilt.

"Perfect. We're both nice and full." Kyle kissed him languidly. "Can you keep yourself from coming until I tell you?"

Paul nodded, huffing against sensation. Years as Arthur Anderson's bed partner hadn't come without any tricks learned.

"Good." Kyle pushed himself up, just a little, and braced himself on Paul's shoulders. "Now fuck me. Hard."

Paul did. Staring up at Kyle like a lost boy finding his way home, he thrust with his hips, crying out at the way the dildo moved inside him as he fucked into Kyle. It slipped, it shifted, eventually sliding out of him with an audible *swuck* as he kept his focus on giving Kyle what he wanted. He watched Kyle's face morph into ecstasy, tense up as he got close.

"That's it." Kyle clutched at Paul, holding himself more and more rigid as Paul hit all the right places. "Perfect. Fuck me good, baby. *Oh. Yeah.* Harder. Faster. Go, baby. Go."

Paul went. He wanted to come so badly he thought it might shoot out his ears, but he held back and pressed on, until Kyle said, *"Come, now,"* and then he exploded inside Kyle's ass, feeling like he emptied his soul into the condom. He held still after he was spent, as Kyle sent ropes of spunk over his chest before collapsing onto him.

"There." Breathless, Kyle kissed Paul's neck. "That's how I can drive from anywhere."

Paul tried to catch his breath. He hissed a little as Kyle pulled off, rolled over, and took care of the condom. He tracked Kyle as he disappeared into the hall, ran water in the bathroom, reappeared with a warm, wet cloth and applied it to Paul's splooge-coated chest.

Kyle covered a yawn as he wadded up the cloth and placed it on the nightstand. "I think I might get a bit more sleep, if that's okay." He slipped under the covers and nuzzled beside Paul. "Can you join me, or do you have to go in to work?"

"The shop is closed, but I'm on call to anyone in town with an emergency. Arthur might bring Gabriel in later on the Ski-Doo, if the weather's okay. But no. I don't have to go in."

"Good." Kyle curled around Paul, drawing him under the covers.

Paul went with him, but he didn't join Kyle in sleeping. He lay there for an hour, staring at the ceiling, a quiet panic building inside him. When the phone on his dresser buzzed, he took the call in the living room, assuring the caller no, he didn't mind at all coming over to help sort out a busted pipe. In fact, he was happy to do it.

He left a note for Kyle on the table, saying he should help himself to whatever he wanted to eat or drink and promised to be home in time to take him to work. Then he bundled up and headed out to his truck, where he huddled in the cab and swam in the confusion of what had just happened between him and Kyle and whether or not he should let it ever happen again.

KYLE WOKE FEELING pretty damn smug.

He was in Paul's house, in Paul's bed. He'd fucked Paul, and pretty well at that. He'd worried he'd gone a little too far a little too fast, but he'd seen how Paul responded. He'd liked it. A lot. He'd come like a fountain. They both had. It had been perfect.

Corrina was so wrong. That had been *exactly* what they needed.

He wasn't surprised to find Paul gone, and his heart melted at the bag of sugared candy and box of green tea on the counter. He sipped some of the latter while he showered and dressed, and ate a piece of candy before foraging through Paul's fridge for sandwich material.

He nosed through Paul's video library after he ate, noting the absence of any porn or the rumored favorite holiday romances. A deeper search revealed both the porn and the cheesy movies, sadly more of the latter than the former. A *lot* more. Paul had at least twenty Christmas love stories, and several of them were multi-movie collections. He had a stack from the library too, hidden in the bottom of the entertainment center.

Kyle stopped snooping, knowing Paul could and would be home any second. He texted his mom to let her know he'd probably stay in town again. He couldn't wait until his shift was over—during his shower he'd imagined all the ways he'd take Paul after his shift, and he was pretty sure he'd spend most of work thinking about fucking Paul as well.

He'd hoped to get some action *before* going to the care center, but at two, Paul still hadn't come home. Kyle was about to text him and make sure everything was okay when someone knocked on the back door. Peering through the window didn't do him much good, only revealed a shrouded figure huddled on the steps.

Frowning, he opened the door.

It was Edna Michealson, who Kyle remembered too late was Paul's neighbor on the other side of the duplex. She huddled beneath a purple parka that looked ready to swallow her whole as she glared at Kyle warily. "Kyle Parks? What on earth are you doing in Paul's house?"

"Good afternoon, Mrs. Michealson. Paul let me stay in town so I could make it to my shift at the care center tonight. Can I help you?"

She flattened her lips. "I have a huge drift on my front steps with an ice patch under it. I'm going to fall and break a hip."

"I can take care of that for you, no problem. Give me a minute to get my boots on."

She nodded toward the front of the house. "He scooped earlier, but it's blowing something terrible. And the back walk isn't done nearly well enough. I almost slipped twice. He never answers when I phone him, so I don't bother calling. I heard someone through the wall, so I thought he was home."

Kyle took note that Paul's neighbor heard noises coming through the walls. "Do you want me to walk you to your door?"

She huffed and waved her hand as if she couldn't possibly, as all the while her face made it clear she wanted that very much. "I'm not the sort of woman who troubles people."

Kyle dealt with the Mrs. Michealsons of the world

on a daily basis. He gave his best old-lady-charming smile. "It's not any trouble at all to help you. I'm only sorry I didn't already have my boots and coat on. I hate to make you wait. Will you come inside? I'll be ready before you know it."

She fussed and clucked, but she came inside, and Kyle hurried to get his winter gear on. While he did so, Edna surveyed Paul's apartment with the eagle eye of a small-town busybody. "Keeps it cleaner in here than I'd have thought. Not terribly homey though. The boy needs a wife." She paused, pursing her lips in a way that told Kyle she'd remembered wives weren't something one discussed in the same sentence with Paul. When Kyle appeared in front of her with his hat in hand, she eyed it speculatively. "That's some fine work. Did your mother make it?"

"I did. Do you knit, Mrs. Michealson?"

She blinked at him in surprise. "I didn't know boys were knitting nowadays." Her gaze fell on the hat, her expression wistful. "I was a master hand knitter. Level three." She touched her weathered, age-spotted hands. "Haven't been able to manage so much as a stockinette stitch for years. Too much arthritis."

The loss in her expression moved Kyle. "I'm so sorry to hear that. A master hand knitter! I'm not brave enough to consider it."

"It takes work and discipline is all." She ran gnarled fingers over his hat. "You have some promise here, but your stitches could be more even."

"You know, Gabriel has talked about having a knitting group meet at the library. I wish I could talk you into coming, giving some advice to us. You have to be the only master hand knitter in the whole county."

She preened over his flattery, and when he got to the actual scooping of her steps, the only way he got her to go inside instead of keeping him company was to promise he'd come in for tea once he was finished. Given how he knew that conversation was going to go, he texted Paul to let him know where he was.

He was a little surprised Paul didn't text back, but probably he was tied up in a job.

As Kyle expected, Edna told him stories about all the knitting projects she'd done over the years, and they commiserated over the lack of a good yarn store in the area. He promised to stop by with a better sample of his work and some of the more delicious skeins from his yarn stash the next time he was over at Paul's.

Edna raised her eyebrows at him with her school-teacher look. "Are you stepping out with him, young man?"

The old-fashioned expression made Kyle grin. "I am." They hadn't discussed it, but they'd had sex, it was great, and Paul wanted a boyfriend. It wasn't a big leap.

"Hmm." She looked like she couldn't quite decide if she should condone the relationship or not.

Kyle decided they should simply avoid that subject. "I don't suppose I could talk you into visiting the care center sometime? The ladies there always love a good chat. If you come on salon day, your ears will burn with how much talk spins around."

As expected, this made Edna prickle a bit. "I don't dare so much as glance at the place. My son is so eager to stuff me away. He'd probably pack me up if I so much as put a toe over the door."

"He'd have a hard time of it. We're full up. Do you know how many people we turn away? I always hate to hear people having to go out of town, but it happens. This says nothing of the need for elder housing in general. People like you who are perfectly fine on their own but need someone to keep their walk clear. A common area where they can meet and catch up on news. A shuttle to the grocery store and help with ordering things online."

Edna huffed. "Sounds like a fairy castle, young man."

No, it sounded like a decent senior care facility, though in a town like Logan it might as well be one.

The sound of wheels on snow made them both look up, and to be honest, Kyle was as sorry to see their visit end as Edna was. He embraced her and promised to come by again soon. "Would it be all right to bring Linda Kay?"

Edna patted Kyle on the cheek, then kissed the spot she'd touched. "You're too *good* for him, you know."

Kyle grinned. "But he's the one I *want*, Edna."

She laughed, looking twenty years younger. "Then best of luck putting a hook in his mouth."

She waved at him as he went out the door, though he quickly forgot her as he saw it was Frankie Blackburn coming up the walk, not Paul.

"Hi, Kyle. Marcus and I are taking you in to work."

"Oh." Kyle frowned. "Is Paul okay?"

"It's a little complicated." Frankie hunched into his red coat as a wave of wind buffeted them. He indicated the door of Paul's house with a nod. "Go get your things. I'll meet you in the truck."

Kyle tried not to be worried. "I won't be long. Just need to grab my badge, and I'm ready to go."

"Ah. Sorry, I should have been more clear." Frankie looked abashed. "You should get *all* your things. Marcus and I will be hosting you tonight."

The worry in Kyle knotted into dread, but before he could ask for clarification, Frankie headed down the sidewalk, back to the truck.

Chapter Eight

KYLE TRIED TO talk himself out of panic while he gathered his few things from inside Paul's house. He hadn't done anything wrong. There wasn't any reason to feel bad. Something had probably gotten complicated, is all.

Except he couldn't invent any excuse that wasn't Paul not wanting to sleep with him again.

Corrina's warning drifted back, and Kyle swore as he stuffed clothes into his bag. It was *crazy*. There wasn't a thing wrong with two healthy, single gay men having sex. Paul hadn't been unwilling.

Had he?

No. Paul had been *very* willing. So what had Kyle done wrong?

Frankie and Marcus drove a smart new SUV, and it was warm and cozy as Kyle slipped into the backseat with his duffel. From the awkward looks they cast his way, it was clear whatever went down *was* all about Kyle, and they didn't want to talk about it if they could get away with it.

Tough.

Taking in the brick wall that was Marcus Gardner, Kyle focused his efforts on Frankie. "Can you at least tell me what's going on?"

Frankie dodged him. "I…ah, will walk you into work. Okay?"

Please work with me on this, he shot Kyle silently with pleading eyes.

Kyle arched an eyebrow and sent a silent message back. *Okay, but this better be good.*

Though Frankie did go with him inside the care center, it took almost five minutes for Kyle to get him through his nest of adoring fans who decided their favorite stylist arriving meant they could get their hair done. When they were finally alone in the break room, Kyle felt like he was ready to explode. "What is going on? What happened? What did I do?"

Frankie looked distinctly uncomfortable. "I don't know what you did to set him off, but he's all freaked out. In your defense, it doesn't take much with Paul. All I know is Arthur called Marcus and begged him to take you off Paul's hands."

The awful, heavy feeling settled in Kyle's gut was so much more than simple embarrassment.

"I'm so sorry." Frankie didn't put a hand on Kyle, but he looked like he wanted to. "This is so awkward. I can't believe I let Marcus make me the yenta."

"No, that's Corrina." Kyle rolled his eyes at himself. "Jesus, she's going to be a piece of work when she hears about this."

Frankie frowned. "Corrina?"

Kyle told him about Gabriel hooking him up with Arthur's mom, about how he'd been following her advice to the letter, and it was working—and then he'd thrown it out the window once he had Paul in bed. Now he was thrown out too.

When Kyle finished, Frankie blinked a few times, then shook his head. "Huh. I can't decide what's weirder, Gabriel thinking that was a good idea, or you thinking the reason he freaked out was because you had sex."

Kyle raised his eyebrows. "You think it was something else?" His heart pinched. *Was it because he's just not into me?*

"I think Paul Jansen is a wonderful man who is more than a little bit messed up in the relationship department." Frankie leaned against the wall and folded his arms over his chest. "He and Arthur were always an awkward couple, but while Arthur was denying they were in a serious relationship, Paul was the one who *wanted* it to be real but never did anything about it except wish. I've watched him date other men for a year, and it's like he has a checklist to make sure guys are a mess before he'll take them home. Then he's upset because he can't find a boyfriend."

Kyle bristled on Paul's behalf. "The dating scene here is abysmal."

"I'm sure that's true, but it's not the whole problem. Gabriel and I plugged Paul into OkCupid and took him for a weekend of speed dating in Minneapolis this summer. Even if you give him a large sample of men, he shoves aside the nice guys and goes in hard for the ones a blind man could see would never work."

"So you're saying I won't work?"

Frankie gave him a withering look. "I'm saying you're a nice guy. A good guy. Stable, kind, decent with other humans. I don't know if it's because he doesn't feel he deserves happiness or if his wiring is screwy on a sub-basement level—but no, I'm not surprised you showed Paul a slice of heaven and he went running."

Which, actually, made Corrina's warning make sense. She could have *said* that, dammit. Kyle threw up his hands. "I don't know what I'm supposed to do now."

Frankie lifted his eyebrows, lips twisting into a wry smile. "What do you mean, you don't know what you're supposed to do? You get up his nose, is what."

"He just kicked me out of his house."

Frankie snorted. "No. He begged his best friends to quietly remove you. Do you have plans to comply?"

Hope bloomed in Kyle, and he smiled. "Frankie, you're the best thing that ever happened to Logan."

"You only say that because your hair has never looked better." His gaze flicked to the top of Kyle's head. "Which, speaking of, I'll text you available times I have for a touch-up on those roots." He pushed off the wall. "I'll do some recon while you're at work, and I'll make sure I'm the one to pick you up at eleven."

Frankie left, and Kyle was a distracted mess all through his shift. He tried to guess what kind of recon Frankie was doing and wracked his brain to think of how he could fail to go quietly. What he *wanted* to do was storm over to Paul's house and demand to know what was going on. He didn't know if that was a good idea or not.

He worried, too, if maybe this was a sign he shouldn't pursue the man at all. The very idea of Paul deliberately seeking out bad relationships made Kyle's head spin. Why would anyone do that? How was Kyle supposed to combat it?

He admitted too, as he woolgathered while helping a resident through her sponge bath, a lot of his pursuing Paul had been about chasing an ideal. His worries that he was attracted to Paul based on a fantasy were entirely valid fears. His own conception of who Paul was and what he could be to Kyle wasn't based on Paul at all, only what Paul could be. Which was…well, juvenile. Maybe he *was* too young to date Paul.

By the time his shift ended, Kyle was a grumpy, self-doubting mess. If it wasn't drifting so bad in the country, he'd have called his dad for a ride. Instead, when Frankie buzzed in through the door, Kyle got ready to tell him to forget the whole thing. Except before he could, Frankie threw him a curve ball. "Marcus and I think you should confront him. Tonight.

Right now."

"What if he kicks me out, this time in person?"

"That's not Paul's style. But if it got awkward, you could call me, and I'd come get you."

Dizzy with nerves, Kyle followed Frankie out to his car. The wind whipped around them, throwing frozen snow into their faces, making conversation impossible until they were inside the vehicle.

Kyle hunched forward in his seat. "I want to do it, but I'm nervous." It would suck to be rejected that hard in person. Especially since he was still sore from Paul's secondhand version.

"You don't have to, obviously." Frankie squinted out the window. "You *do* have to make up your mind, though, because I want to get out of this weather as soon as possible."

Kyle shut his eyes, took in a deep breath and let it out. *What the hell. Might as well make it a fully fucked-up day.* "Drop me off at Paul's."

The drive to the duplex was slow and grueling, though the whole experience matched the turbulent emotions Kyle felt inside. What the hell was he supposed to say? Was this smart? Would it be worse to do it now, or later?

He had no idea. For all he imagined himself a confident, sassy queen who loved to break the rules, right now he felt little more than an awkward mess. When Frankie put the car in park in Paul's drive, Kyle was shaking and almost ready to bail.

He didn't, though. He grabbed his bag, thanked Frankie, nodded at the wishes for good luck and got out of the car. Then he marched up the stairs, pushed aside the queasy feeling in his gut and knocked on the door.

It took Paul so long to open it, Kyle wasn't sure he was going to. When he finally did, he turned on the porch light, illuminating Kyle as he stood there in the bitter wind and swirling snow.

PAUL SHOULDN'T HAVE answered the door.

He'd made the decision being with Kyle was a mistake. He knew if he let Kyle stay, they'd have sex again, and God knew what else. Paul wouldn't want to call it off after another night. Maybe some would see it as cowardly to get Arthur and Marcus to help cut Kyle loose, but it was kinder to everyone in the end. He should stick by his guns and not let Kyle inside, because if he did, all his careful work would fall apart.

But it *was* a blizzard. What if Kyle had walked here? What if his ride had already left?

More important than any other question, and probably the biggest reason Paul opened the door: what if he didn't find out *why* Kyle had come back?

So he let Kyle in.

Kyle looked angry. And nervous, and hurt. He didn't say anything at first, only peeled out of his winter gear and hung it neatly on the coat tree by the door, parking his boots on the mat. When he finished, he kept his arms folded and his gaze fixed on the wall.

"That was really shitty, what you did," he said at last.

Paul didn't have anything to say in reply, because Kyle was right. It had been shitty, kicking Kyle out without telling him why, without even doing the deed himself. He should apologize, but with Kyle in front of him, calling him on the carpet, all he could do was stand still with his back against the wall by the kitchen and wait to hear what happened next.

What happened was Kyle turned to look at him, all that anger and hurt and confusion aimed at Paul. "I can't even make sense of the last eighteen hours, can't decide what I did wrong. Because the last thing I knew, you were having a damn good time."

Paul stared at Kyle's feet, unable to meet his gaze. "You didn't do anything wrong. It's not you. It's me."

"What the *hell*, Paul?" Kyle threw up his hands. "Come on. You're better than this."

The truth was, Paul knew he *wasn't* better than that. And it was the whole reason this had to stop right now.

Kyle paced back and forth in Paul's living room. "I get that you're doing whatever you can to drive me off. Probably I should let you, but I can't."

He stopped pacing and stood in front of Paul, still not touching him, yet drawing Paul's attention up like a magnet so he stared into that pretty, intense face.

Kyle made angry gestures which were, technically,

quite feminine, and yet everything about him was control and command. "Today sucked. Really sucked. I didn't even realize how much until I got here and saw you again. And I finally understand if I keep pushing forward, trying to wheedle you into place, the worst thing that might happen is I succeed." He stopped pacing and aimed all his intensity straight at Paul. "Do you want me here, or not? Do you want me, maybe, but this was too much too fast? Did you fake how much you liked the way I fucked you? Why did you kick me out, and what do you want, or don't want, from me now?"

Paul admitted to himself how much, despite everything he'd said to Arthur, he wanted to try again with Kyle. Not just sex, but…dating. Kyle. Being with him. Maybe carefully. Or maybe not. Maybe crazily. But that bubble of hope quickly crashed into a sea of self-consciousness and doubt. He couldn't tell Kyle he wanted him. He couldn't tell him to go. He couldn't do anything but stand there, helpless, while Kyle glared expectantly.

Kyle remained tense, but eventually his rigidity began to melt away in a slow thaw. He sighed. "Oh, Paul. What in the world am I going to do with you?"

Paul rounded his shoulders, trying to protect the confused ache in the center of his chest. "I'm sorry."

Kyle stepped close enough to touch Paul's hair—a gentle stroke, almost a petting, and it made him burn for more. "Is this really because I'm younger?" His expression tightened. "Or because I'm tall and skinny? Only your type if you close your eyes and pretend I'm Arthur?"

He couldn't meet Kyle's hard gaze. "I don't know why I did it. I…panicked."

The hand on his hair stilled. "Are you panicking right now?"

Yes? No? Paul didn't know anymore. He shrugged, but carefully, so he didn't lose that hand. It dawned on him how ridiculous he was, and he tried to find the words to cut Kyle loose. He deserved better.

Before he could so much as stammer, though, Kyle's delicate fingers shifted to his chin and tilted it up so Paul had no choice but look him in the eye. What he saw in Kyle arrested him, drowned out the whispers that he should try to drive Kyle away. This look had captivated him this morning when Kyle had rolled over and kissed him. How Kyle had looked when he ordered Paul around the bed. Directed him into the crazy place where it was Paul's dick in Kyle's ass, but he still felt like the one getting done.

That, he realized, was what he'd run from. That feeling. The crazy upside-down turning of the world. The way everything kept shifting until Paul was so inside-out he couldn't do anything but be. Because it was so perfect, so right, it scared him. The realization filled him with shame. When had he become such a mess that getting exactly what he wanted most terrified him enough he tried to send it away?

Kyle teased Paul's beard and tucked a curling blond hair away from his forehead. "You love it when I take over for you. You need letting go as much as I need taking control." He kissed the corner of Paul's mustache, teasing the seam of his lips open with his tongue. "Let me take you, Paul."

Shuddering, Paul closed his eyes and swayed toward Kyle, turning his face toward that seeking mouth.

Kyle moved away, whispering kisses down Paul's neck. "There are so many things I want to do to you. Sweet things. Wicked things." He licked at the pulse of Paul's neck. "But I can't do them if you run from me after."

Kyle's touch on Paul's hair became a regretful stroke. Paul chased those fingers. "I know. I'm sorry."

Kyle pulled his fingers out of reach. "I don't just want to have sex with you. I want to *date* you. Go out to dinner without the pretense of Winter Wonderland. Go to a movie. Make dinner at your house. Make you socks and hats. Bring you to my house, let you have a meal with my family. Get to know you better."

Paul wanted that too—well, he wanted it in general. What Kyle had rattled off was pretty much Paul's laundry list of the things he wanted in a relationship. Which meant not only were they great together in bed, they had good odds of being right together out of it too.

So why had he pushed this away? Why did part of him want to push away now?

He needed to distract himself, and sex seemed a good way to do that. But when he tried to steal a kiss, Kyle wouldn't let him. "I can't do today again."

Paul ran fingers across the front of Kyle's scrubs. When Kyle still didn't kiss him, Paul let out a heavy sigh. "I want to date you too. I'm worried I'll fuck it up, but I'll give it a try."

"You won't fuck it up." *Now* Kyle's lips met Paul's. Briefly, a slow, electric brush of lips. "But right now, baby, I'm going to fuck *you.*"

Another sigh, this one dragging Paul under Kyle like a foot sliding into a shoe. "Sounds good to me."

Chapter Nine

K YLE WATCHED PAUL'S eyes flutter closed, muscles go weak, body posture opening—all the signs of surrender. Which would be great, exactly what he wanted.

It was just that *he* was a jagged ball of nerves and doubt.

Sometimes he wished he had some kind of gay bestie or fruit fly like the movies, somebody he could head-shrink with over coffee. If he had that person, one of his first confessionals would be that while he wanted to be a top, *felt* he was one…the reality of topping a guy was a fuck of a lot harder than it should be. Which made him worry whether he was doing it wrong. Maybe he really wasn't one. This would be the point where his mythological bestie would either tell him to get over himself or wince and say, "Well, to be honest…" and proceed to explain his issues.

He didn't have that bestie. His sidekick was his twin, who while wonderful, had her limits in this sort of thing. His friends were the girls at work and a few guys from community college, and none of them wanted to discuss his complicated thoughts about sex. And none of them were here, right now, as he ran his thumb down Paul's cheek, panic rattling through his lust.

Can I do this? Can I actually do this?

What if the reason he bolted last time was because I suck?

What if I suck again, this time so much it's over before it starts?

Kyle swallowed his doubts as best he could and bent to press his lips to Paul's neck.

The shudder this gesture made ripple through Paul did good things for Kyle's confidence. He kissed the pulse point, tracing his tongue over the rapid flutter beneath Paul's skin.

Paul went so boneless he started to slide down the wall.

Catching him by the elbows, Kyle kept up the kisses while his brain raced ahead to sort out where they should move this make-out session to. Bed? Couch? A kitchen chair? To the floor right here?

He was overthinking this. He should just follow his gut. Except right now his gut was mostly frozen, throwing up its hands helplessly when Kyle poked at it.

Punting, he trailed kisses to Paul's ear. "Where should I take you, baby?" He winced inwardly, the endearment feeling a little off. He sucked on Paul's lobe to distract him from noticing. "Should we go to your room? The couch? Your kitchen table?"

He'd meant that last one as a joke, but though Paul murmured, "Wherever you want," it was crystal clear Paul got off on the suggestion of being done while laid out in the kitchen. Which…hot.

Do you really have the chops to pull that off? His gut yanked a blanket over its head at the question.

Kyle pushed past the fear and dug deep into his reserves for bravado. Made *mmm-hmm* and other approving, wickedly suggestive grunts as he hooked an index finger in Paul's belt loop and led him into the darkened kitchen. Slipped a hand into Paul's waistband and scanned the table in question over his shoulder as he made more love to Paul's neck. It looked pretty sturdy. Mostly clean too, just a little bit of mail and a disheveled newspaper. Kyle could all too easily imagine Paul laid out across it. Naked, heels braced against the edge, knees open wide. Cock red and resting on his thigh, balls heavy and swinging above a puckered, flexing hole.

Oh, but he hoped Edna slept like the dead.

Now it was Kyle who shuddered, biting on his bottom lip before turning to Paul and giving his mouth the same treatment. The wave of lust washed over the fear, and he cupped Paul's erection through his jeans.

"Strip," he demanded as he pulled back, breathless and hard as a rock. "Take off your clothes." He drew a chair away from the table and collapsed into it, not taking his eyes off Paul. "Slowly."

Paul didn't hesitate. If he was nervous, he hid it

well. The more direction he got, the calmer he seemed to be. He unbuttoned his shirt, peeling it away to reveal a long-sleeved thermal tee. Skintight, it outlined Paul's body like an invitation. *Here are his biceps, all meaty and toned. Take a look at the pecs too. Nipples already hard. Not super-sculpted abs, but check out the sides of his ribs. Good handholds here. Also, don't miss the taper to his package. You'll want to lick this later.*

Crossing his arms, Paul caught the hem in his fingers and drew the shirt slowly upward.

Spreading his knees open, Kyle motioned impatiently. "Get over here."

Paul obeyed, stepping between the vee of Kyle's legs.

Kyle's gaze was fixed on the bulge of Paul's jeans. "Undo the button. Then put your hands on the back of your head."

Paul did. The motion made his pecs stand out, pebbled nipples rising. Made those unbuttoned jeans hang lower on his hipbones. Kyle ran his hand over the fur of Paul's chest, purring in approval. God, he was so fucking pretty. Kyle traced his thumb down the line from Paul's abdomen to his pubic bone, kneading gently into the dark blond thatch of hair.

He drew Paul forward by his jeans and licked the same line his thumb had traced.

Paul quivered, and Kyle nipped his soft skin. "Hush. Hold still while I eat you up." Paul quivered more, and Kyle swatted his butt playfully.

Paul stilled—all but his ass, which pressed *oh so slightly* into Kyle's hand.

Groaning, Kyle kneaded Paul's ass. Then slapped it again.

Paul gasped and pushed into the slap once more.

The last dregs of fear rolled out of sight, packed away to make room for Kyle's desperate, blinding need to fuck this man. "Let me unwrap you, honey." He pulled the jeans down, taking the briefs with them. The fur of Paul's ass brushed his fingers as the hard length of his cock bobbed a scant inch before Kyle's face.

The scent of dick filled the air, musky and sharp. Kyle stared at it as he ran his hands over the round, soft flesh of Paul's backside. Nice and fat. He remembered the way this thing felt in his ass. He stared at the slit and thought about sticking his tongue into it. Fucking the hole open as he jacked the shaft. Tugging on those *seriously* badass balls, which were hanging heavy and low with their load.

He leaned forward to take the tip into his mouth, and as his lips slid over the glans, he looked up and saw Paul staring down at him hungrily, with his hands on the back of his head.

Kyle hummed as he took the first inch into his mouth, still staring up at Paul. He wrapped his arms around Paul's hips, taking hold of the meat of his ass with both hands, kneading gently while he bobbed languidly on his cock. The smell of Paul—sex, sweat and denim—filled Kyle's nose as he stuffed his mouth full of cock and ground his fingers into firm ass. All the while Paul held still obediently.

Doubt surfaced briefly as Kyle tried to decide what he wanted Paul to do—straddle his legs? Lay on the table? Bend over it? Did he want to eat cock, or ass?

Both. But which first?

He decided to start with what he already had going. With the wind howling and making the duplex shake, Paul trembled in Kyle's grip as a teasing blow job became serious business. Kyle drew that fat cock into his mouth until it tickled the back of his throat and he could bury his nose in the wiry blond hair of Paul's groin. He hummed and sucked hard as he withdrew, rolling his tongue around the shaft until Paul's knees wobbled.

When they wobbled a second time, Kyle popped off Paul's cock with a wet smack, trailing his hands up the sides of his lover's body before leading him to the table and pushing him onto it. The metal groaned but held as Kyle arranged Paul the way he liked: knees up, arms folded back to open his body. He ran his hands over Paul, who was quivering and hard for him, arching into his touch.

"God, but I love this." Kyle's voice was rough, almost raw, and he couldn't stop stroking Paul, except when he paused to tug at his cock or roll his nipples between his fingers. "I want to tie you down and spend an hour oiling every inch of you, then just sit here and stare. Blindfold you so you don't know what I'm doing to you. Take a picture of you and pull it out when I'm on break at work. Make you get on your knees for me, spread open and waiting for me to fuck you."

Paul met Kyle's gaze. "You…could."

Kyle's head spun as all his blood rushed to his dick. "Which part?"

"All of it."

Kyle took a step forward so the bulge in his scrubs rubbed against Paul's balls. *Damn. Hot. Damn.* Need throbbed from a hard, swelling point behind Kyle's balls. "I could fuck you. Here on your table. Right now."

Paul's smile was a delicious cocktail of shy, sly, and utterly debauched as he used his hands to draw his knees up higher, open them wider. "Take the picture first."

Hands shaking, Kyle pulled his phone out of his pocket. He'd taken pictures of hookups before, but this was *Paul*. His boyhood crush. The guy he wanted for so much more than a hookup. He stared at Paul's beautiful, splayed body through the screen. The view was shadowed, though, until he leaned over to the stove to turn on the light above the burners. It cast Paul in a soft, almost angelic glow.

He snapped the picture.

He took another one, closer in. He zeroed in on that fat cock, pinching the slit to make it open and weep precome. He got a picture of Paul's puckered hole, then left briefly to rifle through his duffel and come back with lube and condoms. Paul flinched at the cold, but he flexed to welcome Kyle's finger inside.

Kyle pushed in slowly. Snapped another picture.

It was hot, seriously hot, taking photos of himself fingering Paul Jansen. But what he wanted, he realized, was a picture of Paul's face.

Paul's face while Kyle fucked him.

Withdrawing his finger, he stared down at Paul. The scent of musk hung in the air, wafting off Kyle's hand as well as from Paul's upturned ass flexing eagerly before him. The assault on his senses made Kyle hard even as his belly clutched in nerves he couldn't sort out while he took in the gorgeous vista of Paul Jansen naked and waiting, laid out on his kitchen table.

I want this so much. More than I want anything else in the world.

He tried to get back into the heat and frenzy of the moment, but he couldn't. Oh, he was stiff as iron, and he shook with need as he suited up. But lust didn't drive him. Carnal desire was little more than a mist around a bone-deep wanting, an ache emanating from Kyle's soul. He breached the tight ring of Paul's ass with his heart spilling over. Camera forgotten, he pulled at Paul's torso, urging him to push up from the table and bring his mouth into kissing range. Paul obeyed, lost on a haze of his own need, but he went soft when Kyle kissed him tenderly.

"Don't run from me." Kyle bit gently on Paul's bearded chin, sucking at the bristly hair. His cock had barely breached Paul, stalled in that initial push of discomfort. Kyle didn't withdraw and didn't press forward, only wrapped a hand behind Paul's neck. "Never again."

Eyes drifting closed, Paul nodded. He milked Kyle's cock gently with his ass, seeking his lips in a kiss that was almost shy.

Kyle accepted the kiss, sealing their mouths together so he could swallow Paul's sharp exhale as Kyle fucked abruptly into him. When Paul's legs began to slip, Kyle used his free hand to urge one leg around his waist, and the other followed suit obediently.

It wasn't the sexy fuck on the table he'd meant it to be. It wasn't a display of how rough and slightly kinky he liked his sex. It wasn't an illustration of how toppy he could be or how skilled he was at fucking. It was, despite his efforts to skirt this revelation, an unveiling of his heart.

Soon enough, the waves caught them up again. His thrusts turned rough. Paul let his head fall back and sank to his elbows as his torso became too heavy to hold up. Kyle shifted his grip to Paul's hips, anchoring himself as he fucked harder, faster. As he came close to his climax, he fumbled for Paul's cock and did his best to bring him along too.

"Come for me, baby." Kyle bent forward to kiss skin he could reach, which turned out to be the center of Paul's chest. "Come on."

Paul quavered beneath him, sweaty and gasping.

"H-harder." His eyes blinked open slowly, almost shyly. "Fuck me harder."

Fire erupted inside Kyle at the request. He let go of those hips and wrapped hands around Paul's back, gripping his shoulders from behind, pulling him close as he snapped his hips, trapping Paul's cock between them. Dug his fingers into Paul's skin, thrilling at the way Paul melted into him. He pushed himself faster, no longer trying to be sexy or tough for Paul, but simply riding the heady rush of Paul's submission, letting it unleash everything inside him.

He came almost without warning, erupting inside Paul with a sharp burst, fucking a few times after as he rode out the crest. Before lethargy could set in, he reached between them, grabbed Paul's cock and tugged him until he came too, three wild hot spurts against Kyle's uniform and Paul's naked chest.

This was the photo he wanted—Paul sloe-eyed and sated, sweat dripping from the curls at his brow. Well-fucked and beautiful.

Kyle didn't take a photo. He caught those pale pink lips in his teeth, forced them open with his tongue and kissed Paul with the want and ache that still burned inside him.

PAUL WAS NERVOUS about this thing with Kyle, but he told himself it would be okay.

God knew it felt good. Kyle laid Paul on the table

after they fucked and cleaned him with a warm wash-cloth. Brought him a pair of sweatpants and socks, touched his ass and lower back a lot as they puttered through their before-bed routines. Kissed him when they were in bed, trailed his mouth down Paul's abdomen to lick his cock and suck on his balls. Paul couldn't get it up again all the way, and Kyle couldn't quite either, but they frotted and kissed and fumbled in the sheets until by unspoken agreement they ended in a tangled embrace, Paul behind Kyle. They were still tangled when Paul woke, blinking in the early-morning darkness until he realized the buzzing he kept hearing was his phone on the nightstand.

It was Arthur. Paul padded into the kitchen to answer. "What is it?" he asked in a rough whisper.

"Busted pipe at the café. The plumber can't make it from Eveleth, and they wanted to know if we could give it a patch job before the morning rush. I'm going to bring Gabriel in with me on the Ski-Doo. Can he crash at your place for a few hours? He wants to open the library, but he hasn't eaten or showered or anything yet, and I don't want to make two trips out here."

Paul glanced toward the bedroom. "Uh, yeah, but…" He tried to think of how to skirt the truth, then gave up. "Kyle's here, still sleeping."

"He's *what?*"

Paul winced at Arthur's volume and sharp tone. "He's here. In my bed." Might as well lay it all out.

"Jesus, Paul. Why the hell did we go through all

that shit of getting him out? What the hell were you thinking?"

Paul hated this already. "Bring Gabriel. He can use my truck. I'll be ready by the time you get here." He hung up and turned the phone off so he wouldn't hear it buzz when Arthur inevitably called back.

Worry chased him into the shower, though, blooming up with the steam. He wasn't sorry about changing his mind about Kyle, but he wasn't looking forward to explaining that to Arthur. He barely understood it himself. When he got out of the shower, he stared down at the bed, the worry in his gut tangling with lust and a thin line of growing affection for the young man in his sheets. Towel around his waist, he sat on the edge of the bed and gently shook Kyle awake.

"I have to go out on a job," he said when Kyle looked like he had enough consciousness gathered for comprehension. "Arthur's coming to pick me up. He's dropping off Gabriel, so you might hear somebody in the kitchen."

"Gabriel is coming?" Blinking, Kyle started to sit up.

Paul pushed him down. "Go back to sleep. This is your day off."

Kyle kissed his hand, his gaze on the edge of Paul's towel as it hung low on his waist. "How long will it take them to get here?"

Paul glanced at the clock on the nightstand. "Probably ten more minutes."

"Good." Kyle pulled Paul onto the bed and shifted their positions in one fluid movement. Paul lay with his towel undone and fallen away as Kyle hovered over him. In the shadows of the room, Kyle smiled in a way that made Paul's worry lay down. "I need to kiss you good morning."

Kyle slid along Paul's body, knelt beside the bed and took Paul's cock in his mouth.

The sleepiness of the blow job faded quickly. It wasn't even a minute before Paul buckled and gasped beneath Kyle's onslaught, clutching the sheets as he thrust helplessly into Kyle's mouth. He tried to hold back, but Kyle pushed him too hard, and all too soon he was spasming and coming into Kyle's throat.

After pulling off Paul's dick with a *smack*, Kyle licked Paul's thigh as he rose to his feet. "I'll take a nap later. Thanks for breakfast, though."

Kyle disappeared into the bathroom, and it wasn't until the sound of running water broke his trance that Paul was able to finish getting dressed. He did so absentmindedly, almost putting his briefs on backward and staring into his closet for a full minute before snapping out of his stupor and selecting a shirt. He was buttoning it when the purr of a snowmobile engine cut through the morning stillness, and soon after the back door opened.

"Everybody decent?"

Arthur's shout had an edge to it, like he was trying not to be pissed. When Paul came out to greet him,

Arthur *looked* annoyed too, but he played nice as Gabriel kissed him on the cheek before padding blearily over to the living room couch.

"No coffee?" Arthur glared at the empty pot on the counter. "I figured you'd start some as soon as we hung up."

Paul's cheeks stained red. "I…uh…forgot."

Arthur didn't seem to need a map to figure out what Paul had been doing instead of brewing coffee. He rolled his eyes and jerked his head toward the door. "Come on. They're promising double our usual fee if we can get things sorted before seven."

They said little more to each other as they drove first to the shop to pick up supplies, then to the café, each taking their own snowmobile. The snow had stopped, but the wind blew hard and unforgiving, kicking up snow in glittering whorls across deserted streets. The lights at the café were on as they approached, and Jimmy, the owner, stuck his head out to greet them as they trudged up the steps to the front door.

"Come on in. I'd offer you coffee, but I can't until I get my water. I have day-old muffins, though, and a full-plate breakfast for you once you're finished."

The burst pipe was in the kitchen on the north side, and digging into the drywall revealed poor insulation as the culprit. It took more time to clean up the mess inside than it did to fit new pipe. While Arthur gave Jimmy follow-up instructions for needed repairs, Paul stuffed some towels behind the pipe and rigged up a portable incandescent lamp beside the hole to ensure the ice stayed away. He also installed a valve farther down the line and swapped out another that was rusted shut.

They had the water flowing with fifteen minutes to spare, and as the café opened for business, Arthur and Paul sat in a booth with a fat check and a table heaping with more food and coffee than they could possibly hope to put away. Jimmy sent their favorite waitress to them too, even though they weren't at her station.

"You just holler if you need anything at all," Patty told them. "The heroes of the day get whatever they want, on the house."

It was then Arthur brought up Kyle. "Tell me what's going on with the two of you."

Paul poked at his scrambled eggs with his fork and shrugged. "I'm…seeing him, I guess."

"You really think that's a good idea?"

Paul shrugged again, still not looking up.

"Is he what you want, Pauly?"

He thought of the way Kyle had held him while he fucked him on the table, the shiver his smile sent down Paul's spine every time. "Yeah." Frowning, he made himself meet Arthur's gaze. "That okay?"

Arthur seemed taken aback. "Why are you asking *me*?"

"You said he was too young."

"Well, I didn't mean it was wrong for you to want

him. I just didn't want him annoying you, is all. What's the draw, if you don't mind me asking? Is he that good in bed?"

Paul worried the edge of his toast between his fingers. "I don't know what the draw is. I guess it's what I want to find out." His morning blow job bloomed in his mind's eye. "He's good in bed, though. Damn good."

"I guess I should have seen it coming. The way you looked at him at Marcus and Frankie's that day. The way he looked at you."

Paul jerked his head up. "How did he look at me?"

Arthur's only reply was a smile before he put a fork full of hash browns into his mouth. But after a few minutes of eating in silence, Arthur spoke again. "So does he play?"

Play, Arthur meant, as in BDSM. Paul sipped at his coffee. "Not sure."

"Huh. Well, I guess it was always more my thing than yours. If you do play, be smart and safe. Might be worth me having a word with him."

"I don't think my ex should give kink pointers to my new boyfriend."

Under the table, Arthur's knee bumped Paul's. "How about your best friend does it instead?"

Paul met Arthur's gaze. "I want to give this a try, Arthur. Don't mess it up. I'm liable to do that well enough on my own."

He braced for a wry quip or innuendo, but Arthur's

voice was gruff and gentle as he replied, "I won't. I promise." He took Paul's hand, gripping it tight.

Paul squeezed back and let out a breath he hadn't even realized he'd been holding.

WHEN KYLE CAME out of the shower, Gabriel was in the kitchen brewing coffee.

"Good morning." Gabriel waved Kyle in. "Have a seat. I'm foraging for breakfast."

Kyle started for the table, remembered Paul splayed on it, and rerouted to the fridge, hoping the air would cool him down. "I'll help."

"I take it by the fact that you're here despite Paul's efforts to ship you off to Frankie mean things are better between the two of you?"

"I think so. Though I'm ready for him to try and backtrack on me again." Kyle pulled out a carton of eggs and a plastic bag of bacon. "Frankie says Paul likes to make poor choices when it comes to men."

"Frankie is right." Gabriel saw the bacon and shook his head. "You can put that away. I brought deer sausage."

They made omelets, sighing over the lack of vegetables or spices in Paul's cupboards. When Gabriel learned how much Kyle enjoyed cooking, he declared he was setting up a foodie date in addition to shopping. "Frankie loves cooking more than me, but it's fun when the two of us work together. You'd fit right in,

I'm betting. Oh, hey—what about Thanksgiving? Frankie wanted to host at his new house. Which will piss off Arthur, but I'll deal with that fallout."

Kyle opened and closed his mouth, not sure what to say. He loved the idea in the abstract, but he couldn't imagine what his mother would say if he tried to skip. Or worse, Linda Kay. "I'll think about it," he said at last.

"Speaking of thinking about it—Marcus called me last night and said he'd made some headway on the Winter Wonderland idea we'd had, about using the shuttered storefronts. The city council is all over it. Half of the stores, it turns out, are owned by the bank. Everyone wants to see more businesses opening. And get this—some friend of Marcus's from Duluth apparently has a bid for land just north of here, by Lost Lake. Wants to do something with those summer cabins we keep hearing about. Winter Wonderland could sweeten the deal. The council talked about giving huge tax incentives to any business wanting to extend past the holidays, and I'm looking up some Main Street grants today. That's one of the reasons I wanted to get in to the library early."

The thought of their crazy idea becoming a reality made Kyle buzz with excitement, and he spent a happy hour with Gabriel connecting dots on their brainstorms. When Gabriel declared he had to go to work, Kyle was almost disappointed.

He helped Gabriel dig out enough to free Paul's

pickup, and once Gabriel had left, Kyle took care of the drive and the sidewalk with the snowblower before using the shovel and ice pick to clear the front and back steps of both sides of the duplex. Edna appeared and urged him to come in for a cup of tea.

"Everything going well with the two of you?" She said this as she poured from a ceramic pot, but her hands shook so badly Kyle deftly took it from her, urging her to sit down.

"So far, so good." Kyle frowned as he watched her sink wearily into her chair. "Mrs. Michealson, are you feeling well?"

She waved his concern away. "I'm fine."

She didn't look fine, but she didn't seem ill enough for Kyle to push, so he made a mental note to check on her later. And to drink his cup of tea quickly so she could take a nap.

Once he convinced her to do that, promising to come by with his sister as soon as the roads were clear, he went outside and began packing snow. He went with a traditional snowman, though he used snow instead of sticks for the arms. He was in the middle of sculpting the face when he heard the buzz of a Ski-Doo.

He waved at Paul as he approached. "Just making a little decoration for your yard."

Paul stood beside him, watching him work. "Thank you for not making it a penis."

Kyle pushed playfully at the center of Paul's chest. "You loved them and you know it."

Paul smiled ruefully and rubbed at his cheek with a worn glove. "I gotta head in to the shop. Did…did you want to stay, or go home?"

"I'd love nothing more than to stay, but my mom has already texted me twice this morning asking if I need a ride home. But…maybe we could do something tomorrow? Day or evening. Your pick."

"What do you want to do?"

"How's the weather? You feel like going to Mountain Iron to see a movie? Or we could rent something and stay in." When he saw the way Paul looked at him, his heart kicked up, and he quickly amended his suggestion. "How about we stay in. I'll make you dinner at your place, and you pick the movie."

Paul's smile made Kyle wish they could have their date tonight. "Sounds great. But you bring the movie, in case I pick something you don't like."

Paul tried to give him a ride home, but Kyle's mom had said his dad was coming in to get groceries, so Kyle declined. His father picked him up before going to the store, and while they shopped together for the family, Kyle made some personal selections for his dinner date the next day with Paul.

"Are you seeing that boy, then?" his dad asked as they drove to the farm.

"Yeah." He rubbed his gloves over his jeans. "Hope I don't screw it up."

His dad grinned. "Be yourself, and you'll be fine."

At home Linda Kay greeted him at the door, enveloping him in a tight, teary hug. "You can't ever stay away that long again," she declared.

He kissed her cheek and took her hand. "I'm all yours until tomorrow evening, big sister. What do you want to do with me?"

"Watch movies. *Frozen* and then *South Pacific.* And have a big plate of pizza rolls. Then play Chutes and Ladders and Sorry! with Dad when he's done with chores. Drink lots and lots of hot chocolate."

"Sounds like a perfect day to me," he said, letting her lead him into the family room.

Chapter Ten

PAUL COULDN'T HELP worrying about his date with Kyle, but he didn't try to get out of it. When Frankie offered to give him a haircut and style a few hours before Kyle was due, he didn't turn that down either.

Frankie had been cutting Paul's hair in a longer style, using some gunk and a round brush with a hair-dryer to make it less curly. Paul couldn't manage the style on his own, but he liked how it looked when Frankie did it. Of course Frankie could make anybody's hair better. It felt good to sit in Frankie's chair and get fussed over.

"What movie are you watching?" Frankie snipped the hair around Paul's ears and met his gaze in the mirror. "We have *Guardians of the Galaxy* on Blu-ray if you want to borrow it."

"He said he was bringing something, though I don't know what. He's making the dinner too, at my house."

Frankie smiled at the length of hair he teased with his comb before snipping along the edges. "Look at you, getting pampered. I have to say, Paul, I like Kyle for you. A lot."

Paul did too, which worried him. "We're just trying it out. Probably won't work, since we have so little in common."

"You have more in common than Marcus and I. Definitely more than Gabriel and Arthur. Though that works in their favor. They both love sniping at each other."

Paul hated fighting, which was one of the biggest reasons he and Arthur hadn't worked well together as a couple.

Frankie combed Paul's hair to the other side and kept trimming. "Gabriel said something about all of us having Thanksgiving dinner together at our house. Kyle too. What do you think?"

Paul thought it sounded like heaven, but he knew he couldn't. "My mom would have a fit."

"Honey, your mother will have a fit no matter what."

This was true, but it didn't change Paul's answer. "Better to get it over with in a day. If I skip, she'll make me sorry for a month."

Frankie flattened his lips as he continued to cut. "What if we had our Thanksgiving on Saturday or Sunday? Or on another weekend between Thanksgiving and Christmas? Because something tells me Kyle will have an equal amount of trouble escaping *his* family." He sighed. "Honestly, all our families will be sore if we don't put in an appearance. I'll text Kyle and see what his work schedule looks like, and we'll go from there. Maybe it could even be our Christmas party, for the six of us. Because we'll have an equally difficult time getting together on that holiday too."

Paul thought about the alternate holiday party all through the rest of his haircut. He could *see* it, and it was beautiful. Though Arthur would lobby for his cabin, it would be at Frankie and Marcus's house, all done up nice and pretty. Frankie would make everything sparkle and match and yet it would still feel like home. The food would be great, because Frankie was an amazing cook. But they'd all be there, all helping. Paul could peel potatoes. He was good at that. They'd laugh, drink beer and wine and cider, and...

He let out a sigh full of longing, suddenly wanting the day with his friends and his maybe-boyfriend more than he'd thought he could want something.

When Frankie was done, Paul checked himself out in the mirror, amazed as always at the magic Frankie could work. When Frankie had first tried to do his hair, Paul had worried he'd end up too fancy, like everybody would laugh at him for it. But while Frankie did make him look more polished than usual, he did it in a way that didn't seem too puffed up. His hair had the kind of messy look movie stars got, as if somebody had run fingers through it.

He paid Frankie and hugged him in thanks, then went to his house to do another round of cleaning.

Edna stuck her head out of the door as he came out of the garage. "Paul, could you come inside and change a bulb for me? I tried climbing the step stool, but it's so wobbly."

The thought of her trying to stand on the stool anyway and Paul finding her dead on the floor after a fall chilled him to the bone. "I'm happy to, Mrs. Michealson."

She did, in fact, have five bulbs out, and Paul changed them all, going over to his apartment and fetching his last three. As was often the case, he ended up doing several minor repair jobs, and when she worried over the state of her carpet, he vacuumed that for her too. Even though it meant losing the opportunity to clean his own.

She seemed more tired than usual. She rarely missed a beat to tell Paul what he was doing wrong with his life, but mostly she mentioned how tired and dizzy she was. He left her ten minutes before Kyle was due to arrive, but he didn't do any cleaning, only paced back and forth, worrying, until Kyle knocked on the front door.

Kyle looked gorgeous, all styled and smelling faintly of cologne, full of smiles, but when he saw Paul's face, he sobered. "What's wrong?"

Paul only hesitated a second before nodding at the duplex's shared wall. "I'm worried about Mrs. Michealson. She doesn't seem to be her usual self."

Kyle put down his things. "Get your shoes, and we'll go next door."

It was something to watch Kyle's whole demeanor change as he sat with Edna on the sofa while he took her vitals. He spoke cheerfully to her, but in this patient, careful way that reminded Paul of going to the doctor. Kyle asked Edna questions about her activity level, had her rate her pain on a scale of one to ten and urged her to explain to him where it hurt worst.

He held her hands in his and looked her in the eye. "Edna, I'm going to call your son and have him take you to the emergency room."

For a terrible moment, Paul thought Edna would cry. "They'll put me away. I'll be fine in a day or two. I always am."

"Edna, your pulse is erratic, and I don't have my blood pressure cuff, but I suspect you're low. At the very least you need some fluids and some monitoring." He squeezed her weathered hand inside his. "No one is putting you away. If you go anywhere but home, you'll come to Logan Manor, where *I* will take care of you."

Now the tears did fall. "I don't want to go anywhere. I want to stay here."

"One step at a time, okay? Let's let the doctors give their diagnosis before we get ahead of ourselves." He stroked her hair. "I'll give your son my number, and you can call me at any time, day or night. Even if it's only to tell me you're scared."

She gripped his hand with pressure that made her arm shake. "You said the manor was full. What if they send me to Eveleth?"

"There's actually one opening as of yesterday, and the waitlist is empty. If you want, I'll call over and have them add your name to hold it. You can always take yourself off it later. Would you like that? Would it make it easier for you to go to the hospital?"

Her tears broke Paul's heart. "Would you promise to be there for me?"

The broken bits of Paul's heart shattered as Kyle kissed her cheek. "Of course. I'll help you move in and show you around. I'll pull a favor with Frankie too, and you can have a full spa day at the manor's salon."

She wept, but she nodded. Kyle never let go of her hand as he pulled out his phone, first calling Edna's son, then, with Edna listening in, calling the care center and putting her name down for the open room. Soon after that Hans Michealson arrived from Eveleth, whey-faced and terrified, but Kyle set him to rights too, assuring Hans everything was fine, Edna only needed to be checked out. He gave his phone number as promised and helped get Edna bundled and secured in Hans's car.

Once they were gone, Paul led Kyle to his house, where Kyle gave the unvarnished version of his opinion. "It could be so many things, but most of them are pretty serious. I think she's worked hard to keep anyone from noticing how sick she is."

"Do you think she'll have to go to the care center?"

Kyle shrugged, but he looked grim. "She *should* go. It's not just her ability level. She doesn't get any socialization here. I understand people fear going into a nursing home, call it being *put away* and all that, but honestly, it's kinder than leaving people to hurt themselves on their own. The care staff gets all the grief for not making everything exactly like it would be at home, but what people truly are upset about is their loved one is closer to death than life. We give the best care we can. I'm not saying there aren't some centers fueling the nightmares, but ours isn't one of them."

Kyle's passion stirred things in Paul, though it was weird to get hot for his date while talking about nursing homes. He cleared his throat and nodded at the canvas grocery bag Kyle had left by the door. "Do we need to put anything in the fridge?"

They put the groceries away together, but when Paul admitted he was hungry, Kyle got an apron out of his duffel, pulled the tenderloin out and began patting it with paper towels. Paul stood beside him, trying not to hover. "What are we having?"

"Beef tenderloin with Dijon cream sauce, steamed green beans with mushrooms, and fried potatoes. I brought extra wine, but I won't be offended if you have beer."

Paul's mouth was nothing but water. "It sounds great. Can I help?"

He worried that was the wrong thing to say, but

Kyle beamed at him. "Sure. I love cooking with people. How do you feel about washing the potatoes? I'll show you how to cut them when I'm done tying up the roast."

"I can peel them," Paul assured him, eager to show off his skills.

"Well, I was going to leave the skins on, but we can take them off if you'd rather."

The only thing Paul wanted was to please Kyle. "Just tell me what to do, and I'll do it."

Kyle did. He moved effortlessly between his own prep and instructing Paul in how to slice the potatoes into thin half-circles.

"I'm so glad you have a cast-iron pan." Kyle set his twine-tied, oiled, peppered and salted roast onto the hot surface, sending a delicious sizzle into the air as well as a sharp aroma of seared beef. "How do you like your beef? The recipe calls for medium-rare, but we can make it as done as we want."

Paul preferred medium-well, but he wasn't fussy. "How do *you* like your meat?"

"Honey, I like my meat tickling the back of your throat."

Paul fumbled with the knife, almost slicing his thumb. Kyle slid arms around his waist and moved the utensil out of his hand.

"I'm making you dinner, and I want you to enjoy it, Paul." Kyle kissed his neck, running his tongue along the surface Frankie had so recently shaved clean. "Tell me how you want me to cook your roast."

Paul shut his eyes as Kyle's hand closed over his dick through his jeans. "I... Medium-well."

Kyle squeezed his cock and let him go. "There. That wasn't so hard, was it? Though I admit, it was more fun than a simple answer."

Paul still hadn't recovered by the time Kyle had the meat thermometer in the roast and the pan in the oven. Chuckling, Kyle nudged Paul to the side with his hip and deftly took over the potatoes.

Kyle nodded to the front door. "I'm doing the onion next. Would you get me the latex gloves from the side pocket of my duffel? I don't want my hands to stink all night."

Paul found the gloves easily, though he noted Kyle had more than one pair. He wondered if the others were spares or if Kyle had some kinky purpose in mind. Trying to imagine the latter had him distracted as he came into the kitchen, so much so he startled when Kyle kissed his neck again.

"You make it hard to cook, standing there looking so good." When the comment made Paul lean into him, Kyle laughed and swatted Paul's butt. "Be a good boy and wash the rest of my produce."

Flushed with pleasure over being called a *good boy*, Paul washed the mushrooms and rinsed the beans. After Paul filled a pot with water, Kyle produced a steamer basket from his shopping bag. He filled it with beans, and after setting it on the boiling water, he stir-fried onions and mushrooms in a second skillet. When everything was ready, he piled the vegetables in a bowl beside the stove, washed his hands and set a timer.

"I have to start the last part of dinner in twelve minutes." He put his phone down, took off his apron and leaned against the counter. With a sly smile, he tugged Paul closer. "Let's see how much trouble we can get up to between now and then."

Kyle drew Paul lazily into a kiss. Nipped at his lips, licked the seam, formed a soft seal when Paul opened with a sigh. Paul kept himself upright, but he let his upper body relax into Kyle's hold, let himself be shifted and poised so Kyle could kiss him better. Though Kyle stroked him all over, it never progressed further than kissing. Paul surrendered to it, swimming in Kyle's tender nibbles and licks and nuzzles until he was in a trance. Completely, wonderfully lost. When the timer went off, Paul came lazily awake, remaining in the circle of Kyle's arms, resting their foreheads together.

Kyle shut off the timer, but he didn't move to finish cooking, only kept stroking Paul's face. "We're good together, Paul," he said at last.

Shutting his eyes, Paul nodded. They were. They really were.

He worried he shouldn't give in to that, shouldn't get carried away with fantasies. The more time he spent with Kyle, though, the harder guarding his heart became.

Because for the first time ever, he didn't just want a

boyfriend to date and take to gatherings with the rest of the guys or dream about buying a house with. He wanted Kyle.

THEIR KISS BURNED Kyle's lips all the way through the rest of dinner preparation, and every time Paul brushed against him to grab plates or snag a potholder, Kyle's body radiated with beautiful electricity. Part of him wanted to abandon food and drag the man to a bed, though by and large he was excited to have such a languid evening ahead of them. He looked forward to the intimacy of a shared dinner and movie as much as he did the passion that kiss had promised.

He couldn't help but worry, though, what would happen the morning after. Would Paul truly be okay about the two of them dating? Would it make things easier if they didn't have sex tonight? Maybe, Kyle acknowledged. He hated the idea, but he told himself he was a big boy. He could settle for kisses. For a while, anyway. Give Paul a chance to ease into the idea without freaking out. He'd been masturbating in the shower for months now instead of getting laid. Wouldn't kill him to keep it up a bit longer.

Paul had set up two TV trays in front of the television, and they snuggled together before their steaming plates. Paul nodded to the TV. "What are we watching?"

"*The Shop Around the Corner.* Because a little birdie

told me you love romantic Christmas movies." And because this was one Kyle didn't just tolerate, he loved. Kyle cut some tenderloin and speared a bit of vegetable with it too. On impulse, he turned to Paul. "Open."

Paul ate obediently, and it pleased Kyle to hear his moan of pleasure as he chewed. "Oh my God. That's amazing."

Kyle beamed. "Thanks."

Paul hadn't seen the movie, which thrilled Kyle even more. Kyle's mom had a weakness for Jimmy Stewart, and it turned out so did Paul.

"This is what the movie *You've Got Mail* is based on," Kyle told him as they pushed their plates aside and settled into the film. "I like this version so much better."

"It's so cozy." Paul rested his head on Kyle's shoulder when Kyle put an arm around him. "I love cozy movies. Where everything is safe and okay. This ends happy, right? Everybody gets together and everything is okay?"

Kyle stared at the top of Paul's head, his boyfriend's words ringing in his head. "Yes. It has a cozy, perfect happily ever after."

With a contented sigh, Paul sipped his wine and gave his full attention to the movie.

Kyle, however, couldn't stop watching Paul. *Everything safe and okay.* That's what Corrina had meant about the Christmas movies, cheesy as they were. Because every last one of them had the tidiest, most perfect of endings, tied up in a neat, saccharine bow. Family, romance, and happily ever after.

Oh, Paul. Kyle kissed his hair, shut his eyes and took in a deep breath of his lover.

When the movie finished, Paul was pleased, and soft and gooey in the center. Kyle kissed his neck, massaged his thigh. Felt his cock grow hard through his jeans.

Slow down, he reminded himself. "I should see to the kitchen."

Paul's shoulders fell in disappointment, but he nodded. "I'll help you."

Kyle had intended the cleanup to be a way to dampen his ardor, but with Paul working beside him, close enough to send Kyle whiffs of aftershave, giving a view of his ass as he bent over, kitchen duty was more foreplay than cool-down. At first Kyle tried to draw the chore out, thinking if nothing else time would be on his side, but all it did was outline how miserably he was failing to distract himself from how much he wanted Paul.

"Looks like it's snowing again." Paul leaned on the counter, gripping the edge and drawing attention to his groin.

Kyle tried not to notice, and failed. "I should probably head back, then." He'd meant it to be his noble nod to respecting Paul's need to wade into their relationship, but the comment came out sounding like someone acknowledging they had to go in for a root canal.

Paul seemed disappointed. "Oh—I saw you brought a duffel. I thought you'd stay over."

Originally, this had been Kyle's plan. "I don't want to impose." He mentally eye-rolled himself at his lame defense and sighed. "Okay—it's not only that. I don't want to rush things. I remember what happened the first time I took you to bed."

Paul hunched forward in embarrassment. "That's not going to happen. I swear."

Kyle ran a hand through his hair, massaging his scalp a bit to loosen the right words from his cranium. "It's not a punishment. It's insurance. I'm not kidding, Paul. I want this." He gestured at the kitchen, the living room. "I *liked* this, hanging out with you. Being with you. If having sex too fast is going to screw that up—" He cut himself off, abruptly out of words, though emotions blew up from updrafts inside him, parachutes of confession he didn't dare spill just yet.

I don't want you because you're convenient or because it's been fun crushing on you. I want you because every time we get together, it feels more right, more certain. Except it also means it's going to hurt more if you decide you don't feel the same way or can't do this right now.

Paul pushed off the counter and took Kyle's shoulders in a gentle grip. "It wasn't sex that did it. It was just me being self-conscious." He grimaced, averting his gaze. "I overreacted because it felt good. Which makes no sense, I know, but it's like the better things are sometimes the harder it is for me. I worry a lot about what other people think. I shouldn't, but I do. I've gotten used to bad hookups and failed relationships, and I think the idea you might be exactly who I've been looking for scared me." He blushed and pulled away. "Sorry, that sounded really dumb out loud."

Kyle chased him, drawing him closer. "No. It didn't sound dumb at all."

The kiss started out as slow, lazy nips. But the brush of Paul's mustache and beard sent tingling thrills across Kyle's skin, and he framed Paul's face with his hands, running his thumbs along the rough edge of his hairline. He opened his mouth over Paul's. He flicked his tongue over the edge of Paul's teeth, touched their tongues together.

He meant to be seductive and sweet, and God knows he tried. Skimming fingers over Paul's body, drawing their bodies together, Kyle did his best to keep in the spirit of the evening. To be gentle, sentimental. To make love, not fuck.

But Paul's groans, little moans in the back of his throat, burly rumbles ending in whimpers as Kyle teased his nipples—they roused fires Kyle couldn't dampen fast enough before new blazes erupted. Soon the gentle grind of his hips became rough thrusts fucking Paul's ass into the counter, fueled by Paul's breathy cries into Kyle's mouth.

Even then, Kyle fought to maintain control. He

broke the kiss and nuzzled behind Paul's ear. "Let me take you to bed."

Paul turned enough to kiss Kyle's cheek, stroking it before leading Kyle to the bedroom.

It wasn't enough of a walk for Kyle to calm, and when Paul began undressing as they passed through the doorway, Kyle helped him along. Pulled back the panels of his button-down shirt. Tugged his T-shirt over his head. Shoved his jeans then his underwear to his ankles, and once he was naked except for socks, Kyle pushed his lover onto the mattress.

Shedding his clothes, Kyle grinned as Paul fumbled with his socks in a lust-filled haze, only managing one and part of the other before Kyle was on him, skin to skin, thrusting his tongue into his mouth. When simple friction wasn't enough, he followed Paul's whispered directions for the lube, slicked them both up and captured their cocks together.

Initially he'd wanted to fuck into Paul, to feel his heat and his surrender, but everything was too delicious. The feel of Paul beneath him, shuddering, gasping, those strong arms around him. The perfect evening echoing in his mind. The contact of Paul's head pillowing on his shoulder during the movie a remembered weight—a privilege, a gift. The scent of Paul's hair product mingling with his sweat as they fucked, a silent admission of how much he'd prepared for their evening.

It all tangled and snarled inside him until it became

an explosion of joy, of *having*. Of being, of feeling. Burying his face in Paul's neck, digging fingers into his hair, Kyle fucked against Paul. When Paul's bucks of response threatened to toss them off the bed, Kyle pinned his lover with his knees and latched on to Paul's neck.

Like an animal. The thought burned in his brain, settling loose deeper, darker passion. When he felt Paul erupting beneath him, he stopped holding back and followed suit, shooting into the small space between their bodies, until they were slick with sweat, semen, and satisfaction.

Kyle tucked himself into the crook of Paul's arm, his body buzzing in the afterglow of the most amazing sex of his life. Paul lay beneath him, limp, gasping for air, nuzzling weakly for Kyle's cheek.

"That…was *amazing*."

Kyle grinned through his fatigue, feeling puffed up and proud as much as he was sated. See? They'd be fine. Maybe it wouldn't be a bad idea to be subtle in public, give Paul a chance to acclimate to being in a good relationship. That would just add to the fun, knowing they had to be discreet, had to wait until they were alone. Aware once this happened, they'd be wild together, as if they couldn't help themselves.

But nobody had to know about that but the two of them.

Kyle sank into the blissful aftermath, his whole body glowing. He ran a hand down Paul's meaty, hairy thigh. Over his groin, his belly. He trailed fingers through the hair of Paul's chest, up his neck, through his beard.

Felt his joy crumble into shame as he saw the three-inch-round deep purple hickey beneath Paul's ear.

Chapter Eleven

I T HAD BEEN embarrassing for Paul to go to the shop with a huge, glaring hickey. Especially when Arthur bypassed teasing him and moved directly into arguing more insistently that he should have a word with Kyle about control.

"You're overreacting." Paul touched his neck self-consciously. "He got carried away, is all. We both did."

"Exactly my point. If you're going to play—"

"We weren't *playing*. Not that kind of playing, any-way."

Arthur grimaced. "It's all playing. Some of us are more organized and careful about it."

Paul was absolutely not in the mood for one of Ar-thur's BDSM advocacy lectures. He tugged the collar of his turtleneck higher, hating how hot he already was in it, but it was the only thing that came close to covering the hickey. "Please don't say anything to him. He feels bad enough as it is. You'll only make it worse."

Though Arthur agreed he wouldn't, Paul wasn't

sure he could trust him not to find some other way to bring it up. Which made their time together in the shop distinctly uncomfortable. It wasn't much better out and about, though. The raised eyebrows from people in town and whispers at the hardware store weren't any fun at all. The dead worst, though, was getting home at the end of a long day and receiving a phone call from his mother.

"Pauly, Fran from my circle says you're caught up in some wicked sex ring."

Paul cracked a beer quietly so his mother couldn't scold him for that too and sipped it as he sank into the couch. "I'm not in a sex ring."

"She says you're covered in bruises."

Jesus. "I'm not. I have one hickey."

"A love mark?" Mary made even the pretty euphemism sound like a scandal. But he soon learned her tone was nothing on her next line of inquiry. "Paul, they're saying you're seeing Kyle Parks. Tell me it isn't true."

Paul pinched the bridge of his nose. "We're dating, yes."

"Oh, *Paul.*"

It was hard to guess if her objection was Paul still wasn't dating a woman, Kyle was too young, or Kyle was the kind of guy who gave visible hickeys. Paul wasn't making the mistake of assuming. He kept quiet and waited for her to finish.

"I thought you were past this. You haven't *tried* dating any of the women I've suggested to you."

Paul took a swig of beer and tipped his head back. "Mom, I've told you over and over. I don't like girls that way."

"You haven't *tried.*"

"I did, Mom. In high school. Enough to know it was a horrible idea."

"Well, nobody's any good at it in high school. You need to try again."

Paul drank more, shut his eyes and let her go off on a lecture. He'd done this plenty of times. Eventually she always wound down. When she got to the part about how it shamed the family, she was usually about finished.

Except tonight she had a new verse, and wouldn't you know, she pulled out the one Paul had just managed to put away.

"I can't believe you'd rob the cradle this way. Kyle Parks is barely out of high school."

Paul's hand closed more tightly around his cell phone. "He's twenty-five."

"You're almost forty. You're nearly twice his age."

That was some creative math. Still, he kept silent.

"Your father has a lot to say to you, but he's too angry right now. He's going to sit you down on Sunday when you come for dinner after church."

Paul's headache bloomed. "I won't be able to come to dinner. We're planning for Winter Wonderland."

"You can come on Saturday then. Though the way

that *festival* is going, I'm not sure you should be a part of it at all."

"It's Kyle's day off. We were going to Mountain Iron to watch a movie."

This news sent her back to the start of her lecture and Paul to his fridge to get a second beer, but before he could get one, a tentative knock sounded on his door. He answered it silently, his mother still scolding in his ear.

Kyle stood on Paul's stoop. Naughty puppies appeared less remorseful than Kyle, though not half as cute. The sight of his boyfriend was balm enough to Paul's shitty mood, but when his nose told him the tall, round plastic container Kyle bore was full of cake, his heart swelled. When he saw, perched atop the cake container, the homemade gift bag with delicately handwritten *I'm sorry* surrounded by swirls and glitter, Paul's heart cracked and melted.

"Mom, I have to go," he said, interrupting her mid-rant and hanging up on her as she sputtered in shock.

Kyle looked miserable. "I'm so, *so* sorry."

That had almost been the only thing Kyle had said to him all day, ever since they woke up in the morning and saw Paul's hickey was *worse* than the night before. Seeing Kyle standing there, so cute and hot and carrying cake and a present, Paul thought he'd take a hickey on his *nose*. "I keep telling you. Don't worry about it." Snuffing out the urge to be shy, he pressed a kiss on Kyle's cheek. "Come on in. It's warmer than it's been, but it's still cold outside."

Once inside the door, Kyle took off his boots, but not his coat. His green scrubs scraped the floor. "I can't stay long. I want to get to work early because they're bringing Edna."

Paul felt like an ass for forgetting about his neighbor. "Is she there short term, or for good?"

"Short term for now, but everyone's hoping she agrees to move in permanently." He pressed the cake and present into Paul's hands. "Here. I baked you a red velvet cake." His cheeks stained. "Also, I knit something for you. It's in the bag."

Paul flushed too, though more with pleasure than embarrassment. "You didn't need to do any of this."

Kyle gestured impatiently. "Go on. Open the present. I want to make sure it fits."

Paul set the cake on his coffee table and pulled tissue paper out of the gift bag with an odd flutter in his chest. It was nothing, though, to what he felt when he withdrew a beautiful orange and green knit hat from the bag.

"It has the felt lining, so it's extra warm." Kyle bit his lip and regarded the cap with scrutiny. "I hesitated over what style. I wanted to make you one with earflaps, but you don't normally wear deerstalkers unless you're hunting or it's extra cold. I hope you don't mind the bobble on top. It didn't look right without it."

"It's perfect. Beautiful. When did you do this? Did you even sleep today?"

"I started once I got home the other day, after the blizzard. They really don't take me long, but also I wanted you to have it as soon as possible."

Paul hadn't ever had anyone make anything for him, and it made him melt. "It's so *nice.* I'll have to save it for special occasions."

Kyle swatted his arm. "You will not. I made this for you to *wear.*"

"But what if I catch it on a nail at work or something?"

"Then you tell me, and I fix it. Or make you another one." Kyle sighed, took the hat from Paul's hands and put it on his head.

It fit like a glove, but Kyle still tugged on it, fussing and regarding his creation with a critical eye. Paul held his breath, terrified Kyle would find something wrong with it and take it away. But eventually Kyle nodded curtly and stood back.

"It'll do. I think I might make it slightly bigger next time, so you can tug it lower if it's cold. I brought some yarn with me to work, so I'll get started on it tonight." His cheeks stained. "And a scarf, so you don't have to be embarrassed by my thoughtlessness. I really am sorry, Paul."

It was funny. All day Paul had been frustrated by the hickey, but now he was almost glad for it. Now everyone knew. Everybody would be talking about how Paul Jansen and Kyle Parks were dating. They knew who'd given him the *love mark.*

And Paul knew the man who'd done it was by turns aggressive and sensual and thoughtful and sweet.

"Don't worry about it." Paul touched his new hat. "If hickeys mean I get cake and knitted things, you can give me one every day."

Kyle smiled ruefully, then kissed Paul—on the mouth this time, in a lingering way that made Paul wish Kyle truly didn't have to go to work. "I can't wait for the weekend. I wish I had the whole day off on Sunday and could be part of all the planning."

Paul did too. "We'll get the hard stuff done when you're gone. I worry you'll be too tired from our date the night before, though."

Kyle kissed the bruise on Paul's neck. "Don't worry. I'll wear you out too."

When Kyle finally left, Paul had a stiffy in his jeans and a warm feeling in his belly. It wasn't anything, though, to what his stomach felt like once he had a piece of Kyle's red velvet cake.

As the sugar and cream cheese hummed in his system, his head snug and warm inside his hat, Paul let the gifts from his boyfriend chase away his own doubts and those his mother had sown. He thought about the coming weekend, full of friends and plans and possibilities.

Pulling the hat from his head, Paul shut his eyes and took a deep draught of the smell of wool and Kyle.

Then he had another piece of cake.

EDNA ARRIVED AT the care center five minutes after Kyle did, but he'd had enough time to set out flowers and balloons in her room. After a phone call with her son, Kyle had added three cans of Pringles to the loot. Edna, low on sodium and weight, had been given clearance to eat all the potato chips she wanted.

He'd brought one of his mother's quilts from home as well, knowing he couldn't turn the room into Edna's home, but he tried to make it as homey as possible nonetheless. When she was wheeled in, he beamed at her, and when she beckoned him closer, eagerly accepted her hug.

"How are you feeling?" He crouched so he was level with her gaze. "Did they treat you well at the hospital?"

Edna huffed. "The food was terrible. But the nurses were wonderful."

Good, because Kyle had called over and pulled every favor he had to get her rock-star treatment. "I'll have to work hard to live up to their high standard. I know we can beat them for food, though. And I already stocked your room with contraband."

Edna patted his hand, then drew it to her lips for a kiss. "Thank you, young man." Her grip on his hand tightened a little. "I see you're in your work clothes. How long are you here tonight?"

"I don't go on shift until seven, so you and I have a full forty-five minutes to gossip. I brought my latest knitting project, and I expect you to pull no punches.

I'll never improve if you don't give me an honest critique."

Her son, despite being married with two kids—all of them huddled behind him in the hallway—looked like he wanted to kiss Kyle. "Thank you so much for your help. We couldn't have done this without you."

"I'm only doing my job." Kyle stepped aside so Hans could wheel Edna into the room.

He largely hung to the side as the family settled Edna in, answering their questions and backing up the center director as she gave Edna her orientation. He wasn't surprised, though, that Edna shooed her family out at quarter to seven and planted Kyle in the seat beside her head.

"It's going to be fine," he promised her before she could work up the courage to voice her fears. "No one will keep you here if you don't want to be here, once you're well."

"And what if I don't get well?"

"Then I'll do my best to convince you it's better to let me help you here than come visit and find you're bleeding out on your kitchen floor."

It was blunt talk, but he knew it was what Edna needed to hear. She sighed and smoothed her hand over the quilt. "This is nice work. Your mother's?"

"Yes. She's been showing me how to quilt, but I'm a slow learner."

"I never got the hang of it. Hate the sound of the machine. It's nothing on the click of needles."

Kyle smiled. "Would you let me take my break tonight in here? I'll bring my knitting, and I'll click all you like."

She pulled a haughty face. "I'm not holding back if I think you're doing it wrong."

"Good."

He hated to leave her when his shift started, but he also knew she needed some time to come to terms with her new situation. He also had plenty of work to do, so much that he had to cut a deal with Trina to arrange his break at a time when Edna would still be awake.

"You're so sweet to the little old ladies." Trina waved him off. "Go on. But I want to hear all about this hickey you planted on Paul Jansen once everybody's in for the night."

Edna, thankfully, hadn't heard the gossip about the hickey, or she'd decided it was too scandalous to bring up. She only ate potato chips and ruthlessly critiqued his stitches. She insisted she wasn't tired, but after he helped her through her evening routine, it was clear how exhausted she was.

When he left her room and headed to the nurses' station, Corrina Anderson waited for him.

Unable to help it, Kyle broke out in a deep blush.

She rolled her eyes and waved his embarrassment away. "None of that. No, it's not what I would have advised, but it seems to have worked out okay. Even the hickey. Maybe not quite such a *big* one, but it certainly has everyone talking."

Didn't Kyle know it. "Can I stop watching the movies now? I think I figured it out. He loves happy endings and soft, gooey stories. Right?"

She cinched her scarf tighter around her neck. "I'll have Gabriel pull some more. Though it sounds as if you'll be short on time to watch them, what with work, the Winter Wonderland preparation Sunday, and your big date on Saturday."

And yet she clearly still expected him to do his homework. Kyle sighed.

Corrina patted his shoulder. "It's important, dear. Paul's a complicated man."

"I don't understand why I have to watch bad movies to understand him."

She hesitated, as if weighing her options, then nodded. "Very well. I'll give you one hint. Part of the reason he watches them is because of his family."

"His family? What, the movies are some kind of tradition?"

Corrina's lips flattened. "Oh, no. More of a replacement. The Jansens aren't kind to him in general, and his mother and sister are the worst. Mary's especially always been a stick-in-the-mud. Never gave up hope Paul dating my son was him going through a phase. But no matter who he dates of any gender, she won't be happy until the boy is back under her thumb."

Kyle'd had no idea Paul's mother was so unaccepting. He'd never really paid her any mind, and it occurred to him it might be time to fix that. "And the movies are related to this somehow?"

Corrina touched her nose. "One hint, child. It's all I'm giving you."

She waved him goodbye, and he went on his evening rounds. On break, he and Trina ended up talking about Winter Wonderland, which Trina was excited about because she and her friends had always wanted to open a coffee shop and here was their chance to try. By the time Kyle got off work at three, she bustled with plans, and Kyle felt pretty good about himself.

He fell into bed once he got home, but he woke before ten in the morning, too wired to stay asleep. He helped his mother make lunch and watched a movie with Linda Kay. When the restless impatience got to him, he bundled into his winter gear and went outside for a walk.

It hadn't been his plan to go to Mormor and Morfar's house, but that's where he ended up. The front door was boarded up and the back door locked, but Kyle knew the trick of shimmying open the window and climbing inside.

He hadn't been in the house in years, and he remembered why once he stood in the musty, decayed kitchen. In his mind's eye, the little house looked like Frankie and Marcus's place, only more compact. It smelled of dinner and coffee and sweetbread and his great-grandmother's perfume. The walls were decorated with quilts and painted with stencils his great-grandfather had drawn in by hand. No, the hardwood floors hadn't gleamed, and yes, the plaster had cracked in more than a few places. But the life of the house swelled, enveloping Kyle whenever he visited. Mormor and Morfar were full of stories and legends of his family, of their Swedish heritage, of frontier living.

The house smelled of rot and dust now. When he'd first come home from college, he'd lobbied to turn the house into his home, and his parents had been all for the idea, but when they hired a contractor, they found out they might as well raze the house and rebuild it, as expensive as the upgrades would be. The wiring needed to be redone, the insulation pulled out, the plaster lath repaired or replaced with drywall. They'd talked about doing it themselves, but nobody ever had the time, and somehow the upgrade had never happened.

Kyle feared they'd waited too long as he gave himself a tour, noting new damage, including a large water stain on the second-floor ceiling. He pushed a peeling section of wallpaper back in place, stood in the middle of the bedroom and listened to the scratching sound of rodents in the walls. Then he went downstairs and crawled out of the window again.

As he did so his phone buzzed, and when he pulled it from his pocket, he saw the preview of the message, which was a selfie of Paul, wearing his new hat. Smiling shyly. Adorably.

He sat on the steps of the porch, staring out into the field, thinking. In the quiet safety of the old house, the nagging fears crept slowly out from the corners of his mind where he'd stuffed them. Kyle let them come, facing them like the adult he kept insisting he was.

He was falling in love with Paul. He'd have said so cavalierly a month ago, but now he knew it was true. He knew, too, part of him *had* been chasing Paul because he was handy. Because he fit a script in his head.

As he pulled up the selfie, Kyle's chest ached with longing. He didn't want the idea of Paul anymore. He wanted the man. The shy, uncertain, sweet-hearted man. He wanted to make him smile the way he did in that photo every day. Wanted to see the way he lit up when he saw Kyle. Wanted to make dinner with him. Clean up after. Make love.

Maybe with hickeys in less gossip-inducing places.

Kyle wanted all of it. He'd thought he had before, but he understood now what had been missing. Before, the thought of Paul refusing him had been an annoyance. A challenge. Now, fear of Paul shutting a door on him made him freeze inside like one of his snow sculptures.

He had to be more careful. He had to not be clumsy or hurried or selfish. Because the more he was with Paul, the more he acknowledged it wasn't an option to lose him.

Kyle sat on the steps a long time after, until the cold finally drove him back to the house.

Chapter Twelve

P AUL'S HICKEY FADED quickly enough, but he got knowing looks from everyone in town long after he didn't have any cause to get creative with a scarf. Some people smiled. Some people gawked. A few of them, same as always when someone was caught being gay, glared.

Oh, most people in Logan had decided gay was okay, but there was definitely a Fox News-watching faction who felt gay men and women were harbingers of the end of times. Sadly, Paul's family led the pack of that group. His father never gave him the talking-to his mother kept threatening, but *she* continued to give him earfuls every time he went over to the house. Which led him to go over there less and less. He ran into his sister plenty, however, and each encounter was more unpleasant than usual. She gave him tight-lipped smiles in the grocery store aisles, and when they turned up at the library at the same time, they both developed habits of staring a little too hard at the DVDs.

Sandy, Paul could handle, but it bummed him out to find his niece and nephew gaping at him too. Charity was eleven, David nine—Paul was their godfather, and usually they at least waved. Now they only stared.

Kyle was always touchy-feely, laying his hand on Paul's arm, kissing his cheek. Perfectly normal stuff—if they were a heterosexual couple. But despite Frankie and Marcus and Arthur and Gabriel paving the way, it made a good chunk of Logan uncomfortable, and it made Paul's family turn rigid.

One night Kyle and Paul were enjoying an early dinner at the café before Kyle had to go to work. They held hands over the top of the table, and Paul smiled, listening to Kyle tell a story about something his sister had done. Behind Kyle's carefully styled head, Paul caught a glimpse of his niece, staring at him, unsmiling. Before Paul could read her expression, Sandy turned her daughter away with a glare in Paul's direction and another firmly placed on the back of Kyle's head.

Kyle stopped his story and glanced over his shoulder. "Ah." He turned back to Paul, letting their hands fall apart, his bright expression fading.

Hating the loss of his light, Paul recaptured Kyle's hand. "Ignore them."

Kyle's grip was less sure now, however. "Are they always like that with you?"

"It's new for them to see me out with a guy." His mother's exact words in their last phone conversation had been *throwing it in their faces.*

Kyle raised an eyebrow. "You dated Arthur a long time."

Paul rolled his eyes. "No. Arthur and I slept and lived together. That was part of what I didn't enjoy about our relationship, our lack of dating. That and how he often wanted to bring a third person to bed with us."

He didn't know what to make of the way this statement made Kyle's eyes bug out. "You did three-somes?" He poked his fry into his ketchup, looking boyish and wicked. "I did one, once. It was exciting, but also very tense. I always worried I was doing the wrong thing."

"Arthur bossed everybody around, so that part was easy. Sometimes the ménages were sexy, but mostly I got jealous."

Kyle kept dunking his fry, but he glanced coyly at Paul. "So does this mean you're over threesomes?"

"Um…it depends." He shifted in his chair. "You…want to?"

Kyle shrugged, winked and ate the fry before replying, "Oh, I don't know. I'm curious, I guess. Mine was with these two guys at school. Do you ever run into the guys? The third leg of the triangle? Is it weird?"

"Not really. Just another hookup." He considered the question more carefully. "A few of them I did get with individually. But nothing ever serious."

The next fry Kyle sucked the ketchup off of, which was surprisingly erotic. "See, I've never been good at random hookups. I haven't had a throng of boyfriends, but that's part of where I went wrong. I always *wanted* to have a relationship, so it frustrated me when the guy wanted me to pump and dump."

Paul's heart warmed. "Yeah. It frustrates me too."

"See? That's why we're good together." Dipping another fry, he fed it to Paul. "I'd almost convinced myself I was over you, that I'd made it all up in my head and I liked the idea of you, not the real you, and then I heard you broke up with Arthur because he didn't want a relationship. It was my dream come true. I was sure you were just like me, and all I had to do was show you." He took a sip of Coke. "If I'd have known a snow penis was the way to your heart, I'd have done that a long time ago."

Paul laughed. He had nothing to say in reply, but he did run the toe of his boot along the edge of Kyle's.

Kyle's teasing expression vanished. "I'm sorry if I'm too exuberant. It's only that I love being with you, and I'm not used to hiding how I feel about people. But I've never been on a date in town before either, so maybe I was assuming more acceptance than there is. I don't want to make anything awkward for you, especially with your business."

Paul took Kyle's hand, holding it tight. "It's not awkward to be with you. If people have a problem with me dating you, they must have a problem with Arthur and Gabriel too, so there's nothing gained or lost as far as the shop. But even if it did matter, I'd say screw it."

Pushing aside the remembered glare of his sister, he drew Kyle's hand to his lips and kissed it. "As you said. I've wanted a relationship like this for a long time. And I'm glad it's with you."

Kyle drew their joined hands to his own lips, turning their wrists so he could kiss the mirror of the place Paul had. "Same."

Patty, their waitress, appeared at that moment with a plate of pie choices and a fond smile. "You two lovebirds want some dessert?"

"Yeah." Paul nodded to the chocolate mousse, which he knew was Kyle's favorite. "And two forks to share."

THINGS WERE GOING great with Paul, better in so many ways than he'd ever dreamed. But Corrina's comment about his family haunted him, and after the incident at the café, Kyle felt like he had to take some kind of action. The problem was, he didn't know what that action should be, and no amount of Christmas romance bingeing was going to help him. He knew he should talk to Paul directly about it, but he couldn't figure out how. Not without either rubbing salt in a wound or asking him to address things he didn't want to talk about.

In the end, Kyle split the difference. He texted Gabriel and set up a meeting with him and Arthur.

He was nervous, going to Paul's ex for advice.

Probably he'd been watching too many bad romances, but all the way over to Gabriel and Arthur's house, he couldn't help thinking this would be the part in the movie where Paul walked in at the worst moment possible and there was some Big Misunderstanding. That didn't happen, and when he arrived, once the niceties were out of the way, he sat across from them at their kitchen table and addressed the whole talking-about-Paul-behind-his-back thing full-on.

"I really do want to bring it up to him," he assured them. "But I don't want to step in anything either. I'm not looking for you to tell tales out of school or betray confidences. I only want some advice on how to proceed." Hopefully tips that didn't involve a DVD player.

Gabriel and Arthur exchanged a glance. Arthur looked uneasy, and Gabriel all but threw up his hands, his expression saying quite clearly, *This is totally your turf, hon.*

Arthur rubbed the back of his neck. "I'll be honest, I'm not sure where to start. It's no secret I'm no favorite with the Jansens, and to be honest, some of that I've earned. But yeah, they're conservative, in all the wrong ways. They don't make it easy for him. And yeah, I'm pretty sure they're a big part of his relationship trouble, including the tension you're feeling. Paul can want to be with you all day long, and you can be the best god-damned man in the world for him. The real threat to the two of you is the shit his family has put in his head. And nobody in the world can take that poison out but him."

Arthur's warning left Kyle cold and impotent. He didn't like it. "What do you mean? What poison?" This sounded so ominous. "Did they…abuse him?"

"Probably some would say so, but it's one of those gray lines. Not so much physical but emotional. They hate that he's gay, to start. But he could marry a woman tomorrow, and they'd still find crap wrong with him. It's as if they need him to be the boil they poke at. Their resident asshole, bearing all their shit so they can feel better about themselves."

A tidbit from college lit drifted into Kyle's mind. "Like the story where the villagers keep the kid in the basement, alone and abused and starved, because his suffering keeps the village safe?"

"'The Ones Who Walk Away from Omelas' by Ursula K. Le Guin." Gabriel pursed his lips and nodded. "I haven't had much contact with the Jansens, but from what I know of them, the analogy holds pretty accurately."

The thought filled Kyle with rage—and helplessness. "What do I do to stop this?"

Arthur grimaced. "You can't. You'll have to bury this idea you can be good enough for him. That you screwing up is what will drive him away. He'll drive *himself* away."

Kyle wrapped his hand around his mug of tea, hating this conversation so much. "So you're saying I can't help him at all?"

Arthur looked flustered, but Gabriel simply grimaced. "Speaking as someone coming from a similar background, no, there's not much you can do. Not the way you're asking. That sort of stuff hangs with you. Love helps, but it's not an eraser. Pain has to be carried and processed. Some of it will never go away. With Paul, though, your first step is letting him get used to the idea of having something good. He doesn't need his family around to make him second-guess it. He'll get through it, though. What you need to do most is be patient and willing to wait."

Arthur took Gabriel's hand in his, kissed the knuckles and kept hold of it on top of the table. "The more I watch the two of you together, the more I think you're right for one another. He's always been a hot mess of wanting to be the boss right up until he doesn't want to be in change anymore, and I can tell you, it's a real bitch to sort out. Yet you seem to ride that tiger no problem. So stop worrying he's going to change his mind about you. He wonders the same damn thing. We all do, when we're faced with the one we want most."

"I'll second that." Gabriel smiled at him. "Up to and including the part where you're right for Paul, and he for you."

Kyle flushed, mostly with pleasure. He hadn't realized how much he'd wanted their approval of him until he had it. "I just want everything to be okay. With every day that passes, I feel more and more like if he decides he doesn't want me the way I want him, it'll devastate me."

Gabriel bumped his head against Arthur's before winking at Kyle. "Welcome to a serious relationship."

Kyle groaned. "Can you at least feed me some pap about how it gets better?"

Arthur ran a thumb down his fiancé's cheek. "It gets different."

Not exactly the world's most winsome reassurance. The glance Arthur gave Gabriel, though, packed enough punch to make Kyle look forward to finding out what *different* meant.

DATING KYLE WAS tricky, Paul quickly realized, but not for the reasons he'd fretted about ever since he'd seen the man putting the finishing touches on the snow penis. The age difference was only a problem when he thought about it. The bedroom wasn't any kind of an issue. They had no problem agreeing on what to do for their dates, usually agreeing to stay in and watch a movie.

The problem Paul hadn't seen coming was how difficult it was to arrange so much as a meal together at the café. Kyle's schedule was erratic, but he was largely evenings and overnights. This meant if Paul got a call for a late repair job, he was likely to miss Kyle entirely, or they'd have to settle for a quick fuck against the door before Kyle hurried off to his shift. Every so often Paul suggested Kyle sleep at his place if he got off at three in the morning, but they tended to stay up for hours fucking when they did that, and Paul ran the risk of hammering his thumb the next day.

Arthur, surprisingly, had stopped all objections over Kyle and liberally offered to take late jobs alone so Paul could go home. Paul tried to reserve his acceptance of those offers for nights Kyle went in at eleven or had the evening off altogether. Usually Kyle let himself into Paul's place and had dinner waiting when Paul got home, though a few times Paul had surprised him with dinner waiting in the Crock-Pot. He loved how grateful and moved Kyle was whenever that happened.

Sometimes their whole date was cooking together. Paul's favorite evenings in were ones where they went to the grocery store together, selected what they'd eat, then worked side by side in his kitchen to make the meal.

It blew Paul's mind how little they fought. Outside of that night of the blizzard after Paul had kicked Kyle out, they never really so much as raised their voices. After so many years with Arthur, always fighting over things as simple as who drove the truck to work, it was good but slightly unnerving for Paul to feel so easy with Kyle. It wasn't so much that Kyle was laid-back, more that he was sneaky about how he convinced you to go along with his idea without conflict. Kyle was graceful in all things. Charming. Flirty. Funny.

The only times Paul didn't care for Kyle's manner

was when they were out in public together, because he noticed sometimes other people seemed to write the script for Kyle on how he should behave, and all too often Kyle let them. Paul suspected Kyle didn't fight because it was easier to give in, though it could also be because he was too polite to point out they were being assholes. Sometimes Kyle played up the camp, yes, but for him to *not* do that meant actively resisting other people's assumptions and expectations.

Paul got a bit of eyebrow over being gay, mostly comments running from teasing slights against his manhood to awkward glances and frowns in the men's restroom. Kyle got something different. For that matter, so did Gabriel and Frankie. Gabriel got testy when women assumed all he wanted to do was go shopping, and even Frankie was known to grumble about how everyone talked like he was the woman in his and Marcus's relationship. Kyle got all that too, but Paul quickly realized why he'd panicked about Kyle being too young. People treated him like he was teenage Kurt from *Glee*, some kind of gay Peter Pan. They might treat Gabriel and Frankie as if they were women, but they treated Kyle as if he were a *boy*. A sexless boy.

It chafed Paul every time he noticed it. It fucked with his head, because *his* vision of Kyle was someone who took charge, who made him feel safe without being suffocated. And absolutely he fucked like a man. It upset Paul to see his vision of Kyle so neutered and…well, mocked, in a way. Eventually one night as they ate dinner he said something about it.

Kyle shrugged as he stabbed a bit of salad. "They don't mean anything by it. I tell myself it's better than being told I'm Satan's spawn or going to hell."

"They shouldn't dismiss you, though. You're not a boy. Sometimes I think you're more man than I am."

Kyle's smile made Paul shiver, and something about the way Kyle wiped his mouth with his napkin had Paul wanting to skip the steak on his plate and ask for an entirely different kind of meat. "So long as *you* don't see me as a boy."

Paul pushed his lust slightly to the side, because it was important to him to tell Kyle how he felt. "I don't. I'm sorry I ever did."

Kyle reached across the table and stroked Paul's beard. "It's okay. Really. It's easy to fall into stereotypes in a small town. I think it's less that people want to see me as sexless and more they don't like things moved too far out of their boxes. It's a miracle, given the voting demographic, we're accepted at all. It's hard for people to make room for something other than the standard male-female dynamic. If I started dating a girl, they'd move me into the *man* slot with a happy sigh and start asking when I'll have kids. It's not so much that they think that's right, but it's what they *know*. Since I've been out forever, they put me in a kind of sexless state." He picked up his knife to cut his steak, smiling ruefully. "Now that I'm dating you, they've pretty much decided I'm a young lady with a dick."

Which was almost word for word what Frankie had complained of. "It isn't *right*, though."

"What in this world is fair? I'm not saying I don't want to change their minds. Mostly I'm acknowledging it'll take a lifetime to do so." When Paul still frowned, Kyle touched his lips again. "Thank you for being outraged on my behalf."

It was things like that which got Paul. Because with Arthur they'd have argued and ended up having angry sex. With Kyle, the discussion turned into a deeper connection. Kyle touched him a lot as they did the cleanup, and while Paul did the dishes, Kyle stood behind him, fondling his ass until he finally undid Paul's jeans and groped his cock. The number of times he'd had sex in his kitchen were now too numerous to count. And yeah, the sex was great.

But the companionship was what he was there for, what he cherished. What made his heart soar and ache with fear of loss by turns.

Best yet was the way Kyle folded so effortlessly into his friendship with Marcus, Arthur, Frankie, and Gabriel.

One weekend, Marcus, Arthur, and Paul went hunting, and as they set off for the tree stand, their men went to Duluth for a day of shopping. When the hunters arrived at the cabin, they rendered the meat and started some stew, and when the shoppers returned in time for dinner, they revealed their discoveries. All three of them had bought something for their partners.

Marcus got several packs of new socks and a new tie. Arthur got a six-pack of his favorite local beer and a Terry Pratchett novel, which Paul knew Gabriel would read to him aloud.

Paul received a DVD of *While You Were Sleeping*.

They ended up watching it the next day instead of heading to the movie theater. Paul hadn't seen it in years, and he'd forgotten how much he enjoyed it.

"I wonder what it would be like to live in a big city," he said once it was finished.

"Loud and busy." Kyle settled his head into Paul's lap and smiled up at him as he teased fingers through his beard. "I prefer small towns. *Our* small town."

Paul didn't always, but he'd become awfully fond of it lately.

Kyle kept petting Paul's beard. "Hey, I've been meaning to ask you. Gabriel and Arthur got engaged last year, Marcus and Frankie this spring. I haven't heard of any dates set, though. What's going on there?"

"Oh, I don't know." Paul looked away, fighting a bloom of embarrassment. And losing.

Kyle sat up, studying him a moment. "Now *that* was an interesting reaction. I want to hear all about it."

The more Paul hemmed and hawed, the more Kyle petted him, urging him gently but insistently to spill the beans. Paul sighed. "I don't know for sure. I really don't. But I think, sometimes, they're waiting for me." His blush heated his whole body. "To find my own somebody."

The pause between that confession and Kyle's reply wasn't overly long, but it felt like an eternity to Paul all the same. He felt ridiculous with the words hanging in the air. He worried what they would make Kyle think. He worried what Kyle might say. But then Kyle shifted on the sofa and straddled Paul, taking his head in his hands, holding his face firmly in place. He brushed a kiss over Paul's mouth before he replied.

"I'll have to work harder, then, to show them you already have."

A second kiss turned sultry, and after a break for air, Kyle stripped them both out of their shirts and pushed Paul onto his back before trailing kisses down the fur of his chest. When he took Paul in his mouth, though, he kept things tender, never driving their passion into a frenzy. He paused often to kiss Paul all over his body, stroking, licking, sucking, but with a reverence that made Paul feel worshipped. Adored.

Loved.

By the time they came together, mouths fused, cocks rubbing together inside Kyle's sure grip, Paul floated in a perfect haze of tenderness and surrender. It lingered long after he came, and as he drifted to earth again, it occurred to him Kyle was the first man who had ever given him everything he wanted in one package: aggression, tenderness, domination, equality. Affection and delight. Rough fucking and wild passion. He was everything.

He was perfect.

As they lay twined together in bed, listening to the wind blow against the house, Paul shut his eyes and said a silent prayer.

Please let this stay. Please, if I get nothing else in life, please let this stay.

Chapter Thirteen

P AUL HADN'T REALIZED how much work Gabriel and Marcus had been doing behind the scenes for Winter Wonderland until he saw it spread across Frankie's dining room table.

For weeks now, there had been public meetings at the library, notices in the paper, and all manner of repair work for Arthur and Paul on the abandoned storefronts on Main Street. Kyle had turned part of their workshop into a design studio, where he and Frankie huddled together to discuss colors, motifs, and other mystical things for the look of the project. Paul had felt the fever of the festival for some time now, and he was excited for it the same as he was for any public event.

Now it was a week before Thanksgiving, a little more than a month before the festival, and everyone who was anyone in Logan was crowded into Marcus and Frankie's house along with the Winter Wonderland planning committee, finalizing this year's project and making big plans for festivals to come. Standing over the mass of applications, permits, and licenses, however, drove home the depth of what they were doing in a way nothing else had. This wasn't some little party the library was throwing to raise money. This was *big*. Or, rather, it could be.

It made Paul excited. And terrified.

Frankie and Marcus's house buzzed with people. The six of them—Frankie, Marcus, Arthur, Gabriel, Paul, and Kyle—but also Corrina, the library board, the mayor, and city council, and the small business association. Marcus led them all, using a PowerPoint presentation projected on a fold-out screen Frankie set up in front of the dining room's picture window.

"Here you can see the Winter Wonderland venue sites." He hit a button on his laptop, and the image of Logan Main Street morphed names and images into the buildings previously marked VACANT. "We've randomized applicants for the demonstration, but it's important to know we have three times as many potential businesses than we have space to house them. Even filling the gymnasium will leave some leftover."

The mayor shook his head in disbelief. "Where are all these people coming from?"

"Everywhere." Marcus poked at the computer again, and the PowerPoint shifted to a graph. "Here's a breakdown of which cities the applications have come from. This will clearly be a regional event. Bear in mind these are mostly established or recently folded businesses—if we'd put this application out in July, it'd be a different story entirely."

"This is only interested *businesses*." Frankie reached around Marcus to pull up another slide. "We took out a few Facebook ads offering a link to a mailing list for when information was available. Here's how many people signed up." The slide loaded, and the room gasped. Frankie's smile was sly. "We targeted users in the Twin Cities as aggressively as we did Duluth and the local counties. We almost got a *better* response from urban areas."

Gabriel spoke up from the back of the room. "It makes sense. Everyone wants nostalgia at Christmas, and that's what Winter Wonderland sells."

One of the council members nodded, her expression something between stunned and excited. "This could be what finally gets the contractors to stop telling us they might build vacation homes here and actually get around to buying the land and starting construction."

"Which would help the mill," Arthur said from the other side of the table. "Which would create jobs."

"And the seasonal businesses would become year-round businesses," the head of the small business association said in a near whisper. "But how do we make sure this is what happens?"

"We have some ideas about that. What the city needs to decide is how big we want this to get. Because it could get pretty big." Marcus advanced the next slide.

It showed a picture from the year before with Arthur in his Santa suit on a sleigh, but underneath it were the boldface words: *Logan: Minnesota's Year-Round Christmas Village.*

The mayor blinked. "All year?"

"Yes." Frankie gestured to the packet of paper he'd distributed before Marcus had started his presentation. "We need a hook, something to set us apart from the other small towns relying on tourism. Our lake isn't the best lake in the area, and let's face it. It's Minnesota. Everybody has a lake. We aren't close to a major city. We don't have anything particular to draw people here, not on a regular basis. But everyone loves Christmas."

"We'll hate it soon enough," one of the library board members said.

Corrina, though, had stars in her eyes. "No, we won't. Because this won't just bring jobs. This will bring *people*. We won't be a dying town anymore. We'll be the Christmas village."

"We could even get our school district back," someone said.

Marcus held up a hand. "Nothing magical will happen overnight. We need to let this year be the test case and carefully nurture the idea throughout the next couple of years. And we must start planning next year's Winter Wonderland in February."

The various city agencies and councils began talking at once, and Marcus ceded the meeting to the mayor. It was less exciting pretty quickly once Marcus and Frankie's slideshow ended, and Paul was glad when Frankie declared it was time for cocktails and hors d'oeuvres.

Since he'd been separated from Kyle when they took their seats, the first thing Paul did when it was acceptable to move around was locate him. Kyle turned out to be in the living room, sipping punch and talking to Corrina. Arthur's mother saw Paul first and waved him over, rising and insisting he take her seat.

"I need to ask the mayor something anyway." She kissed Paul's cheek and bustled away.

Paul sat beside Kyle, who smiled at him in the way that made Paul's belly get butterflies.

"What did you think of the meeting?" Kyle offered his plate of food to Paul, who took a cheese roll mostly to be polite. "It's all very exciting, don't you think?"

Paul nodded, chewing the roll before he answered. "If it works, it could be something else, that's for sure."

"I think it'll work."

"I don't know. Wouldn't another town have done this already, if it's that easy?"

"It's not easy at all. But we're not afraid of hard work. Plus Logan has all of *us*." He squinted at Paul's mouth. "Oh, hon, you have a—Here."

Paul held still, cheeks staining as Kyle wiped cream cheese out of his mustache with all the bigwigs of Logan looking on.

Soon people started to leave, everyone wearing smiles on their faces. Corrina was the last to go, hugging and kissing and carrying on about what a *wonderful group of boys* they were. She pulled Paul aside though, asking him to help her carry her things to her car, which turned out to be an excuse to give him a pep talk.

"Everything going well with Kyle?" She blinked up at him beneath the streetlight as if studying his face to find the answer there. "You seem happy. Are you happy, Paul?"

Paul nodded, blushing, ducking into the scarf Kyle had knit for him. "Yes, thank you."

Corrina didn't stand down. "Is your family giving you a tough time? I know how they can be." When Paul's only answer was a shrug, she pursed her lips. "Don't listen to them. If you're happy, *be* happy, Paul." She patted his arm. "Oh, I wanted to tell you—we're having Thanksgiving as usual, and you're welcome to come. Kyle too."

"Thank you, but my family expects me. Kyle's probably does too."

Corrina lifted her eyebrows. "You haven't asked him what his plans are? You should plan to go together, wherever you decide."

"We've barely dated a few weeks. It seems a bit…big to do a holiday together."

"Are you telling me you don't *want* to have Thanksgiving with him?"

Paul blushed, stammered. "No, I—I just mean, it's so soon, and my family…"

Corrina wagged a finger in his face. "You won't know what Kyle will say until you ask. As for your family, don't bother with what they think or don't."

That was all well and good, but inviting Kyle to Thanksgiving meant involving them. Or inviting himself over to Kyle's, which was worse.

Paul worried Corrina would do the asking for him. She didn't, thank God, though he suspected she said something to Kyle, because on the way home, *he* brought it up.

"Do you have plans for Thanksgiving?"

Paul shifted his grip on the wheel. "Yeah. Going to my parents' place at noon, like usual." He chewed his lip, then made himself add, "What about you?"

"Work, unfortunately, though as usual Mom's a rock and moved the family dinner until after my shift." He tugged at his ear and smiled. "You're welcome to come, if you can handle a second dinner. I'd say you could not eat, but Mom won't let you out without *something*."

"Oh, I wouldn't want to put her out."

"You wouldn't. She's been after me to bring you to dinner, in fact." He messed with his ear again. "But there will be a lot of people there, so I won't pressure you if you don't want to come."

Paul honestly couldn't decide if he wanted to go or not. "I'll think about it," he said, as a compromise.

Kyle smiled. "You do that."

Paul dropped Kyle off at his house shortly after. As

usual, Kyle's father and brothers were working outside, and they waved to Paul in a friendly way. They were always glad to see him, inviting him to come in for a cup of coffee.

He thought a lot about going to the Parks house for Thanksgiving. About how good it would feel to be truly welcome somewhere, to spend a holiday with people who didn't inject a judgment into every conversation. Weirdly, that made Paul less inclined to accept Kyle's offer, though he couldn't articulate why. Not until Arthur brought up the holiday at work and asked Paul if he and Kyle were getting together. Paul told him about Kyle's offer and his failure to accept or deny.

"I want to go, and I don't." He rubbed his beard and frowned at the workbench. "His family seems great. I do want to get to know them. I just...I don't know. I don't want to rush. And to be honest, I don't want to get attached."

Arthur's smile was rueful and understanding. "For what it's worth, I don't think he regards you as a passing phase."

The observation spawned something warm in the center of Paul's chest, but it also increased the gnawing doubt in his gut. "He doesn't know all my faults yet. Could change his mind. I'd rather hold off, keep some cards back. I mean, one hot young cub walks in, and what have I got to counter that?"

"A *lot*." Arthur nudged Paul in the arm. "You're a great catch. And the two of you are perfect together.

Maybe I worried about the age difference too at first, but I don't now. He's good to you. Good *for* you. You're not convenient. You're what he wants."

"For now."

"He wants it to be for a lot longer than a lark, bud. He's a long-hauler."

Paul wanted to believe this. "It's just easier to hold back. Safer."

Arthur sighed and held up his hands. "You do what you need to do. Let me tell you, though, you won't get anywhere by playing it safe. You need to open up to him. Take a risk. I get that the more you want it, the harder it is. I threw up twice before I put on that Santa suit and asked Gabriel to marry me. Part of me knew he'd say yes, part of me was equally sure he'd slap my face. And look at Marcus and Frankie. They almost walked away from each other, and now they're playing house and picking out invitations. Sitting on the chamber of commerce together. Wouldn't have happened if Frankie hadn't risked it all to come back up here and open his heart."

Paul pursed his lips. "It doesn't work like that, you know. It's no guarantee you get a happily ever after if you put your heart on the line."

"True enough. But it *is* a promise that if you don't take a risk, the happily ever after will *never* happen."

The warning hung in Paul's head all the rest of the day. Arthur was right, he should go. As risks went, it was an easy one to take. The worst thing that would happen was he loved Kyle's family and later Kyle broke up with him, cutting the Parks out of his life. He convinced himself, as best he could, he could guard against falling for Kyle's family too hard. It was his baby step toward getting his own happily ever after.

Yes, it also fed the crazy part of him that was aware Marcus and Arthur had both found their husbands-to-be in this very season. They'd known they were forever before the church bells rang on Christmas morning. He knew it wasn't rational to think that just because it had happened for them it would happen for him.

It wasn't rational, but Paul couldn't stop hoping it would happen anyway.

HOLIDAYS WERE THE rare times Kyle wished he worked in a regular hospital: while nurses still could expect to work on special occasions, major holidays meant less surgeries and zero voluntary admissions and therefore less census and less staff required. Nursing homes tended to need the same staffing regardless of what day of the year it was. As such, holidays were granted on a rotating schedule. They each had to work one major and two minor holidays a year. They did work with less staff, but it was only slightly less than a regular day.

Kyle's mother always scheduled her meal around his shift, a pleasantry he did his best not to take for granted. He did what he could to help her with preparations in the days before, baking pies, doing the shopping, especially those little trips for things she didn't realize she was out of until the last possible moment. It was during one of those occasions on Monday when he ran into Corrina at the grocery store.

"How are your mother's preparations coming?" Corrina nodded at her overflowing cart. "As you can see, I'm late to the game myself. But then I don't have nearly as many guests as she does. How many this year?"

"Thirty." Kyle nodded as her eyes went wide. "A cousin got married out of state last month, and we're using the holiday as a way to have an informal reception for the family who couldn't make it. Everyone's bringing a dish, but Mom can't stand the idea we might not have enough of the staples. I have the feeling we'll be able to feed the entire county before it's all said and done."

Corrina gave an approving nod. "And is Paul one of that number?"

"He says he's thinking about it."

"Keep after him. He'll say yes eventually. Especially if you ask him the right way."

"Well, what's the right way?"

She winked and patted his arm as she pushed her cart away.

Kyle thought about Corrina's comment the rest of the day. He wasn't against it at all, but it felt weird to offer when he'd already done everything from subtle hints to out-and-out wheedling. He absolutely couldn't get the job done "the right way" via text, and since he wasn't due to see Paul until Wednesday night, he couldn't see how it was going to happen before then. Which at that point might possibly be too late.

When Kyle stopped at Paul's on Wednesday, Kyle was beat from a long day, with a long night of food prep ahead of him before more work in the morning, and Paul was equally exhausted from a long repair job, but they didn't even wait for Kyle to get his coat off before they started. Paul slid warm, work-rough hands under Kyle's coat hem, and Kyle fucked his tongue into Paul's mouth as he peeled out of his parka and abandoned it with his boots. When Kyle groaned and pushed on Paul's shoulders, Paul smiled into the kiss before sinking to his knees, opening his mouth as Kyle shoved his scrubs down enough to free his cock.

It was still a rush to see that curly blond head bobbing on his dick. Part of the thrill came from knowing Paul would do pretty much whatever Kyle told him. Like tonight, when he told Paul to put his hands behind his back, Paul did so without hesitation. The dregs of Kyle's long day evaporated as Paul moaned around his cock, drooling and gagging as Kyle fucked deep. But when Kyle pulled out, some of the shadows crept in.

Kyle threaded his fingers more gently into Paul's hair. "Something wrong?"

Paul shook his head, as much as he could with Kyle

holding it hostage. "No." He deliberately kept his gaze from Kyle's.

Kyle rubbed the tip of his cock teasingly along Paul's beard, ignoring the thrill of sensation that brought him. "Come on, baby. I know when you're lying. Tell me what's wrong."

Paul's shrug broke Kyle's heart. "It's nothing, really. Just not excited for tomorrow."

"You aren't? Why?"

Another shrug. "My family. They're never great, but they've been especially rough lately."

"Why? What's happened?" Kyle let go of his cock and touched Paul's face in concern. "I know you don't like to talk about your family, but you do know I'd be happy to listen about your struggles with them. Including right now."

"Nothing happened, really. Nothing new. They never like when I date, but I haven't been serious with anyone since Arthur, and I guess they were hoping I'd grown out of being gay or something."

Kyle ached for him. "I'm sorry."

Paul shrugged. "Arthur keeps telling me to skip out, but it would be worse after. Plus…well, they're my family. And it's not *all* bad."

Kyle stroked Paul's cheek with his knuckles before cupping his chin. "I wish I didn't work. I'd volunteer to go with you."

Paul shuddered, and his laugh was bitter, sad. "That would be worse, unfortunately."

"Then come to my house after. It's a little crazy, but it's a good crazy. And we can escape to my room if it gets to be too much. Though I can't promise Linda Kay won't insist on escaping with us." He couldn't stop a smile. "She thinks you're handsome. She told me to tell you if you ever switch teams, she wants to be first on the list for tryouts."

"I like your sister. Tell her it's doubtful I'll change my mind, but she can have that first place in line."

Kyle swayed on his feet, his smile faltering, though not because he was unhappy. Quite the opposite, in fact. Holding his pants up with one hand, he crouched to Paul's level and touched his face.

Paul regarded him warily. "Did I say something wrong?"

Kyle shook his head. "I don't think you understand what a gift it is to have you accept Linda Kay so easily. I've had boyfriends who thought she was weird. Others who I could tell only tolerated her."

Paul shrugged, embarrassed. "She's your sister. And she accepts me, so why wouldn't I do the same?"

Kyle couldn't say any more, not right away, so he kissed Paul, slow and sweet. When it began to turn into the same fire that had started the blow job, he broke the kiss and pressed their foreheads together. "Please come to Thanksgiving with me."

Paul nodded and put his hands on Kyle's arms. "Okay."

"Will you text me during the day? Let me be there

for you that way, since I can't be with you in person?"

Another nod and a nuzzle. "I'd like that. Thank you."

Kyle wished as he'd never wished for anything else to be able to get out of work. He gave a moment's thought to begging the late-shift person to swap with him, even if it meant telling his mother he couldn't go so he could be with Paul. Except he knew Paul wouldn't let him.

He kissed the corner of Paul's mouth regretfully. "I wish I could be there for you. I wish I could fix it. I'm sorry I can't."

Paul kissed him back, a tender, tentative brush of lips. "It's okay. I'm not asking you to."

"But I want you to ask me to do those kinds of things for you."

Paul kissed Kyle again, this time with tongue, and while he did so he reached for Kyle's now-soft dick, stroking it to life. "You do all kinds of things for me. Which is why I'd like to do something for you."

Kyle smiled, biting his bottom lip as Paul's hand job became more intense. "But I want to help you tomorrow. I want to be there with you. In whatever way I can."

Paul moved his lips to Kyle's neck, teasing the skin with his beard. "Maybe…maybe we could text. But I know that can be tricky sometimes at work."

Kyle was going to work like hell to keep himself available. "What if I stopped by before I went in? I'd stay the night, but I have to help my mom get ready. I can stop by for breakfast, though." He nipped Paul's chin. "Maybe some dessert too."

Paul leaned into Kyle, shutting his eyes. "I don't want to put you out," he said, in a tone making it clear he wished he could anyway.

"It's never putting me out to be with you, to take care of you." Kyle pulled away from Paul, then laughed as he realized his cock was still hanging out of his pants.

Paul closed his hand over it, his grip firm and sure. "Let me take care of *you* right now, then."

Grinning, Kyle rose to his feet, shutting his eyes as his boyfriend's mouth closed over him again.

WHEN KYLE ARRIVED the next morning, Paul had breakfast ready and waiting.

It was only oatmeal, hash browns, and bacon, but he set the table up as pretty as he could, wishing he could have put flowers in the center or something. Kyle didn't seem to mind the place settings weren't as fancy as Frankie's, kissing Paul hard on the mouth before digging in.

"I'll be by as soon as I'm off, and I'll text you as much as I can." He slugged some orange juice and wiped his mouth with the paper towel Paul had laid out as a napkin. "What time will you go to your parents' place?"

"Probably around eleven."

"Oh, that works out. I get a break just before. We could text or talk on the phone, if you wanted. And please do text me anytime you want. If I can't reply right away, I will as soon as I can."

Paul hated how pathetic this all made him feel, until he thought about what his day had in store for him, and then he mostly wished he could crawl back into bed.

Kyle took his hand and leaned across the table to kiss him. "Don't think about how awful they'll be. Think about how crazy fun my family will be. They're all so excited you're coming. Mom was peeling Linda Kay off the ceiling when I left."

Paul smiled, but even the vision of Linda Kay couldn't chase away all his shadows.

Pulling him to his feet, Kyle placed his next kiss just below Paul's ear. "In case it's not enough to get you through, let me give you something to carry you into your oncoming hellscape."

They stumbled together to the bedroom, tearing at each other's clothes, and as soon as Paul was naked, Kyle pushed him to the bed. He did the trick where he rode Paul for a bit, but he didn't let either of them come until he had Paul on his hands and knees, gripping the headboard as Kyle pounded into him. He went in hard, riding the edge of too much too fast, and the rush made Paul come like a fountain. When they collapsed onto the bed, he felt spent and as weak as a kitten. And a hell of a lot more mellow.

That glow faded, however, when it was time for Kyle to go. Paul put briefs and pajama pants on, going with Kyle to the door to kiss him goodbye.

Kyle wrapped his scarf around his neck and smacked Paul's sore butt with his mitten. "I'll be by to get you at three. Text me as much as you want. And if something goes really bad and you need to talk, call."

"I will," Paul promised, and kissed him on the mouth.

Kyle went to work, and Paul watched a movie on the couch until it was time to go. He'd tried to time it so he arrived an hour before the meal, and he'd leave a half an hour after pie—basically the minimal amount of time required for him to be present. He didn't plan to eat much since he wanted to be able to eat again at Kyle's place. But as he got ready to walk out the door, the looming criticism, judgment and general censure he knew waited for him made him wish he could get away with not going at all. His family's cloud overwhelmed him in a way the memory of his morning with Kyle couldn't counteract.

He was even more nervous to call Kyle, but he did it anyway.

Kyle answered on the first ring. "Hey, baby. Are you on your way?"

"Yeah." The heaviness overwhelmed him, and Paul attempted to distract himself. "Tell me about your day. What were you doing before break?"

"Trust me when I say you don't want to know what I was just doing. A nurse's job is seldom glamorous and often full of bodily fluids."

Paul gripped the phone. "I'm nervous. I'm sure they're going to start shit, and I'll have to sit there and take it."

"You don't have to take it. If they're terrible, leave. Go home and wait for me, or go to my house. My mom and Linda Kay can have you smiling in three minutes flat."

Paul knew he couldn't do that, but the thought was nice.

Kyle wasn't done, though. "Don't let your family drag you down. You don't have to be rude to them, but you don't have to stand there and take it either. You have other family. You know you could go with any of the guys, and they'd fold you right into their holiday. And you have me. For as long as you want to have me."

Paul shut his eyes. "I can't wait until three. I wish you were with me now."

"I am, baby. Every step of the way."

They hung up shortly after that. Tender-hearted feelings buoyed Paul out the door, all the way to his parents' farm. They faded slightly as his sister met him in the hall with a thin smile. But he smiled back, touching his phone through the front pocket of his jeans, reminding himself Kyle was only a text away.

He helped his father put extra leaves in the table,

sat with Tim and problem-solved the sticky gearshift in his tractor while their mom and Sandy set the plates out. Paul's niece and nephew raced old toys down the hallway until they were all called to wash their hands and come to eat.

The turkey was dry, the gravy bland. The biscuits weren't great, but they were familiar, his mother's staple. Sandy had brought the green bean casserole, and it wasn't bad. None of it, though, was even half as good as what he and Kyle cooked on a regular weeknight in.

Mary frowned with disapproval at Paul's plate. "You're hardly eating anything. Are you coming down with something?"

Paul cleared his throat and focused on poking at his lumpy mashed potatoes. "I'm fine. But I'm heading over to Kyle's parents' place later for another dinner. I wanted to be polite and save room."

He knew he'd just lobbed a bomb into the middle of the table, and most days, he'd have avoided that at all costs. But his ass still throbbed from being with Kyle, and his heart brimmed with his encouragements and promises. As his family gaped at him for daring to mention his boyfriend at the Thanksgiving table, Paul was ready for someone to berate him, but all that happened was Sandy gave him a glare and asked her husband in a too-bright voice to tell everyone about the plans for the remodel. Paul's imminent date wasn't brought up again.

When he was in the living room waiting for pie,

texting with Kyle, his niece, Charity, planted herself in front of him.

"Mom says it's wrong for boys to be boyfriends with other boys and girls to be girlfriends with other girls."

She delivered the line dutifully, as if repeating something learned by rote. She'd never brought up the subject of Paul's orientation before, and it dismayed Paul to hear her parroting her mother. But as he floundered with possible replies, something prickled at the back of his mind, made him pause and take a second look at his niece. He tried to think not of how *he* would respond to her, but how *Kyle* would.

"I don't think it's wrong," Paul said at last. He did his best to keep his tone patient, kind, but not judging or defensive either. "A lot of people don't."

"Jesus does."

Maybe he was making it up, but something about the way she looked at him, the edge in her voice, made Paul wonder. He put his phone aside and gave Charity his full attention.

"He doesn't, actually. He never said anything about it. I know because Marcus looked it up when we were in high school. And he's a lawyer, so he's pretty smart about that kind of stuff." After daring a glance at the kitchen to make sure his sister was out of earshot, he got brave. "Pastor Michaels doesn't think Jesus says so either. And he says the parts of the Bible saying homosexuality is a sin are from the same bits saying we shouldn't wear mixed fibers or eat pork. We're supposed to care more about what Jesus says, as Christians. And he never said a word about boys having boyfriends."

"But we *raise* pork."

"Exactly."

Charity frowned. "What's a mixed fiber?"

Paul smiled and rubbed his beard. "To be honest, I've never been able to figure it out."

Charity didn't smile. She worried her bottom lip with her teeth, and then she too glanced at the kitchen. When she spoke next, it was in a quiet voice.

"Sometimes…sometimes I think I don't like boys. At all. Not even to have a baby."

Paul didn't look away from Charity, trying to appear as natural as possible, not freaked out over the gravity of their conversation. "You're only eleven, so it might be too early to know if you like boys or not for sure. But if you do decide you only like girls, or girls as well as boys, you can come to me, if you need to talk to somebody about it. Or Corrina Anderson. She'd be good too."

Charity grimaced. "She's bossy."

"Yeah." Paul grinned. "She can be." He put a hand on her shoulder. "Don't worry much about it right now, okay? And don't listen when your Mom says bad stuff about gay people. She doesn't know everything."

Charity didn't say anything, but she did nod and look a little teary. She briefly threw her arms around

Paul's neck in an awkward hug, and then she hurried out of the room.

Paul watched her go, thinking of Kyle and wishing he'd been present to hear the exchange.

Chapter Fourteen

T HE HOURS UNTIL the end of a shift had never crawled by at a more glacial pace as they did for Kyle Thanksgiving Day.

There was plenty of work to do—a holiday was the same as any other day in a care center, as far as residents' needs went. The census was down slightly, with some people out with family for lunch or dinner, though not many were able-bodied enough for such an adventure.

Edna Michealson was one of that number, unfortunately. She'd made a great deal of improvement and was off her oxygen treatment, but she exhausted far too easily to brave a journey to her son's house, especially in the cold. Her son had been by on the weekend, but he didn't stay long in deference to her need to continue resting. This meant on the holiday Edna was in a particularly foul mood, fighting with the aides and other residents. Kyle was the only one she would tolerate, and even him not very well.

"Might as well roll me out to the parking lot and let me die." She waved a weathered hand at Kyle, a weak attempt to shoo him away. "Go take care of someone else. I'm not in the mood for your cheerfulness."

Kyle didn't budge, holding up the blood pressure cuff. "I can't leave until I take your vitals, I'm afraid. And I was told you didn't take your medicine, which means that's my job too."

"I don't *want* my vitals taken, and I'm done with that medicine. It hurts my stomach."

"Oh? I'll say something to the doctor, see if he can make a change. In the meantime, I'll make a note you're to be given as much vanilla ice cream as you like before your medicine is administered."

He didn't let himself smile at the way this made her pause, unwilling to snipe at the offer of her favorite treat. But he did think, *Gotcha.*

She sighed in a tight huff and held out her arm. "Very well. You win. Not like it matters. I'm going to die here. I'd rather it be sooner than later."

"If you've decided you're staying permanently, we should see about bringing more things over from your house. I'd be more than happy to help you make your room more comfortable." He sat beside her on the bed and wrapped the nylon cuff around her arm.

She watched him. "You're the only one who puts up with my foul mood. And you're the only one who's gentle when they put that thing on."

He glanced at her. "I'll speak to the staff. About the

cuff." He winked. "You'll have to work on your foul mood yourself, I'm afraid."

She *humphed* at that but kept quiet as he put his stethoscope in his ears and took her blood pressure and pulse. Once he swiped her forehead with his thermometer, however, she spoke again. "You shouldn't be here, fussing with me. You should be home with your family."

"No, I should be here, taking care of you. I'll be with my family later tonight." He waggled his eyebrows at her. "Paul's coming with me."

That made her smile. "Progressed far enough to have him at a holiday meal? Goodness, you're fast."

"Yes, well—it might be a bit quick, I'll admit. But his family is horrid. I wanted him to have a decent holiday, at least in part." He couldn't stop a besotted sigh. "I really like him, Edna."

"You certainly brighten when you speak of him. Which is saying something, as you're usually bright as it—"

She broke into a fit of coughing, having exerted herself too much, and Kyle took her hand, putting his other palm on her back, patting gently. "All right, young lady. You've had enough excitement for a bit, I think." He passed her the plastic mug of water from her bedside, nudging the straw to her mouth and urging her to sip. "Rest up, and I'll be back at noon with your holiday meal. If you want, I'll take my lunch break then too, and we can have our turkey together."

Releasing the straw from trembling lips, she fell back into her pillow, eyes closed with exhaustion. After a few breaths, she opened her eyes just enough to peer at him. "You…are so good…to us." She drew a few more breaths. "Why?"

There were a lot of answers to give, but she didn't want to hear this was his job or that he genuinely cared for her as a person. She wanted to know why a cheerful young man worked horrible shifts at a small-town care center.

So he told her.

"When Mormor and Morfar got too ill to live at home, even with us next door, they came here. It was the first time they were apart from one another since they were children. I watched the nurses rush about, seeing them only as patients, not people. Or at least, not Mormor and Morfar. I came by after school every day to see them, cajoling nurses to get them out of their rooms to be together in the lounge. I noticed how much better they both were when I came, how much brighter they were. When they finally passed away, within days of each other, I kept coming because I'd made friends with the other residents. I came by so much the head nurse guided me through the steps I'd need to become a CNA, then helped me apply to school." He smoothed her hair away from her face. "I like taking care of other people's grandparents. That's why."

She caught his hand weakly and drew it to her lips

to kiss it. "You're a treasure."

Kyle kissed her cheek, squeezed her hand and let it go as he stood. "I'll be by at noon. You get some sleep."

He did go by at noon, and they enjoyed a lovely meal. The food wasn't as grand as Kyle would have that evening, but it was good enough, and the company was wonderful. He stopped by her room again before the end of his shift, getting her to smile, letting her know he'd had the doctor change her medicine and made sure she'd get ice cream whenever she wanted it.

Eventually he was in his car, heading for Paul's house. They'd texted throughout the day, and he knew Paul hadn't had a terrible time, but not a wonderful one either. He also knew, after a series of increasingly flirtatious texts, the first thing they were doing when he walked in the door was fucking.

On the way to the door, though, he stopped to make a quick sculpture. Not his best, not by half, but the hastily assembled mini-snow penis still did the job, making Paul laugh and kiss him hard on the mouth when Kyle appeared on his doorstep with the snow cock perched in the palm of his mitten.

"Nice," Paul said, setting it off to the side where it wouldn't get knocked over by the door.

"Don't worry." Kyle nipped at Paul's chin. "I'll fuck you with something a lot warmer."

They went inside the house, kissing and grasping at each other until Kyle ended up on his knees, taking

Paul in deep. Paul didn't last long. All too soon he gripped Kyle's hair, his hips thrusting until his body seized and he came down Kyle's throat. He shuddered a moment after, his fingers relaxing against Kyle's head. He nudged Kyle to his feet and kissed him long and languid.

Then he pulled Kyle's shirt off, pushed his scrubs and underwear to his feet, and led him to the bedroom.

He made love to Kyle's whole body, nipping at his shoulder, teasing and sucking at his nipples until they were tight buttons. He licked Kyle's abdomen, his thighs, his taint. He took Kyle's cock into his mouth. Kyle swam in the sensation. He shut his eyes too, until the bed shifted with new weight. Paul kneed his way up Kyle's body, slicking him with lube and quickly working on a condom. Kyle watched Paul reach behind himself and work lube into his hole. Then Paul positioned himself over Kyle's cock and slowly sat down.

Kyle rode the blissful waves of tight heat as he pushed into Paul's ass. He tried to open his eyes to watch, because it was a glorious sight, Paul working himself over Kyle's body, but it was too overwhelming. All too soon he screwed his eyes shut tight, body heaving as he rode out his orgasm.

Paul collapsed on the bed beside him, lying face-down in deference to his sore backside. Kyle kissed him languidly. "Doesn't that make you sore, being fucked after coming?"

Paul shrugged. "It's a little intense, yeah. But sometimes I kind of like it." He kissed Kyle again, but quicker this time. "When are we due at your place? Because it's after four."

"Shit. We better get going. They'll start as soon as we get there, as some of my family needs to travel to get home."

They hurried to get their clothes back on, though they stopped to kiss and giggle a lot. Kyle convinced Paul to not only ride with him but bring a change of clothes and his toothbrush. "I'll take you in if you have to go to work, but I'd love it if you could stay all day. I have it off, and we're putting up our tree."

Paul rubbed his chin. "I'd have to ask Arthur if he minds covering. I might have to be on call if he gets a big job. But I've covered for him before. A lot, actually. He owes me. Yeah, I can stay."

Kyle smiled. "Perfect."

The house was full to bursting as they arrived, and it smelled like heaven. His siblings and their spouses were all there, and a handful of aunts and uncles and cousins from both sides. The whole counter over-flowed with food, and the buffet in the hall groaned with pie. The dining room table had every leaf inserted, and card tables dotted every room on the first floor. Even with all that seating, though, Kyle knew some people would end up sitting on the couch and eating off their laps.

Kyle introduced Paul as much as he could, but once Linda Kay jumped them, he spent most of his time trying to keep her leveled out. She loved family gatherings, but she got a little too excited and tended to get herself in trouble. He worried Paul would feel slighted, but if anything, Paul seemed happy to join in corralling Kyle's twin.

"Thanks," he said once Jane had taken Linda Kay to get her plate while Kyle and Paul stayed back to save the three of them seats at the big table. He waved at her and smiled, but once she was out of sight, he let his shoulders sag. "She can be…intense."

"She's okay." Paul caught Kyle's fingers briefly, looking at him in concern. "Aren't you tired?"

"Exhausted." Kyle ran a hand through his hair before leaning on Paul's shoulder while he watched his family file by. "But I love Thanksgiving. I love the noise and the chaos and the too much family." His belly rumbled. "And the food."

Soon it was their turn to fill their plates. He led Paul to the end of the line, and he told him about Edna as they wove their way through the living room and down the hall to the kitchen. "She's doing okay, healthwise, but it's bothering her a lot to be in the care center."

"Will she be able to go home once she's better?"

"Yes, but I don't think either her doctor or her family wants her to. I wish she'd get connected with the care center community. Is it an ideal place to live? No. But residents who find a way to make it a home get the best of both worlds. Friends and care."

They reached the food and heaped their paper plates high with mashed potatoes, stuffing, Jell-O salad, turkey, ham, sweet potatoes, creamed corn, and steaming-hot rolls. Paul volunteered to carry both their plates so Kyle could get them silverware and drinks—coffee for Paul and fruit punch for Kyle. When they returned to the dining room, it overflowed with people and noise, but Linda Kay stood, waving her stubby arms frantically at them.

"I saved your seats." She bounced on her heels as they put down their food and drinks, and Kyle had barely cleared Paul's coffee cup before Linda Kay clamped him into a bear hug with a squeal. "I love Thanksgiving!"

Kyle hugged her back, then extricated himself and urged her into her seat. "Come on, squirrel, let me eat before my food gets cold."

He joined his aunt in badgering Linda Kay to eat too so *she* could finally get a few bites in, and then they worked out a natural rhythm. Of course, Linda Kay wanted to ask Paul a thousand questions, so he ended up part of the gentle redirection as well.

"A lot of people," Paul observed, once Linda Kay had settled into her food for a bit. "Is it always like this?"

"This is an unusually big crowd, but it's often intense, yeah. We're kind of a central location for the family, and we have the biggest house." Kyle took a bite of sweet potatoes and closed his eyes on a groan of pleasure. "Mmm. These are my Aunt Fiona's. Nobody does them like her. I was afraid they'd all be gone by the time we got through the line. A little bit of heaven every November."

Paul forked another bite of stuffing. "This is my favorite, I think. Who made this?"

Kyle beamed. "Me, yesterday. Mom cooked it for me, but I put it together."

Soon enough they finished their meal, and after a few minutes to let things settle, they went back for pie. Paul got apple and a scoop of ice cream, Kyle pumpkin with whipped cream, but they swapped bites back and forth so that by the time they finished they'd each eaten half of the other's.

"Look at you two lovebirds." Linda Kay leaned over the remains of her brownie and blinked coquettishly at Paul. "So. Are you staying overnight, sexy pants?"

Paul laughed. "Yeah, I'd planned on it. That okay?"

Linda Kay snickered and waggled her eyebrows at Kyle, who gave her a warning glare, but she only laughed darkly and got up to beg their mother for a second brownie.

Kyle's relatives began to drift out one family at a time, hugging Kyle and shaking Paul's hand, telling him with a smile it was nice to meet him. Once most had left, Kyle and Paul worked together to help tear down tables, pile tablecloths by the washing machine, put food away, and do the dishes. By nine thirty, the two of them cuddled in the living room. Linda Kay was in bed, and Kyle's parents talked quietly in the kitchen as they finished the last of the tidying up.

Paul teased Kyle's hair idly where it rested on his thigh. "You seem tired."

Kyle was exhausted. But he caught Paul's hand, drawing it to his mouth to kiss. "I like being with you. I don't want to go to bed yet."

Paul paused. "Am I sleeping somewhere *other* than your bed?"

"No, but once I hit the pillow, I'm passing out." He wrapped Paul's arm around his side, snuggling into Paul's leg. "I love this. Sitting with you after a big family gathering. I hope you had as much fun as I did. Hope we weren't too overwhelming."

"Not at all." Paul stroked Kyle through his shirt. "It was a perfect tonic to an otherwise disappointing holiday."

The words buoyed Kyle, making him turn onto his back so he could gaze up at his boyfriend. "I like being with you, Paul Jansen."

Paul bent to kiss Kyle's lips tenderly. "Me too."

PAUL HAD WOKE next to Kyle many times before he stayed overnight at Kyle's house, but waking up with him the morning after Thanksgiving still felt like uncharted territory. It wasn't just that it was a different bed, a bigger room. It was that he kept hearing people shuffling through the hall, talking quietly. In the case of Linda Kay, not so quietly. He heard the sound of tractors outside, muffled shouts as Kyle's father and brothers did chores. When Kyle woke and wanted to make love, Paul was so distracted by the thought of someone hearing, his paranoia about noise became part of the game, Kyle trying to get Paul to moan, cry out, or in general give away that they were getting it on.

He managed to cling to his dignity, though only barely, and he blushed like a furnace when they went down for breakfast, worried someone might have heard. If they had, they didn't remark on it. Daryl saluted Paul on his way out the door with a refilled thermos of coffee, and Jane smiled brightly, wiping her hands on a dishtowel as she asked how he took his eggs.

Linda Kay bounded into the kitchen shortly thereafter, and while he sipped coffee, Paul watched the Parks twins carry out what he knew from Kyle's stories were daily rituals: hide-and-seek, stealing bacon from the platter in a tag-team effort, plotting mischief for the day. As Kyle's guest, Paul was included automatically in the latter, and he was helpless against getting roped into a snowball fight and snow-sculpture contest in the backyard.

"We have to finish by lunch." Linda Kay wagged a finger at her brother and Paul. "The afternoon is for putting up the tree and the decorations."

"Do you get a real tree?" Paul had fond memories

of fetching trees with Arthur, and of course the one year Frankie and Marcus were there too.

Kyle shook his head. "We keep it up so long, it's a fire hazard. Plus our house is too dry with the wood furnace. We have a pretty good artificial one though."

"It's the most beautiful tree in the world." Linda Kay stuck out her tongue and clapped her hands before continuing. "Decorating is the best. We put on the lights, and the ornaments, then we sing Christmas carols." She leaned back in her chair and spoke with a thespian's exaggeration toward the kitchen. "Maybe somebody will make us some Christmas cookies, since we have a *guest*."

"Maybe somebody should clean her room before she asks me for favors," Jane replied back without looking up from her dishes.

Muttering under her breath, Linda Kay left the table. While she cleaned her room, Paul and Kyle went outside. The sun shone, though it was plenty cold. The snow glistened, crunching as they marched through it.

"Your grandparents' house?" Paul indicated the cottage with a nod. "It's pretty cute."

"That's Mormor and Morfar's house, yes." Kyle sighed. "It's gotten so rundown. It makes me sad."

"The external structure looks pretty good from here. Can we poke around?"

"I'll take you inside, but don't let Linda Kay know how we got in. That's the last thing we need, her getting stuck with her foot through a rotten board."

Once Paul was inside the little house, he doubted very much she'd be in danger of something so dramatic. Sure, there was work to be done, but the foundation was solid. When he told this to Kyle and remarked every last bit of it was the kind of work he and Arthur did all the time, Kyle seemed delighted, but surprised.

"We were told it was too much work to fix." Kyle gestured to a light switch. "The wiring alone would be more than the place was worth."

"What? No. Who told you that?"

"Knutson, I think."

Paul rolled his eyes. "Yeah, that's not surprising. He's real pissed at us for what he calls scamming all his customers. Never mind he's been the one giving everyone in the county a raw deal."

"So you're seriously telling me you could fix this place up?"

"Sure. It'd take a bit of patience and some creativity, but it could be done."

Kyle pressed his mittens to his mouth briefly. "Oh my God." He hugged Paul tightly, pressing a kiss on his cheek. "You might live to regret saying that, because now I'm going to be determined to hire you."

Paul laughed. "Hire me?"

"Yes. I've always wanted to live here, and now you're telling me I could." His cheeks stained with more than the cold. "I know it sounds silly, only moving this far from home—across the yard, basically. But every time I think about moving out, I realize I can't bear to leave my family. They need me. Especially my sister. And as she gets older, she'll need more care. I always imagined myself here with—" He cut himself off and looked away, tucking his hands under his armpits. "Here. I always imagined myself here."

Paul blushed too, because he was pretty sure what Kyle had been about to say. *I always imagined myself here with you.*

Trouble was, Paul could see it. Not only living here, but doing the repairs. Making it just right. Taking the time to do things properly like Marcus and Frankie. Making it not only a house but a home.

Kyle's home, and his.

He cleared his throat and nodded at the door. "We should go, before she gets outside."

The silence between them as they went across the yard wasn't awkward, but it was a bit heavy, both of them circling around something they wanted very much, so much so they didn't dare disturb it before it was time. They started a snowman instead—a repairman snowman, Kyle insisted, in honor of Paul. Paul watched, enchanted, as Kyle mixed water with snow to make slush, then added dry powder until he had sculpting material. While he worked, Kyle rattled off ideas he had for the Winter Wonderland sculptures and where to station them. He promised to show Paul his preliminary designs for the snow queen's palace once they were in his room.

"That reminds me," Paul said as they dug through a shed for some props for the snow-handyman. "When I talked to Arthur yesterday to ask if I could have today off, he said Marcus connected with some friend in the Cities. A developer who loves our Christmas village idea. He's coming to the council meeting in a few weeks to talk about what it would take to make that a reality."

Kyle beamed. "Who would have thought this all would come out of Corrina Anderson maneuvering her son into a relationship with Gabriel?"

Paul blinked at Kyle. "What?"

Kyle's smile faded, and he turned away quickly to fuss with the snowman, though not before Paul caught a look of guilt. "She set them up. I thought everybody knew that."

"I didn't, and I'm one of Arthur's best friends." Paul frowned at Kyle. "How in the world did *you* know?"

Kyle tensed for a moment, then let his shoulders sag. "I know because she and Gabriel told me." He didn't hide his guilty expression this time as he met Paul's gaze. "When they offered to help set me up with you."

Paul stared at Kyle, trying to understand what he'd just said. Gabriel and Corrina had... "Did they tell you to put a snow penis on my porch?"

"No, no. That was all me, but it was the snow dong that got their attention." Kyle tucked his arms over his belly. "Please don't be angry."

Was he angry? Paul pushed aside his shock and searched around. "I'm not mad. I'm just… I had no idea any of it had happened."

"All she did was tell you we were working together on Winter Wonderland and gave me some advice."

Advice? "What did she say?"

"To watch romantic Christmas movies, and to hold off on kissing you." He blushed scarlet. "That one I had a little trouble with."

Paul shook his head, stunned. They'd set him up with Kyle.

The way Corrina had set up Gabriel with Arthur. Apparently.

The way he and Arthur had set Marcus up with Frankie.

Paul laughed.

Kyle bit his lip. "You're not mad? You're sure?"

Paul drew him close and kissed him. "Yeah. I'm sure."

Linda Kay appeared then, dissolving their tender moment with a poorly molded snowball. They tossed some back at her for a few minutes, then got to work on a second snowman—a male nurse, at Linda Kay's insistence, to go with the repairman.

Paul thought they looked pretty damn good together.

Lunch was leftovers from Thanksgiving, which Paul had no complaints about, and after that he helped

Kyle and Daryl bring the boxes of decorations down from the attic. While Kyle and his mother helped Linda Kay put the boughs into the tree stand, Paul hung lights from the eaves with Daryl and draped them over the front bushes. When they came inside, coffee had brewed and the others had not only the lights but half the ornaments on the tree. Linda Kay, however, had saved a pile for Paul, and he couldn't help smiling as he added the colored balls, store-bought and homemade ornaments to the branches.

Daryl appeared in the doorway of the living room as they finished. "Paul, could I borrow you for a bit? Dennis had to go home, and my back gets powerful put out stoking that furnace."

"Sure thing." Paul nodded at his boots and coat by the door. "Is the wood outside or inside?"

The wood, it turned out, was both. Daryl proudly showed Paul his wood chute near the giant woodpile out back that fed logs into a steel basket in the basement. He handed Paul bundles for a bit, but soon Paul ordered Daryl to let him do all the lifting and bending. He discovered this wasn't half as bad as reaching into the basket and hauling the wood to stuff into the blazing maw of the furnace itself, but Paul rather enjoyed feeding the fire, and he felt the heat still kissing his skin as he followed Daryl up the stairs to the main floor once the chore was finished.

The kitchen smelled of chocolate and sugar, the countertop boasting a few dozen spritz cookies and the stove a saucepan of homemade cocoa. Music drifted in from the living room, and as Paul followed the sound, he realized it was Kyle playing the piano, singing Christmas carols along with his sister.

He stopped in the hall, where he could see and hear them without being seen, his heart swelling at the sight of them. They sang "Do You Hear What I Hear", Kyle's bright tenor blending perfectly with the effortless dance of his fingers on the keys. Linda Kay landed nowhere near the notes, but Kyle smiled at her as he sang, as if the sounds she made were the most beautiful tones anyone could make. He led her through the song, slowing his playing when she got lost, letting her watch his mouth to help herself find the words.

Paul watched his boyfriend love his twin sister, and as he did so, he fell in love too.

He'd known he was falling for Kyle for some time, but in that moment not only did he finish his tumble, he grabbed the rest of Kyle's family on the way. He never wanted to go home to his sad duplex, never wanted his holiday to be suffering through another disappointing Jansen gathering. He wanted *this* family. He wanted the little house in the backyard. He wanted to be the one to fix it up.

He wanted to live in it with Kyle. He wanted *Kyle*, period. Wanted him, loved him with an intensity that frightened him. He didn't run from it, though, only sat with the terror, shaking off his sorrow, letting himself be vulnerable enough to believe.

Jane appeared beside him with a cup of cocoa and a plate of cookies, which she pressed into his hands. She smiled at her children. "He's wonderful, isn't he?"

Paul smiled at Kyle too. "He is. He really is."

Chapter Fifteen

THE WEDNESDAY AFTER Thanksgiving, Kyle ran into Paul's sister at the grocery store.

It wasn't a literal collision, but when he rounded the corner of the cereal aisle and saw her waiting in line at the meat counter, they both stood a little straighter and went on guard, smiling thin smiles at one another. Once he was out of her line of sight, Kyle shuddered and tried to shake off the creepy feeling her gaze had given him, and he did his best to finish getting supplies for his dinner with Paul. But in the parking lot when he shut his trunk with the groceries inside, Sandy stood beside his car, not smiling in the slightest.

Kyle was determined to play nice, but before he could work up what to say, Sandy aimed a finger at him. "Stay away from my brother."

Blinking, Kyle turned away from the car, widening his stance and putting his hands on his hips. "Excuse me?"

"You heard me." She lifted her chin, her blue eyes

flinty. "Stay away from my brother. You're no good for him. None of you are."

The parking lot was empty of people, only a few cars here and there, but something about the way Sandy confronted him made him think she'd have thrown down even with an audience. She was more than a little disturbing in her zeal. Normally Kyle would be happy to engage, but something about the way she went after him threw up all kinds of red flags.

"I'm dating your brother, and what we do with one another is our business, not yours."

He said the words calmly, but she fumed as if he'd shouted them at her. "You won't get away with this." She gestured toward the town square. "Not with what you're doing to Paul, not what you're doing to the town. You're ruining a wholesome community. And the people of Logan won't let it stand."

Her ire was now so off-putting and uncomfortable Kyle worried how this would escalate. So he decided to end it. "I'm leaving, Sandy. I hope you have a nice evening."

She stood beside his car with her arms folded, glaring after him as he left the lot.

The encounter left Kyle rattled, and he wondered what to do about it. He thought about bringing it up to Gabriel or Arthur, and he told himself he might, later. He decided he didn't want to tell Paul. He worried about whether or not that was the wrong decision, despite his gut telling him he'd done the right thing. He wasn't absolutely sure, though, until Paul opened the door to greet him, beaming and relaxed and happy.

No, there wasn't any reason to burden him with this. Not unless something else happened.

God, Kyle hoped nothing else happened.

They made chicken parmesan together, and once the dishes were done, they watched *A Boyfriend for Christmas*.

The movie had been lying on top of the DVD player, and spurred by a wild hair, Kyle put it in while Paul was in the bathroom. When he came out, the menu screen was cued up and ready.

Paul blushed and hurried to take it out. "Sorry, I thought I put that away."

"It looks like a cute movie," Kyle said, trying to smooth the moment over.

Paul was adorable when he was bashful. "It's my favorite." He fumbled with the DVD case. "Silly, I know."

"It's not silly." Kyle put a hand on Paul's, stopping him from opening the player. "Let's watch it."

"You don't want to." But Paul's tone made it clear he wished Kyle did.

"I most certainly do." Kyle took Paul's hand and led him to the love seat. "Let me get my knitting, and we'll snuggle under the blanket."

That's exactly what they did. Paul was nervous at first, but Kyle settled in and acted as if this was the best date ever, and eventually Paul relaxed. During the movie, Kyle continued to work on the pair of wool socks he was knitting for Paul. Normally he didn't like people to watch him make something for them, but Paul always regarded even a simple stockinette stitch as an amazing feat, and it was fun to let him observe his present appear. Kyle kept offering to teach him to knit, but Paul said he liked watching Kyle better.

The movie wasn't anything amazing. It was better than most of the pap Kyle had endured in his Paul homework packet, but it still wasn't anything he'd seek out on his own. The premise of the movie was that when the heroine was a young teenager, she'd told Santa—a mall Santa who the viewer was led to believe was the real deal—what she wanted most was a boyfriend for Christmas. He gave her a magic snow globe and told her when both hearts were ready, the wish would come true.

But the wish was never granted, and now she was older and bitter about Christmas. The same Santa was now working a tree lot and charity kitchen, and when he sees her, he sends a good-hearted lawyer to be her present. She thinks it's a game, that the "boyfriend" is a setup by one of her friends, and she plays along, going so far as to take him to her family's Christmas. Like all these kind of movies, there was a rival boyfriend who was clearly the wrong choice, an ex who wanted back in her life.

What was notably different about this Christmas movie viewing, however, wasn't the movie itself. It was that it was the first time Kyle watched one with *Paul.*

As the movie played, Paul surrendered to its spell. He settled deeper into the couch. His body went soft and pliant. Moved, Kyle reached around Paul's back to ruffle his hair, and Paul shifted so his head rested on Kyle's shoulder.

It was such an unconscious gesture, full of so much trust and peace, that for quite some time Kyle studied the golden tousled curls of Paul's head, his face in the dim flicker of the television.

Paul had such boyish, handsome features. Kyle had lain awake more than once studying it as Paul slept. Paul was pretty on the worst of days, but when he slept, his features smoothed out into perfect innocence. His expression as he watched his favorite cheesy Christmas romance was similar, but this one stood out for a different reason: this expression was full of want. Longing. Hope. As the movie boyfriend fought for his fated beloved, as treachery was dispatched and true love conquered all, Paul was laid bare, the naked yearning emanating in waves from his face.

Kyle figured it out, why the movies were so important to understanding Paul. He also knew exactly how and when their own dark moment would come, how Kyle could—and would—slay the enemy for his boyfriend.

He was all the more glad he hadn't told Paul about Sandy. The way to defeating her wasn't with a shouting match or pitting Paul against her. It was by simply loving Paul. Over and over. In every situation. Turning the other cheek if he had to when the Jansens got nasty.

Holding Paul when they'd been nasty to him, reminding him he'd made other, better family.

Kyle stroked Paul's hair as the credits rolled, each of them caught in their respective spells. When the DVD went dark to shift back to the main menu, Kyle slid his hand down Paul's arm and captured his fingers.

"I'd like to go with you to your Sunday dinners with your family sometime, if you'll allow me the honor."

"Probably a bad idea." The soft glow around Paul wavered, clouds threatening at the mention of his family. "They'll be awful."

"I know." Kyle kissed Paul's hair. "That's why I want to be there for you."

Paul's hand, resting on Kyle's leg, tightened. "It's not your place to have to put up with them."

"But, Paul, don't you see? That's exactly the place I want."

Paul regarded Kyle with confusion. "Why? Why would you *want* to be there with them being awful?"

"Because I don't like the idea of you facing them alone. Because I'm not dating you because you're convenient. Because I don't want to simply have sex with you or hang out with you." He stroked the line of Paul's beard. "I want to be *with. You.* I want to watch gooey movies with you, and laugh and play and figure out new ways to enjoy sex, but I want to help you through the rough parts of life too."

Paul went soft and leaned forward, his forehead touching Kyle's. "I still don't know what I did to deserve you. Sometimes I get nervous you'll realize you have no business with a sorry sack like me."

Kyle kissed Paul's hairline, shut his eyes, and drank in the scent of him. "When I was in seventh grade, I knew I was gay and so did everyone else. There wasn't any marriage equality anywhere. I was teased horribly, and the teachers didn't do anything. They made fun of me because Linda Kay always yelled at them, and they thought it was hilarious how my Down syndrome sister was my bodyguard. They called her retarded, called me a fag. I felt so lonely and confused and sad. Until one day something changed."

He shut his eyes with a smile, remembering. "I'd heard there were some guys in town who were older and out, but it was mostly rumor. I knew it was you, Marcus, and Arthur who were supposed to be gay, but you seemed like regular guys to me. I was pretty down on myself by that point, so I decided you'd make fun of me too because I was so femmy. But then one day I was running from bullies, and I fell and slipped on the ice. Everyone laughed, even though I'd bit my lip and it was bleeding. I was trying not to cry—and then *you* came up to me."

Paul turned to look at Kyle in surprise. "I did?"

"You absolutely did. You helped me up from the

ground, made sure I was okay. Gave me your handkerchief to wipe the blood from my face, and you let me keep it. I still have it, in fact. Because in front of everyone, you stood there, so handsome and big and kind, and told me not to care what a bunch of idiots thought of me. Then you ruffled my hair and went away."

Paul appeared stunned. "I have no memory of *any* of this."

"Not surprising. That was what impressed me the most, how you seemed to feel this was all no big deal." Kyle bit his lip against a shy smile. "I had *such* a crush on you, and it never went away, because the more I watched you, the more I wanted you. I loved how quiet you were. You reminded me of my dad. Big and gentle. I liked how you didn't move away, either, once you graduated. I wasn't wild about you being with Arthur, but I was sure I could woo you away. I knew we were supposed to be together. So, no. I'm not going to wake up one morning and decide this was a bad idea. I've wanted you for most of my life. Now that I have you, I'm not going anywhere."

When Paul ducked his head to hide a blush, Kyle chased him, catching his mouth in a kiss. Heat rushed through him as Paul yielded, letting himself be pushed back into the sofa. Kyle kissed his way down Paul's neck, rucking up his sweater so he could nuzzle the fur of his chest. When he laved his tongue over Paul's hairy abdomen, Paul shuddered and gripped Kyle's shoulders, and Kyle felt a thrill at the power of their connection.

He sucked Paul for a few minutes, but it wasn't long before Kyle spit on his palm and jacked them together as he plundered Paul's mouth. They came quickly, but after a cursory cleanup with tissues, they snuggled half-dressed together on the couch for a long time after, holding each other, drinking in the moment.

The next day Kyle went out to Corrina's house. "I know why he likes the movies."

"Oh?" Corrina raised her eyebrows and folded her arms. "Tell me, then."

"Because he wishes his life were one. He wants all of it—the cheesy romance, the family reconciliation, the happy ever after once a tension is resolved. To feel wrapped up and cherished, yes, but more than anything, he wants someone to go *through* the darkness with him. And make everything okay, just in time for Christmas."

"Well done." Corrina's smile was soft, approving. "You passed your test with flying colors."

Not yet, but Kyle fully intended to see that outcome. "Do you think Gabriel has more?"

She kissed him on the cheek. "I'll buy them for you myself."

BY THE SECOND week in December, Winter Wonderland preparations were in a frenzy, and the whole town was abuzz with dreams of a better tomorrow. Marcus's friend the developer was due to meet with the city council on the seventeenth, and he'd be staying with Marcus and Frankie through the festival that following weekend. Rumors flew wild around town over what magic the big-city developer might work on Logan. People dreamed of fancy coffee shops and a revamped town square, and some even dreamed of having a school in town again.

Paul thought people were getting carried away. But when the six of them met up at what Frankie had declared The Three Bears' Christmas, Marcus told them while nothing was guaranteed, it wasn't beyond the realm of possibility.

"This is what Dale does best: reimagines something and outlines the steps to make it happen. He's done it to businesses, buildings, districts. Never a whole town, but that's what excites him. Plus he's originally from somewhere as small as Logan. In Wisconsin, but we try not to hold it against him."

They sat, all six of them, in Marcus and Frankie's living room, sipping cider and cocoa and coffee beside the roaring fireplace while Christmas music played in the background and a ham roast, green bean casserole, and cheesy potatoes baked in the kitchen. All three couples sat together: Marcus and Frankie in the recliner and a dining room chair borrowed for a spare seat, Gabriel and Arthur on the big couch, Paul and Kyle in the loveseat. Everyone was easy, happy. It was all so beautifully homey and idyllic, that Paul wanted to marinate in the moment and never leave it.

Gabriel lay with his head in Arthur's lap, listening to Marcus while Arthur toyed with his curls. "How invested would he be in the project? No offense meant to your friend, but I'm always leery of situations like this where the coordinating party lives not only out of town but in a different *type* of commercial area. What sort of businesses will he promote? Local? Or will Logan become some kind of company town for a Minneapolis subsidiary?"

"My instinct would be an emphasis on local, though he'd have to bring in outside industry or it'd never work." Marcus sipped his cider. "Feel free to ask at the city council meeting, though."

"You'd want significant change, if you were attracting tourists." This remark came from Frankie, who looked thoughtful. "Visitors would want local charm, but city amenities. Frankly, I could go for some of those too. I can't imagine Starbucks would open a chain here. But it'd be great if I didn't have to go all the way to Duluth to have a fix."

Beside Paul, Kyle raised a finger. "No, remember? They opened one in Virginia a little bit ago."

"Write down your questions and bring them to the meeting." Marcus rose to his feet with a stretch. "Right now I'm going to go snitch some ham from the Crock-Pot."

"Oh no you aren't," Frankie admonished. He chased Marcus into the kitchen, laughing all the way.

The rest of them followed less hurriedly, ostensibly coming into the kitchen to help, but mostly lingering over the delicious smells. Frankie put them to work setting out condiments, filling water glasses, opening bottles of wine. Paul was charged with taking the dinner rolls out of the warming drawer and arranging them in a wicker basket lined with a dishtowel before carrying them to the table. When they all finally sat to eat, everyone fawned over Frankie, telling him how good it smelled, then how wonderful it tasted. Frankie beamed and said it was nothing, and Marcus puffed out his chest, a proud fiancé. Gabriel smiled over the edge of his wineglass, elbowing Arthur when he made a rude remark.

Kyle touched Paul's arm whenever he said something to him, and under the table he ran his stocking feet beneath the cuff of Paul's jeans.

Dessert was a hefty assortment of Jane Parks's legendary Christmas cookies, which they all said they were too full to eat and yet decimated anyway. Nursing full bellies and happy hearts, they reconvened in the living room, where Arthur put on a Santa hat and passed out the presents. Gabriel gave everyone a book. Arthur gifted everyone with his favorite local beer, except for Kyle, whom he gave a liter bottle of locally made hard cider. Marcus and Frankie gave gifts together, assortments of things from people's Amazon wish lists arranged in pretty baskets. Paul gave each person something he knew they loved: a cooler full of venison for Gabriel, a new tool cabinet for Arthur, a pretty ceramic teapot for Frankie, a duplicate of the heavy wrench he always borrowed for Marcus. An apron for Kyle covered with pinup lumberjacks.

The best gifts of all came from Kyle. He'd knit them each a pair of woolen socks, one of his knit/felt hats, mittens, and neck warmers. He'd given everyone the colors they loved best too. Everyone declared how amazing they were, and they put on their socks then and there. Arthur donned *all* of it, and wore his knitwear the rest of the evening.

They played cards after that, and a few party games, laughing and teasing and in general having the time of their lives. It was a perfect, wonderful moment. It was everything Paul had always wanted: the three of them, Marcus, Arthur, and Paul, settled and happy. Paul tried to admonish himself not to get too attached, because things could still unravel with Kyle. But it was hard to remember.

Especially when Kyle sighed, leaned into Paul, and said, "This was the best Christmas ever. Can we do it again next year?"

Eventually they had to go home. Kyle and Paul went to Paul's house, where they kissed languidly on the couch for half an hour, smiling and touching each other's faces, nuzzling noses and recalling their favorite parts of the evening. When they finally went to bed, the slow, sweet feeling remained. Kyle made love to Paul, but there was nothing rough or hard about it this time.

He kissed Paul all over his body and sucked his cock with tenderness. He let Paul return the favor, but not for long. They tangled face-to-face, Paul on his back, legs wrapped around Kyle as he kissed Paul and pumped away inside him. Afterward, they spooned together beneath the comforter, listening to the sound of the snowplow clearing away a new round of snow.

"I love you." Kyle kissed Paul's ear, running fingers down the fur of his chest. "I do. I love you. I hope it's not too soon to say that, but I do."

Paul shut his eyes, letting the words wrap around him. Then he kissed Kyle's hand and whispered back, his voice rumbly, "I love you too."

For days, everything was wonderful. Paul worked hard with Arthur to finish construction on Winter Wonderland in-between jobs, and once they finished, they worked each day with Frankie and Marcus, filling in the stencil designs Kyle drew for them. They also helped Kyle make his snow sculptures, putting them on pallets and storing them in the old meat locker until it was time for them to be displayed on the big day.

The whole town was abuzz with excitement. The hardware store was over the moon with its uptick in business and gave everyone associated with Winter Wonderland a discount. The temporary shops were decorated and filled with things to buy and activities for the attendees to do. Someone had set up a coffee shop, complete with espresso maker and a blender for frappés. A bakery in Eveleth had signed on for a space in a long-defunct donut shop, and they made it clear if the big city developer got things going, they wanted to buy the space outright. Everyone in the grocery store, the library, the church narthex, the counter at the café, and the bar at the muni could talk of nothing but how Logan was about to change for the better.

The day before the council meeting, Marcus's friend the developer came into town, and one of Dale Davidson's first stops was to Logan Repair.

Dale stood in the center of the shop, grinning, his big, burly body taking up a great deal of space and, to be honest, stirring more than a little appreciation in Paul. Dale was sandy-haired, polished and handsome as hell. He looked like a cross between the Brawny paper towel man and Chris Evans. But when he winked as he shook their hands, he was John Barrowman all the way.

"Great place you have here. Both the town and your shop." Dale's gaze lingered on Paul appreciatively, and he did the same to Arthur as he shook his hand. "I've heard a lot about both of you."

"Same to you." Arthur leaned on the workbench the way he did when he wanted to show off his package. "What can we do you for?"

"I've interviewed a lot of people around town already, and I've heard all kinds of ideas and plans." Dale pulled out a stool and straddled it. "But as Marcus's best friends, I want to hear yours, and hear what you think of mine, before we head over to the meeting."

Paul and Arthur told their ideas, about the tourism

and the Christmas village, about the cottages by the lake, about making the temporary shops on Main permanent ones. Dale nodded and took notes, then shared his own thoughts.

"I like how you're thinking, and we're on the same page, by and large. A long, slow, careful growth arc. The Christmas Town angle is a good one, though it has to be nurtured carefully. Probably have to start with a Christmas in July festival to go along with the one in December. Keep building slowly. Build smart." Dale rubbed a meaty hand over his beard. "Everything depends on how this inaugural festival goes, and how the council receives my offer. But I have to tell you, what has me most excited is the six of you. I don't want to spook the council by bringing it up too quickly, but—well." He grinned, slightly sheepish with a dab of mischief. "To be frank, there's a real market in drawing the LGBT community to Logan. Many of us are from small towns, and some of us can't go home, even at Christmas. If it gets out that Christmas Town, Minnesota is gay-friendly? You could reopen the school everyone seems so attached to resurrecting. Possibly with some new residents making up same-sex families sending their kids there."

The idea was shocking—but appealing. Paul had been imagining the new, improved Logan for a while now, but with this one speech from Dale, the fabric adjusted, and the couples wandering the streets weren't all straight couples from the suburbs. There were some gay and lesbian and trans couples from the suburbs.

A small town, his *hometown*, an LGBT mecca. It seemed crazy.

It seemed like a miracle.

"That's an awful lot of pie in the sky," Arthur said, but Paul could hear his friend longed for the image too.

Dale nodded. "It's not a sure bet, no. And as I said, I'm not bringing it up to the council. But it's in the back of my mind." He clapped his hands together and grinned. "All right. I have to head over to this library and meet Gabriel. Arthur, you want to tag along and introduce me?"

Paul ended up going along too. Gabriel liked Dale as much as Paul and Arthur did, and though they'd never seemed interested in inviting a third before, Paul half-wondered if Arthur and Gabriel wouldn't end up inviting Dale to their cabin at some point during his stay for a little recreation. Kyle met Dale when they all went to Marcus and Frankie's for dinner, and while he seemed to like Dale well enough, he bristled when Dale's flirtations included Paul.

Pulling Kyle aside, Paul kissed him and smiled into his hair. "Don't worry. He might be handsome, but I prefer toppy nurses."

Laughing, Kyle kissed him back. And whispered an idea he had for role-play into Paul's ear until he blushed.

It was another great evening, one that promised a weekend full of excitement, possibility and friendship.

When Paul arrived to the council meeting the next day, he watched Dale interact with the city leaders and felt like nothing could possibly ever go wrong again.

And then Paul's family, full of frowns and fury, stormed into the room.

Chapter Sixteen

Paul hadn't been to his parents' house since Thanksgiving, partly because he was busy, partly because he didn't want to go. It was easy to pretend they didn't exist at all, except for those uncomfortable run-ins about town. He'd enjoyed the break from them, to be frank. But when his sister and mother came into the city council meeting flanked by ten of the most conservative members of Logan, hate and vengeance burning in their breast, Paul wished he'd kept tabs enough on his family to see the blow coming.

Sandy led the pack, lips pursed in a thin, tight line. "This meeting must stop immediately!"

The room buzzed with confusion and chaos, everyone looking at one another, trying to figure out what was going on. The mayor stood up, frowning at the interruption. "What's going on here?"

Sandy was different than the last time Paul had encountered her, her fury pushing outward instead of pulling in. Like she'd stopped stewing in it and was using it as fuel instead. "We're Concerned Citizens for Logan, and we've been investigating this *developer*. He isn't who he says he is." She aimed an angry finger at Dale. "He's a *homosexual activist*."

Horrified, Paul hunched over the table, cupping his hands around his nose and mouth. This wasn't happening. This *wasn't. Happening.*

Except it was totally, absolutely happening.

A retired teacher who flew a Don't Tread on Me flag above his garage sneered at Dale. "He's on the board of *three* homosexual rights groups. He was part of that campaign where people drove around Minnesota with gay marriage propaganda on their cars. Three of his projects in the last year were developing LGBT crisis centers. He's given interview after interview with press about how homosexuals should be able to go anywhere they want, how small towns need to be more accepting. He doesn't want to rebuild Logan. He wants to make us more homo than we already are!"

The room was both bustling and uncomfortably awkward at once. Arthur and Marcus stood, speaking angrily at the intruders, and Gabriel used that tight, clipped voice he usually reserved for misbehaving children at story time. Frankie looked a little green, and Kyle kept quiet, digging his fingernails into the tabletop.

Paul continued to shrink into his seat, but he was keenly aware he sat in a line of six openly gay, partnered men. That Dale was gay too, and had admitted yes, he wanted to make Logan a gay-friendly destination. When he'd said as much in the shop, it had sounded innocent and wonderful and hopeful to Paul. Regurgitated and thrown down as an accusation from *Concerned Citizens for Logan,* it made him feel queasy and uncertain and sad.

"*Order!*" This wasn't a city council meeting, and the mayor didn't have a gavel, but he banged his palm on the table until the room rumbled to a reluctant quiet. He glared at Sandy and company. "I do *not* appreciate people coming in to a private gathering uninvited and shouting wild accusations. Mr. Davidson is a guest in our town, offering to help our city, though I can't imagine why he would with this kind of dramatics being thrown in his face." The Concerned Citizens tried to interrupt, but the mayor quelled them with a glare and a raised hand. He turned to Dale. "Mr. Davidson, I apologize."

Dale had kept quiet during the outburst. He gave the mayor a curt nod, and didn't give Sandy and company so much as a second glance as he spoke. "Not at all. This is an exploratory venture, my coming to the festival. If Logan decides it doesn't want development, my company certainly can go elsewhere."

"We don't need *your* kind of development," one of the protesters cried, and then chaos broke out again as Marcus, Arthur, the mayor, and Corrina rose to shoo the Concerned Citizens out of the room.

Grim, weary, Gabriel turned to Dale. "May I apologize on behalf of my town. They're not normally quite this agitated. I think what you're experiencing is bottled-up backlash over the rest of us being so public." He gestured to the four of them: himself, Frankie, Kyle, and Paul. "LGBT people have been out in Logan for quite some time, though I suppose it's only recently that we've been in relationships. I didn't realize things had become this organized, but I'm fairly sure it will burn out soon enough."

Dale didn't smile as he gestured to the door. "I won't lie to you. I don't put up with that kind of nonsense lightly."

Frankie had paled, hunching in his seat. "It's never been like this, ever, in the two years I've lived in Logan. I've had a salon almost that entire time, and Marcus a law practice. It's true we've seen our share of cold looks, but I got those occasionally in Minneapolis. This is entirely new."

The mayor and the others returned, effusing apologies to Dale, assuring him this was a fringe element and such rude interruptions wouldn't happen again. The meeting resumed, somewhat stilted now, but lurching steadily forward.

Paul, however, couldn't bring himself to engage. All he could do was replay Sandy and his mother's faces in his mind, hearing their accusatory words. It hurt that they would do this to him. To hurl those words at him—not exactly directly, but they didn't mean to miss him, either. The stunt had embarrassed him in front of his friends and the city leaders. In front of Dale, who could do so many good things for Logan. It had hurt him both as Paul Jansen, their son and brother respectively, and as a gay man.

What burned in his gut, though, eating his insides like acid, was the knowledge that Gabriel had been wrong. This wasn't about Gabriel and Frankie and Arthur and Marcus. Not for Sandy and Paul's mother. This was about him. About Paul dating Kyle. About him not showing up to Sunday dinners to accept their abuse. His punishment for getting away was that they'd focused their bile on the town and gathered up anyone else who felt *the gays* were an acceptable scapegoat for the ills in their lives.

Paul knew, too, they wouldn't stop. They might have already cost Logan Dale and the Christmas City project. They'd unquestionably stage something to ruin Winter Wonderland.

They would drive Kyle away from Paul, or make Paul utterly miserable and uncomfortable in their efforts to try.

Paul didn't excuse himself from the meeting. He simply stood, grabbed his coat from the rack by the door, and left the building. He heard Arthur and Kyle calling after him, but he ignored them, hurrying into his truck and peeling away before they could reach him, not even bothering with his seat belt.

Kyle would be upset at being ignored like that, he knew, and justifiably so. He told himself he'd apologize later, though he couldn't bear to think of talking to anyone right now.

He went home to his duplex, where the lights he'd hung with Kyle twinkled hopefully. Paul shut them off, locked the door and went to his room, barely bothering to kick his boots off before collapsing onto the bed.

He didn't cry, but he sagged into the mattress, clinging to the numbness that kept those tears at bay, ignoring the buzz of his phone inside his pocket until it stopped and he was able to surrender to the black quiet inside his mind.

KYLE WATCHED PAUL pull out of the parking lot with his heart in his throat and Arthur's hand firmly attached to his collar. "Let me go, dammit. I need to go to him."

"Give him a minute, okay? That wasn't easy for him to watch his family lead that nonsense."

Kyle struggled out of Arthur's grip. Paul's mother and sister were with the other idiots on the other side of the parking lot, huddled together in conference, though a few of them watched Kyle and Arthur.

Setting his teeth, Kyle turned away. "I *know* that killed him. Why do you think I want to comfort him?"

"He's all wounded bear right now. Give him a minute to lick his wounds."

"I'm not going to stop him from licking his wounds. I want to *be there* while he does it." Kyle folded his arms over his chest and set his jaw. "I want to punch the Jansens out. Yell at them. Swear a blue streak. Drown them in the lake."

"Yeah, well, that's *exactly* what they're after. They crave a big scene, a showdown. They want to point to the crazy faggots and say, 'See, look how unstable they are.'"

"We aren't the ones bursting into meetings and spewing mean-spirited garbage."

Kyle had shouted that, loud enough to get the attention of more of the group across the parking lot. Arthur stood between Kyle and them, a somewhat futile move as Kyle could see over the top of Arthur's head by barely standing on his tiptoes. Arthur's stern expression was enough to draw Kyle's focus, though. "This isn't the way, Kyle. I'm not telling you to smile and eat the shit. I'm saying you can fight back, but not here, not now."

The fire in Kyle's breast became a lump that made his voice waver when he replied, "They hurt Paul."

"Yes. And believe me, I'm holding myself back as much as I am you. But they've hurt a lot of people right now. You. Me. Gabriel and Frankie and Marcus. My mom. Everyone in that room. The *whole town*, because Dale won't take this lying down."

Kyle was all too aware. "While you guys were outside, he flat-out said this kind of crap was a game-changer."

"Exactly. With one outburst they turned him from

engaged and eager to invest to seriously rethinking his position. And that was their whole goal. That and riling us up. They want to turn Winter Wonderland into a shit-storm, not a celebration. Don't give them what they want."

Kyle wanted to throw up. "I can't believe they'd sandbag the whole town because we're gay. I mean, I know Logan's not perfect…" He couldn't finish the thought. Because no, he'd never thought it was like this.

For the first time in his life, Kyle questioned his passion for insisting on living in Logan. Not for long. But he questioned it all the same.

Arthur led him inside, promising him they were all going over to Paul's house as soon as the meeting was over. Kyle let himself be led, feeling slightly out of body and utterly unable to focus on something he was so eager to discuss such a short time ago. He couldn't stop thinking about what the Concerned Citizens for Logan had said, with how much hate and cruelty they'd delivered their message.

As he drove over to Paul's house with the others, he wondered what the protesters would try next. Dale had agreed to let the awkward incident slide, but the elephant in the room had been everyone knowing that wouldn't be an aberration. The Concerned Citizens would unquestionably show up at the event itself and be embarrassing. Would they do more than that? Would they try to dissuade the business owners?

Would they coordinate more scenes?

How could they be so willing to destroy all the good in the event? Why were six gay men such a threat?

How could Sandy and Mary do this to Paul?

At Paul's duplex, Kyle had to use his key to let them in. Paul came out of his bedroom as they entered, looking wrecked but wooden. "I don't want to be with anyone right now."

"Tough." Arthur spoke before Kyle could. "Get out here and let us comfort you. We know who was hurt most in that scene."

Paul clearly wanted them to go, which made Kyle feel unsure of himself and how to behave. In that moment he was so glad for the presence of the others, for the way they shuffled him next to Paul on the couch, began caring for him as much as for Paul. Kyle wanted to put his arm around Paul, to reassure him, but to his shame he didn't know how to react. What to say. What the hell *was* there to say? Kyle wanted to tell Paul his family was horrible, but that wasn't news to him, and in any event, everything in Kyle had come unplugged and he was suddenly unsure of how to do that. He wanted to be a supportive boyfriend, but right now when Paul needed him most, Kyle had no idea how to behave. It was ridiculous. But the more he tried, the more he failed.

When he got up to go to the kitchen to try to get a grip on himself, Gabriel followed him and put a hand on his shoulder. "What's going on? You're a frayed nerve."

"I don't know what to say to him." Kyle shoved his hands into his hair. "I don't know what to do."

"Be here for him. Love him."

Gabriel was right, obviously. Kyle went back out into the living room, but he couldn't get himself together, and he knew soon he would make it worse. It didn't help anything that Paul gave him exactly nothing to work with. He didn't lean into Kyle. Didn't do anything but tense up when Kyle touched him. When Kyle tried to kiss Paul's cheek and he recoiled, Kyle couldn't take any more. He disappeared into the kitchen again, this time snagging his coat and boots on the way by.

This time Frankie followed him. "What's going on? Why are you being so weird?"

Kyle had no idea. "I have to go. I'm making it worse, clearly."

Frankie's expression softened. "Oh, honey. You're not. We told you, he gets funny about his family."

"I know but I—can't." He hated that he couldn't. But it didn't make it any less true. Kyle shook his head, averting his gaze in shame. "I need to get out of here for a little while. I'm sorry."

Frankie sighed. "Call me later, okay?"

Kyle nodded, accepted a hug and got the hell out of there.

He wiped tears away from his eyes as he drove

home, but once he entered the kitchen and saw his family standing there, surprised to see him, Kyle burst into tears. That they dropped everything, circled the wagons and plunked him at the kitchen table and tried to soothe him only opened his wounds further. He relayed the story of what had happened at the meeting, which from the looks on his parents' faces, they'd already heard about. He told them about Paul leaving, about the parking lot with Arthur, and then, sobbing so hard snot ran out of his nose, he confessed his utter failure to be there for Paul when he needed him most.

"I had to leave because I was only making it *worse*." Kyle stopped to hiccup and blow his nose in the handkerchief his dad passed over, a soft blue bandana that smelled of diesel oil. "The others kept telling me to stay, but I wasn't making him any better. He didn't want me to touch him." Kyle tossed the hanky away and buried his face in his hands. "It's like they said all along. I'm too young for him. I'm not the right man for him. I'm not even truly a m-man."

"Stop right now." Daryl's sternest voice was still full of gentle, wrapping around Kyle and soothing him the same way it always had. "You're upset, and that's understandable. But let's back up before you start undoing what to my mind is a positive, good relationship despite whatever differences you might have between each other, age and otherwise. Especially over something you had no part of."

Jane had her arms full of a tearful Linda Kay, who

always wept when someone else did, but she managed to comfort her daughter and speak to Kyle at the same time. "If you're guilty of anything, it's being unable to stand it when other people hurt. You're always at your worst when someone you love faces something you can't fix. Plus those fools who burst into the meeting hurt you too."

"I want to go yell at them, but Arthur says that'll only make it worse."

Daryl nodded curtly. "He's right. The way to fight hate is with love."

Kyle tensed. "I *don't* love them. Not right now. I don't know if I ever can. I was all set to get to know them for Paul's sake, but I don't know that I can. Not now."

"Not *right* now, no." Jane smoothed Linda Kay's hair. "Let's focus on getting you put back together right now. The Jansens can wait. All of them but Paul. Take a moment and text him, sweetheart."

The thought made Kyle queasy. "I don't know what to say. I feel ridiculous now, leaving. He probably thinks I abandoned him."

"Then tell him the truth. You got overwhelmed and sensed he needed his space. Tell him you love him, that you're here for him if he wants to talk with you. Or simply be with you."

Kyle got out his phone.

I love you. I'm sorry I had to go. I thought you needed space, but if I'm wrong, tell me and I'll be over in a heartbeat. I do love you. So much. We'll get through this. I'll be with you all the way. I love you.

He put the phone down, sure he wouldn't get a response, which was why he was so surprised when his phone buzzed less than thirty seconds later. Paul's response was brief, but warmed Kyle all the same.

It's okay. Thank you. I will. I love you too.

When he relayed the message to his family, they smiled. "See?" Daryl ruffled Kyle's hair. "You two kids will come through this just fine."

Kyle wasn't sure how, exactly, that was going to happen right now. But when Linda Kay slid her chair over, wrapped her arms around his midsection and squeezed, Kyle shut his eyes and leaned into her and let himself trust somehow, some way, it would.

Chapter Seventeen

P AUL PUT HIS phone on the coffee table, Kyle's text still visible on the screen for a few seconds longer before fading away. Arthur had been monologuing reassurances, but when he saw the phone, he stopped. "Everything okay?"

Okay? Paul huffed a bitter laugh. "Yeah. Everything's great." He stroked the phone, though. "That was Kyle."

"Where did he go?" Marcus looked around with a frown. "I thought he was here."

Gabriel started to answer, but Paul spoke over him. "He got overwhelmed and needed to be alone. Which is what I've been trying to tell you all for an hour is what I need too."

Arthur scowled and folded his arms over his chest. "If you think we're leaving you alone after your family pulled a stunt like that, you've got another think coming."

Paul pinched the bridge of his nose and forced his

breath out in a measured release, not a sigh. "I appreciate the support. But I really do want to be by myself right now."

It took another hour to convince them he was fine, or at least that being alone was the medicine he needed. Frankie was the one who got them to go, urging everyone to give Paul space, giving him a sad smile over his shoulder as he herded them out the door. Once they were gone, Paul let the quiet press against his ears for a moment. Then he leaned forward far enough to gather his remotes.

He'd left one of the ten-pack Christmas romance DVDs in the player, and he fired up *The Most Wonderful Time of the Year*.

He only half-watched, mostly trying to absorb the happy Christmas feeling, to get enough of a hit to bleed off the pain of the afternoon. When it failed, he pulled out *A Christmas Kiss*, and soon after that, *A Boyfriend for Christmas*. In the middle of the prologue flashback where the hero and heroine met first as teens, he snapped off the TV and picked up his phone. Kyle answered before the first ring finished.

"Hey, you."

Paul shut his eyes, the beautiful sound of his boyfriend's voice welcome even as it, like the movies, made everything all too real. "I'm sorry I couldn't…react right today. It had nothing to do with you."

"I know. I'm sorry I had to leave."

Paul sank into the couch, reveling in how much

Kyle's voice was *home*. He wasn't sure when that had happened. It felt dangerous. And wonderful. "Sometimes…when I'm upset, I need to be by myself. You leaving was actually good. I wish the others had listened like you did."

"I'm so sorry, Paul." Kyle sighed raggedly, gathering himself. "I'm sorry they did that. It was so hurtful to you. It makes me so angry. But mostly—" His voice cracked. "I just…God, I want to make it all go away. I want to be everything for you. I want to be your white knight. But I can't. Not all the time. And I hate it." He made a frustrated noise. "Sorry. I'm making this about me. As I said, I suck at this."

No, he didn't suck at all. Paul shut his eyes and gripped his phone tighter. "You *are* my white knight, Kyle. My beautiful, swishy, fierce, toppy, tenderhearted white knight."

"I hate when you hurt." Kyle wept now, drowning in all the rage and helplessness Paul was too numb to feel. "I want you to have your Christmas movies in real life. I want to help you find the plot device in the last ten minutes that fixes everything and makes what was horrible okay." He choked on a sob before forging forward. "But I can't. I can't, because life isn't a movie, and even men with money and power and abs like Dale Davidson can't erase people who hate and families who disappoint. And I'm sorry. I'm so sorry I can't be magic enough to give you that."

Tears ran down Paul's face, and he had to swallow

a lump in his throat before he could continue. "I never asked you to do that."

"I know." The despair and frustration in Kyle cut Paul so he could bleed with his lover. "I know you didn't. *I* asked me to. But I can't." He paused to blow his nose, then whispered, "I love you so much, Paul. *So much.*"

The words wrapped around Paul, tugging him open and pouring love into the place he'd been trying not to notice was so full of pain. "I love you too, Kyle."

"When you're done being by yourself, you come find me, okay? You come be with me. I'll be your family. For as long as you'll have me."

Despite the tears still falling, Paul smiled. "I will. I promise." He swallowed. "Thank you."

"I love you."

"I love you too."

Once he hung up, Paul sat in the silence again. He stared at the movie screen, which was frozen in the middle of a scene. He replayed Kyle's words in his head. Shutting his eyes, he willed them to do what the movies had failed to do, to override the pain.

It worked, but something else happened, a side effect the movies had never given him. Paul felt better, but he also felt *angry*. Betrayed. Cheated.

Hurt. He felt so, so *hurt*. And for the first time in his life, he felt that pain, held it in his hand, and said, *I don't deserve to feel this way.*

He got off the couch and paced to the small tree,

beneath which were all his presents for his family. Gifts he'd purchased, like a fool, out of duty and even a small bit of love for the people who had humiliated him that way, hurt him and his friends. People who had never and would never call him up to bleed with him the way Kyle just had.

That is not a real family.

Paul picked up his mother's gift—a music box she'd been eyeing, which he'd spent fifty dollars on—and threw it against the front door with a roar. He heard it shatter, but that wasn't enough. He stomped on it, ripping the paper, destroying the box, pulverizing the beautiful china into dust and the music box apparatus into broken gears. He yanked on the silk scarf he'd ordered for Sandy until it tore, using his teeth and then scissors when it didn't want to yield. He couldn't destroy the tool set he'd bought for his brother-in-law or the fancy level he'd gotten his father, but he threw them out the front door into the snow, watching the wrenches and the ruler sail into the drifts, knowing they'd rust and ruin before anyone found them.

It wasn't enough. It wasn't nearly enough.

He tore through the house like an animal, ripping apart magazines his mother had given him, cutting up the blanket she'd crocheted for him, taking a hammer to photos in frames, breaking hand-me-down plates and crockery—anything his family had given him, he tore into with all the rage and hurt he'd never allowed himself to feel until there was nothing left to destroy.

The rage died away, but the hurt and the pain lingered as an ache he feared would never go away.

He tried to go to Kyle. He got in his car, armed with an overnight bag and a toothbrush he intended to *leave* at the Parks house. But when he got to the edge of town, when he saw the care center, his car turned into the lot almost as if Paul had no say in the matter. He wasn't even sure where he was ultimately headed until he saw the nurses' station.

"I'm here to see Edna Michealson."

She was in her room, lit by a lamp Paul recognized as one from her side of the duplex, which Kyle must have brought over. The TV was on, but when she turned blearily to Paul, he knew she hadn't been watching it. Only keeping it on for company.

Edna frowned at him. "Paul? What in the world are you doing here? Your young man isn't working tonight." Her tone said she understood Kyle couldn't work every night, but she resented his absence all the same.

"I came to see you, actually." Paul braced a hand against the doorway. "I had a pretty terrible afternoon and evening. I've spent the last hour tearing my house apart, wrecking everything my family has ever given me and everything I intended to give to them, but you know, it didn't really help. I still feel pretty lousy."

She raised an eyebrow at him. "Oh? What did those fool Jansens do now?"

Paul shook his head. "I don't much care to talk

about it, if you don't mind. I came here…" He let out a heavy breath. "I've decided I need a new family. And I came here to see if you were at all interested in being part of that."

Edna stared at him for a long time. He thought, briefly, her eyes might have glazed over with tears. Then she blinked, sighed as if very put upon, and motioned to her dresser. "There's a deck of cards there. Bring them over, and we'll see how well you play bridge."

After grabbing the cards, Paul brought over a chair and sat. As Edna pulled over a rickety hospital bed table, he frowned. "That thing is a piece of junk."

She rolled her eyes. "They keep telling me they'll fix it, but they never do."

"I'll bring my tools the next time I come. But that'll only be a patch job. I could build you something better than this in a long weekend." He shuffled the cards and laid them on the stand. "Cut?"

Smiling, a little sadly, a little happily, Edna waved the offer away. "Deal."

Paul did.

WHEN THE KNOCK at the front door turned out to be Paul, Kyle dropped his knitting and ran to throw his arms around him. They hugged, they wept, they kissed each other until Kyle's mother scolded him to let the poor man come in and sit down, and did Paul get dinner? Because she had some beef stew still left in the Crock-Pot.

Paul looked weary, but much better than he had when Kyle had left him. He let Kyle touch him too, first in the kitchen as he ate, snuggled together as they let Linda Kay force a viewing of *South Pacific* on them, and finally as they went to bed together, they touched like crazy as Kyle made sweet, tender, then intense love to Paul. Afterward, Kyle held Paul close, until the gentle up and down of Paul's chest told Kyle his boyfriend had gone to sleep.

Kyle, however, found he couldn't easily follow.

In the quiet of the night, fears rose like shoots from dark ground. He worried about how easy the lock on the butcher's was to cut off, how simply someone could get inside and destroy his week's worth of work on the snow sculptures. He worried what Paul's family and their horrible companions would do during the festival—because they'd absolutely do *something*. He worried Dale was disgusted with Logan and already writing them off.

Most of all, he worried Paul's family would find new ways to hurt him, that they'd find a wound they could make fatal and drive Paul back into his cave, no longer willing to let Kyle or anyone else in.

He knew, intellectually, that last one wasn't going to happen, but in the darkness with the wind howling outside, it was hard for him to trust that truth emotionally. His fears scrambled and drifted inside him like the

Minnesota snow, until he had to get out of bed and into his clothes or risk drowning.

His intention had been to drive into town and double-check to make sure the lock hadn't been damaged. He figured the outing would put to rest his paranoia, and the drive would wear him out enough he could sleep. Once he got to the shop, though, he couldn't leave until he didn't simply see the undamaged lock, he had to open the door and check the statues for himself.

The butcher's locker wasn't huge, which meant the statues were all crammed in tight, hardly any room to move between their wooden platforms. They were ready to roll out at eight the next morning to be stationed around the square. The mayor wanted to make it a big reveal, so the plan was for Marcus and the mayor and a few other men in town to wheel them into place before putting up a big canvas curtain on a PVC structure around the perimeter—a curtain Kyle had helped stencil and paint with Dala horses. Standing in the locker, Kyle saw for himself the statues were safe. The Concerned Citizens for Logan would have to find some other way to embarrass themselves, some other way to spread hate.

Kyle was about to leave, but to get out, he had to navigate around his masterpiece, the snow queen's palace. True to his promise, he'd made no reference to *Frozen* and hadn't named the beautiful snow queen Elsa, but anyone who'd seen the movie would know who she was. Kyle smiled at her frozen sassy expression as he passed, remembering how fabulously fierce she'd been in the movie. Remembered how good the movie had been, right up until the commercialization had made every adult on planet Earth set their teeth every time they went through a department store. He kept thinking about his conversation with Paul.

If only he *did* have magic like the snow queen. If only he *could* melt those bigots' frozen hearts. With love, or a blowtorch, or *anything*.

And then, standing there in front of his butcher's locker full of statues, he had an idea. A crazy, barely conceivable idea. One that might work, or it might not. But it would sure as hell be fun to try.

He grinned back at Elsa, meeting her sassy smile and raising her a smart salute and click of his heels. Then he stacked the last four pallets on top of each other and pushed them off into the night.

Chapter Eighteen

P AUL WOKE UP in Kyle's bed alone. Or rather, he
was in the bed alone, but a pair of eyes and the tip
of a nose peered at him from the edge of the bed,
blinking rapidly. He tugged the sheet higher up his
naked body and cleared his throat. "Good morning,
Linda Kay."

Linda Kay rose to her knees. She looked worried.
"Kyle isn't here. His car is gone."

"What?" Paul sat up straight, wrapping the sheet
around himself as he searched for his pants. "Where'd
he go?"

"I don't know." Linda Kay seemed upset. "Mom
says I'm not supposed to worry, but *I'm worried.*"

Paul relaxed a little. "Does she know where he is?"

"No, but she says Kyle has a surprise for us. Except he's been gone *all night.*" She pursed her lips and
shook a clumsy fist at him. "If your crazy family kidnapped him, there's gonna be blood."

It was a sign of how much better Paul was doing

that he was able to smile at that. "I promise you they haven't kidnapped him. Besides. If they tried, Kyle would punch them out. Or stick them with his knitting needles." He ruffled her hair. "How about you let me get dressed, and we'll go talk to your mom together. Okay?"

"Okay. But if you don't come out in five minutes, I'm coming in with an Uzi."

Paul was, in fact, out of the room in less than two minutes, and he let himself be led down the stairs by an anxious Linda Kay. Jane waved at him from the stove.

"Good morning, Paul. Don't let Linda Kay worry you. Daryl went in to see what Kyle was up to, and he called me all mysterious, saying he won't give the surprise away, but Kyle's making a new sculpture. He worked on it all night, all by himself, in the city square. He's still at it, apparently. We get to see it when we go for the unveiling at nine." She motioned to the table. "Have a seat. I remember how you take your eggs."

Linda Kay took a little mollifying, which Paul eventually solved by whispering he'd take Kyle's place at bacon-stealing. He wasn't terribly good at it, but luckily Jane helped him by being deliberately oblivious. They ate their breakfast together, the three of them, and while Linda Kay and Jane finished getting ready, Paul checked his messages. There was one from Marcus, assuring Paul that Dale wasn't upset. The mayor had been over at their house until midnight doing backflips as he promised to never let anything like that happen again. Arthur had left a voicemail asking Paul if he was doing okay, and Paul replied with a text, letting his friend know he'd stayed the night at the Parks' place and was just fine.

The ladies weren't yet ready, so Paul wandered outside, winding through the backyard until he stood in front of Mormor and Morfar's house. He took deep breaths of the cold as he imagined what it would look like painted and re-shingled, with the shutters repaired and stenciled. He thought of how wonderful it would be to wake up with Kyle inside that house, to have breakfast together there, unless they went over to the main house and let Jane spoil them. Thought about Linda Kay arriving armed with the DVD of *South Pacific*, swinging on a swing on their front porch singing "Valley High" at the top of her lungs because the overflowing joy in her heart demanded it.

Thought about living in that house and building a life together with Kyle. Forever.

"Hey, you!" Linda Kay's voice belted across the yard from the garage, and she waved frantically at Paul with a hand-knit red mitten. "Come on, slowpoke, we don't want to miss the big show."

Grinning, Paul hurried across the yard to ride into town and see what the fuss was all about.

A large crowd had gathered already when they arrived, but the mayor himself greeted them, hugged Paul and Jane and Linda Kay, and ushered them to the front of the crush. "I was instructed to give Kyle's family a front-row seat. Hello there, Dale." He waved at the developer, who lifted a scarf off the bench beside him and motioned for Paul and the women to sit.

"This is so fancy." Jane beamed as she nodded at the huge curtain circling the square. "That whole thing is full of Kyle's snow sculptures? Have you seen them?"

"I have. Most of them." Paul watched the curtain, eager to see this new one. He couldn't imagine what it might be.

Marcus and Frankie wove their way through the front-row seats and took up the tail end of their bench. Frankie hugged Paul and kissed his cheek. "Wait until you see. Kyle outdid himself this time."

"What in the world is it?" Paul asked, unable to stand it any longer.

"Love," Marcus replied, his voice rumbly with emotion.

Before Paul could ask what he meant by that, Gabriel and Arthur stepped out in front of the curtain. Gabriel raised a microphone and began to speak.

"Ladies and gentlemen, if I could have your attention." He used his story-time voice, smiling at the townspeople the way he did children at the library, mesmerizing them with his secret librarian powers. "We're so glad you could come out on this cold morning. We're hoping to have quite a crowd later today, and as I see some new faces, I think some of our city's visitors have already arrived. Welcome to you all. We hope you enjoy this grand opening and all of the first annual Winter Wonderland festival. After this ceremony the shops will open, including the coffee shop and bakery, which I suspect will be doing some very brisk business. For those of you here from neighboring towns, I want to make sure you meet our guest of honor, Mr. Dale Davidson of Davidson Incorporated. He's interested in helping us make not only this festival but this whole valley a vibrant hub of tourism and community. Please don't hesitate to introduce yourself to him. He wants to hear *all* your ideas."

Gabriel sobered. "You might have heard, sadly, about a little incident last night, where a few people said some insensitive things as they barged into a planning meeting for this festival. We, the planning committee and the mayor and the city council, want you to know this isn't something you need to worry about. We understand some people have a hard time with change and aren't afraid to embarrass themselves in an effort to keep it from coming. We want you to know change *is* coming—in fact, it's already here. It's a change for the better, though. It's a change for hope and unity and possibility. And most of all, love. That's what this festival is about after all, isn't it? What this season is about? One of our festival volunteers certainly thinks so. He stayed up all night to craft the centerpiece of our sculpture garden, which it is my great pleasure to reveal to you now." He smiled at Arthur. "Darling, will you do the honors?"

Grinning, Arthur tugged on a cord at the edge of the curtain—making it crumple to the ground in a rustling heap to reveal...

Magic.

The entire audience gasped collectively, all but Paul, whose heart filled to overflowing with affection as he stared at the man in the center of the amazing sculptures.

There was the Santa and Mrs. Claus, yes. And the town library, with Gabriel in front of it, welcoming a herd of children to story time. There was his and Arthur's fix-it shop, the two of them waving in front of it. There was the beautiful snow queen, complete with a platform where children could pose for a picture with her. There were elves and candy canes and a nativity, and a little church at the end of a lane. Every statue he'd seen Kyle working on for a week, some he'd helped him craft.

But in the center of it all was Kyle, standing proudly behind a four-foot-high snow message.

Logan is love.

He hadn't simply carved out the letters. He'd filled each one with people. Intricate, snow-and-ice-chiseled people. Men and women, children, the elderly, the newly born. Mothers and fathers and sisters and brothers, cranky neighbors and best friends. There were couples everywhere. Men with women, women with women, men with men. There were figures who could easily be Paul's cranky, uptight family, scowling and frowning, unaware of the same-sex couple sneaking up behind them with a smile and a warm blanket to wrap around their shoulders. The old man shaking his cane at two men snuggling on a park bench had a woman who looked a *lot* like Corrina smiling as she offered him a cup of coffee.

Love. It was twenty feet of snow and art and love.

Oh, Kyle Parks. You're brimming head to toe with magic.

As the crowd clapped and cheered his lover, Paul rose and navigated his way through the garden of snow, until he reached the wall of love and was able to take the man he cherished more than anything in the world into his arms. In the distance the church bells pealed, signaling the official start of the festival with the same peals they'd sound on Christmas morning.

Kyle beamed, his cheeks red with cold as Paul brought him in for a kiss. "You like it?"

"I love it." Paul kissed him again. "I love *you*."

Kyle's smile turned wicked. "I hid a tiny snow penis behind the sculpture of your mother. No one will see it, but I know it's there."

Paul took Kyle's face in his hands, the love over-flowing and making the words tumble out of his mouth. "Kyle Parks, I really need you to marry me. As soon as possible."

Kyle looped his arms around Paul's neck and beamed at him. "As long as we can have the ceremony on Sandy's birthday."

Paul's laugh cracked through the town square like a

whip. A blissful, giddy whip. "You've got a deal."

In front of everyone, Paul kissed his fiancé, sinking deep into the joyful, perfect throes of his very own Christmas happy ever after.

About the Author

Heidi Cullinan has always enjoyed a good love story, provided it has a happy ending. Proud to be from the first Midwestern state with full marriage equality, Heidi is a vocal advocate for LGBT rights. She writes positive-outcome romances for LGBT characters struggling against insurmountable odds because she believes there's no such thing as too much happy ever after. When Heidi isn't writing, she enjoys cooking, reading, playing with her cats, and watching anime, with or without her family. Find out more about Heidi at heidicullinan.com.

Did you enjoy this book?

If you did, please consider leaving a review online or recommending it to a friend. There's absolutely nothing that helps an author more than a reader's enthusiasm. Your word of mouth is greatly appreciated and helps me sell more books, which helps me write more books.

Other books by Heidi Cullinan

There's a lot happening with my books right now! Sign up for my release-announcement-only newsletter on my website to be sure you don't miss a single release or re-release.

www.heidicullinan.com/newssignup

Want the inside scoop on upcoming releases, automatic delivery of all my titles in your preferred format, with option for signed paperbacks shipped worldwide? Consider joining my Patreon.

www.patreon.com/heidicullinan

OTHER BOOKS IN THE MINNESOTA CHRISTMAS SERIES

Let It Snow (*also available in German*)

Frankie's malfunctioning GPS sent him to Logan, and a blizzard ensures he won't be leaving anytime soon. Being rescued by three sexy lumberjacks is a nice fantasy, but the biggest of the bears seems cranky…and ready to gobble Frankie right up. Once a high-powered lawyer, Marcus has no interest in a sassy city twink who might as well have stepped directly out of his past. Yet as the snow falls, the deeper they fall in love. Though all they want for Christmas is each other, the gift of forever may be too much to ask.

Sleigh Ride (*also available in German*)

Arthur wants nothing to do with romance, and he certainly doesn't want to play Santa in his mother's library fundraising scheme. He knows full well she really wants to hook him up with the town's lanky, prissy librarian. It's clear Gabriel doesn't want him, either—as a Santa, as a boyfriend, as anyone at all. But as their arguments strike sparks, two men who insist they don't date wind up doing an awful lot of dating. And the sleigh they're trying not to board could jingle them all the way to happily ever after.

Santa Baby

A one-night threesome becomes more when Dale Davidson joins already coupled Arthur Anderson and Gabriel Higgins, which is complicated enough in their sleepy northern Minnesota town, but when Dale's abusive ex draws him into a dark web, the whole community must put aside their preconceptions of relationships, come together, and help bring their Santa home.

More adventures in Logan, Minnesota, coming soon

THE ROOSEVELT SERIES
Carry the Ocean (also available in French)
Shelter the Sea
Unleash the Earth (coming soon)
Shatter the Sky (coming soon)

LOVE LESSONS SERIES

Love Lessons (also available in German, French
coming soon)
Frozen Heart
Fever Pitch (also available in German)
Lonely Hearts (also available in German)
Short Stay
Rebel Heart (coming fall 2017)

THE DANCING SERIES

Dance With Me (also available in French, Italian
coming soon)
Enjoy the Dance
Burn the Floor (coming soon)

THE SPECIAL DELIVERY SERIES

Special Delivery
Hooch and Cake
Double Blind
The Twelve Days of Randy
Tough Love

CLOCKWORK LOVE SERIES

Clockwork Heart
Clockwork Pirate (coming soon)
Clockwork Princess (coming soon)

TUCKER SPRINGS SERIES

Second Hand (written with Marie Sexton)
(available in French)

Dirty Laundry (available in French)
(more titles in this series *by other authors)*

SINGLE TITLES

Antisocial
Nowhere Ranch (available in Italian)
Family Man (written with Marie Sexton)
A Private Gentleman
The Devil Will Do
Hero
Miles and the Magic Flute

NONFICTION

Your A Game: Winning Promo for Genre Fiction
(written with Damon Suede)

Many titles are also available in audio and more are in production. Check the listings wherever you purchase audiobooks to see which titles are available.